# Above the Mistletoe

# *Above the Mistletoe*

**A Haven Creek Romance**

## Michele Arris

TULE
PUBLISHING

Above the Mistletoe
Copyright© 2022 Michele Arris
Tule Publishing First Printing November 2022

The Tule Publishing, Inc.

ALL RIGHTS RESERVED

Second Publication by Tule Publishing 2022

Cover design by LLewellen Designs

No part of this book may be used or reproduced in any manner whatsoever without written permission except in the case of brief quotations embodied in critical articles and reviews.

This is a work of fiction. Names, characters, places, and incidents are products of the author's imagination or are used fictitiously. Any resemblance to actual events, locales, organizations, or persons, living or dead, is entirely coincidental.

ISBN: 978-1-957748-85-6

# Chapter One

"HAPPY HOLIDAYS, AND have a safe trip." As her last drop-off went on his way, Reyna let go a deep breath. Her day finally liberated, she slid in behind the wheel and removed the earpiece, head resting back against the comfy leather seat, eyes closed. Ah.

An incoming call flashed on the car's dashboard screen. She measured for a long moment whether to ignore Frank Rasino as she threw the car in a pin circle and caught sight of the jet taxiing away in her rearview mirror. Frank never bothered her when she was working unless he needed something. Another ring. And another. Respect for the man won out. Still . . .

She connected. "Frank, whatever it is, don't ask. I'm officially off work as of a minute ago. Lily is away with her father, so I'm taking a much-needed night off. See you tomorrow. Goodbye."

"Wait, don't hang up! Rey, you know I wouldn't ask if I had anyone else available. Are you still at MIA? Your schedule shows you have a drop right about now."

"I'm just leaving."

"Don't. Mel is stalled on Highway 836. The tow is on its way, but his fare should be arriving where you are any minute. Mind scooping them up?"

"Yes, I mind," Reyna grumbled, but she was already catching the on-ramp to circle back.

"Come on. I'll sign over the full fare, no split . . . pick up and departure all yours, which, by the way, is tomorrow, Sunday, at noon. I see here you're free from eleven thirty to one. All good there."

"That's because I left it open to grab lunch. My schedule is pretty tight tomorrow."

"Yes, I'm looking at it. North Star is reserved solid through the first week of January. Good. Very good, indeed. It pleases me to see your company is thriving. As for today's pickup, the reservation was fully paid in advance at booking. Ace doesn't get many private airline clients. I wouldn't want to get a bad review on Yelp. Say yes to an old friend, why don't ya? And it's the Christmas season. You wouldn't want to find a lump of coal in your shoe, huh?" A hearty chuckle, no doubt his round belly rolling animatedly with it.

Reyna was pulling into the airplane hangar as they spoke. She could never say no to Frank. When she was first starting out in the private car service business and searching for a parking lease, he'd been the only person willing to offer space in his company's garage hangar.

Unlike Ace Car Service, which primarily reserved commercial passengers, North Star was exclusively private flight travel. Two years ago, Reyna poured every dime she had, on top of a small loan, into the purchase of two custom Bentley luxury line vehicles. She was slowly building her client list, having found a niche in the high-dollar private car rental sector. On occasion, Frank sent work her way, and in return, they had an eighty/twenty split in her favor.

"Well, will you do it?"

"Yes, I'll take the fare. No splits. Now, you said *them*. How many are there?" The Bentley seated five comfortably—three on the front-facing bench seat and two in the rear-facing bucket seats. Plush accommodations outweighed practicability with Reyna's usual clientele, who didn't tolerate being sandwiched together, knocking elbows.

"Reservation says three. Name—Julian Swan. They're headed to the Edition hotel downtown. Not a far haul. Check your email. You should have the contract."

"This is your third car stall this month." She grabbed her electronic pad from the passenger seat to confirm receipt but didn't bother reading through the typical jargon. "Your cars are decent, Frank, but they could really use an upgrade."

"Yeah, yeah, I know. I'd love to have my entire line decked out like the Mulliner chariots North Star has, but that would cost me a small fortune. On that note, when you park later, stop by my office. There's something I'd like to discuss with you."

Reyna could never tell by Frank's forever-monotone voice whether he was happy or disturbed about something. The building could be on fire and he'd sound as though a piece of paper was merely singeing hot in a small, metal waste can. "What is it?"

"Just business. We'll talk when I see you. Call if you have any issues with the pickup."

She closed the line. *Just business.* Her lease of Ace's garage space was coming due at the start of the new year. An increase in rental fees—the first uptick in two years—likely would be the topic of discussion. Putting the matter aside for now, she got out and disposed of the empty peppermint schnapps bottles her last passenger had imbibed. *Who drinks straight schnapps?* You could tell a man by the liquor he drank, according to her friend and employee, Danielle. Reyna stuck the used glass with several others in a case kept in the trunk compartment, set to give them a scalding dishwasher spin later. She then placed four clean glasses in the rear cup drawer between the bucket seats. The back cabin of the car was otherwise tidy. Still, with sanitizing wipes from her utility bag and air freshener, she swabbed down the camel-leather seats, followed by a good buffing with a soft microfiber cloth, a quick run of the cordless hand vac, and a couple of mist pumps of Febreze Ocean Breeze. It did its work just as jet wheels met the tarmac with a slight bounce and slowed to a smooth stop.

The ground crew went to work guiding the plane forward. She waited until the airstairs lowered before she slid her sunglasses in place and drove out to meet her clients.

"I THINK THAT'S our ride." Noah jerked a look over his shoulder. "Hawk got us riding in style. Sweet."

His cell phone to his ear, Hawk paused in his note-taking. "Hold on a moment," he told the parties on the conference call, then pressed mute. "Noah, what are you going on about?" He got up, crossed the cabin to his brother, and gave a look out the window. Their cousin, Asher, did the same. They watched as the sleek black vehicle, its high-polished finish reflecting off the late sunrays like smudge-free glass, slowed to a stop a short distance away from the plane.

"Maybe Mason ordered it. You know how he likes to do everything at level ten," Asher remarked as the attendant handed him his luggage.

"I told Mason I'd handle our transportation and hotel," Hawk groused on his way back to his seat, aware their friend tended to overindulge. "Flying us out here on his private plane was enough."

"Dudes, our driver's a woman!" Noah grinned, his face practically plastered to the glass.

Hawk and Asher pivoted back to the window. Decked out in all black, her stylish leather jacket flapping about at the knees, legs slightly spread in her trimmed-fitting slacks, sheen patent leather heels firmly planted, and hands linked at her back, she looked as though she belonged on the set of the *Matrix*. Especially with those opaque wraparound shades. Even the stoic expression on her face gave off a dark, sexy vibe.

She turned her face, chin angled upward toward the setting sun. The way the pink rays illuminated her brown skin stole Hawk's breath.

"Today must be my lucky day." Asher grinned wide and adjusted the tuck of his button-down shirt, then hurriedly ran his fingers through his intentionally mussed, blond-tipped, dark hair.

"There has to be a mix-up with the reservation. I'll work it out later." Feeling somewhat enchanted by the woman as well, Hawk centered himself and returned to his seat to finish up his conference call.

"In the meantime"—Asher was already heading for the exit before the stairs had been properly secured—"the lady awaits."

Noah, wearing his Santa hat, followed him. He paused and looked back. "Hawk? Hey, what happened to no work this weekend?"

Hawk brought his eyes up from the notepad. "I'm right behind you." He continued scribbling, trying to keep up as he listened to his accountant, his architect, and his attorney go over the exorbitant dollars it would take to acquire the vacant business property next door to his custom woodworking retail store. His current square footage was bursting at the seams. But since he was still on the fence about moving forward, and the fact that the flight attendant stood at the exit with his carry-on, her patient demeanor belied by her glance at her watch, he cut the meeting short. Best to get into that *holiday party mode* as Asher had drilled the entire flight out.

On exit, Miami's unexpected chilly breeze struck Hawk's face as he watched Asher's big body crowd the lady, chatting . . . charming her in the way Hawk had witnessed his cousin do with women more times than he cared to count. Yet, aside from the small smile she allowed, their driver maintained that military pose beside the passenger-side rear door, her professional mien in full form.

"I was expecting three, the reservation under the name, Mr. Julian Swan, to be precise."

"Good afternoon," Hawk announced behind them. The men turned, both grinning like ridiculous hyenas.

"Hawk, meet our driver." Noah stepped aside, revealing

the lady in a way Vanna White would turn letters, fanning an exaggerated hand up and down her slender black-clad frame.

Up close, Hawk understood why both behaved like drooling idiots. Wind whipped her long ponytail about like the smooth ebb and flow of ocean waves, slashing across attractive features the color of rich, buttery cashews. Beneath that sleek leather coat, her silk blouse accentuated the perfect swells of her breasts and were neatly tucked, sketching the contour of her waist. The dark shades and scarlet lipstick pulled the whole superhero, don't even think about crossing me, look together.

She was smoking hot, and Asher had gotten to her first. Noah, at six-one and almost as big as Hawk himself, had recently turned twenty-one. The young man had a few years before he could swim in the big-boy pool.

"I see you've met my brother, Noah, and my cousin, Asher."

"I go by Ash." He flashed her his bright white smile.

With her hands still clasped behind her, she inclined her head, not revealing anything in her steadfast visage, and centered on Hawk. "Good afternoon, sir. I'm Rey. Your original driver, Melvin, was detained. I'm afraid you're stuck with me instead."

That was just fine with Hawk as he studied her, trying to see what lay behind those opaque lenses. Her eyes would speak far beyond her words if only he could see them. The soft, breath-catching smile touching her lips when he was slow to respond snapped him swiftly back to the moment at hand.

"It's Julian, but everyone calls me Hawk."

"He means he prefers it," Noah supplied.

Another nod. "I should get you all on your way."

She clicked the car's key fob, springing open the trunk, and they piled in their luggage, then settled in their seats.

Hawk elbowed Ash beside him. "Dibs. Back off," he whispered and tilted his head at the lady circling the front of the car with graceful strides. "You'll have plenty of women at the party to disappoint."

Ash chuckled with an unperturbed look back at him. "Are we in sixth grade? What about you and Francesca? She'll be looking for you tonight," he whispered. "How about we flip a coin?"

"No." Hawk glowered. "And there is no me and Francesca. It was one date," he murmured, then rushed out, "Heads," as his cousin gave a flick of his thumb, sending a quarter a short flight upward and caught it just as their driver—Rey—slid in behind the wheel.

"You might want to tell Francesca that," Ash muttered under his breath amid revealing the winner of the coin toss.

Hawk smirked, triumphant. He took the branded good luck piece and stuck it in his pocket, taunting, "Merry Christmas." Staking claim to their driver in such a way was infantile, barbaric even, but he didn't care. "Fair play, my friend."

"Pardon? I'm sorry, I didn't catch that."

Hawk looked up. Rey removed her sunglasses and gave a look over her shoulder. Her head tilted to see past Noah in that obstructing Santa hat, situated in the bucket seat directly behind her. "Um, I said Merry Christmas." His awkward smile was met with yet another nod.

"Oh. Yes, Merry Christmas to you all. By the way, it's usually an easy twenty-minute ride to downtown, but traffic on a Saturday and with holiday travel, my route is showing major bumper-to-bumper. I'll do my best to detour where I can."

"It's not a problem. I have no doubt we're safe in your capable hands," Ash quickly piped in, wearing his perfected suave grin.

Hawk shot him a narrowed side-eye before turning back to her compelling brown eyes. "There's no hurry." She made a slight adjustment to the rearview mirror. He shifted left ever subtly in his seat. It provided him an optimum angle of her face. And, consequently, her view of him.

"Fellas, how sweet is this?" Noah started opening compartments and pressing buttons. "Heated seats. Dudes!" He held up an assortment of travel-sized liquor bottles. "Cool!"

Rey met Hawk's gaze in the mirror. "You'll find glasses in—"

"Got 'em." Noah pinned two plastic-wrapped shot glasses between his fingers. "Now this is how you start off a holiday party."

"Please help yourself."

The privacy glass began a slow roll upward. Hawk hastily tapped the button on the console, commandeering control, sliding it back down.

Rey looked back. "I thought I'd give you all your privacy. The rear cabin is virtually soundproof with the partition closed and the intercom on mute."

"No need." He reached across and snatched two whiskey

mini bottles from Noah after watching him practically inhale his first drink straight from the head. "One's enough." Again, he met Rey's stare in the mirror. "You'll have to excuse my brother. We don't let him out of his cage often."

"Yeah, he's a new twenty-one," Ash added while already tossing back a second bottle of the dark liquid in a glass himself.

"She said it was okay," Noah grumbled, but did exactly as ordered, relinquishing his empty glass to the drawer compartment. "Hawk, are you going to be a buzzkill the entire trip?"

He shrugged. "It's looking that way."

Slouching with arms crossed at his chest, Noah aimed his scowl at the dark-tinted window. "I should've gone skiing with Tuck and Rob. Fresh snow on the ground in the Berkshires would be better than this."

"North Star Private Car. Reyna Star, Proprietor." Hawk held up a business card he found in the cupholder, completely ignoring his brother's sulk. "My reservation was with Ace Car Service."

"I own North Star. But on occasion, I assist Ace when asked. It's our busiest time of year. All hands on deck."

"A business owner who doesn't just sit behind a desk. Is your company strictly private charter?"

"Yes. So, what brings you all out to Miami for such a quick turnaround? I have you leaving out tomorrow afternoon."

"Ash's and my college roommate is throwing a Christmas party." As Hawk stuck her card into his pocket, he kept eyes on her reflection, appreciating how the dipping sunset seemed to glow in her eyes like pink flames behind warm embers. "Is it Miss or Mrs. Star?"

"Ms." A slight smile twitched back at him.

He confidently returned the gesture, noting how she continued to watch the road, then him, back and forth, provoking a sudden quickening of his pulse. "Ms." He grinned. "I can work with that."

"Hawk, it doesn't mean she's single," Noah cut in as he texted on his phone.

"Noah, shut up," Ash growled low.

That brought the get-to-know-you to an awkward pause. There was a somewhat remote look to her features. Her attention now stayed planted on the cars ahead. Hawk wanted to toss his brother through the window into slow-moving traffic.

"Nice plane," she said after a stretch of silence. "Helps to have it with quick trips, I'm sure."

Hawk blinked. "Pardon?" He was glad their dialogue had resumed.

"Your jet. Is it a Bombardier Challenger or a Citation X? I see plenty of them in my line of work. I've gotten pretty good at identifying what they are. But the nose on the Challenger 604 and Citation X are very similar."

"Oh. Um, I—"

"It's a Citation X, right, Hawk?" Ash delivered a subtle prod with his elbow while rapidly nodding his head.

"Ash, what are you talking about? Hawk doesn't—ow!" Noah groaned and rubbed his leg. "Hawk, man, you nearly cracked my shin."

Hawk cleared his throat. "Ms. Star—"

"Reyna."

Another smile. He couldn't contain his own because hers was so lovely. "Reyna, any holiday plans?"

"Nothing out of the ordinary."

"Maybe I can change that. At least for tonight. How about you join me? We're allowed to bring a guest to the party."

She held his stare with short hesitation. "No, but thanks."

"I know we just met, but I promise, I'm a gentleman. One might even say"—still smiling, he scratched the neatly cropped hairs on his cheek—"straitlaced." He winked and was rewarded by a soft chuckle.

"Sadly, he really is," Ash unceremoniously vouched for him. "He's as narrow-path as a saint."

"Yeah, he's a stickler for following the rules," Noah muttered. "Trust me, you have nothing to worry about with my brother. That's if you don't mind being bored to death." He jerked his legs to the side, laughing. "Hah, you missed me that time."

After sending a quick threatening look at Noah, Hawk leaned forward, putting a strain on the seat belt strap to its full capacity, and observed Reyna's watchful eyes shift between him and the road. "A copy of my driver's license was supplied with the reservation. You can easily look me up." He grinned alongside an innocent flutter of his lashes. "I'm as harmless as a kitten."

"Their sharp claws are hidden." She hadn't taken her focus off the road, yet a touch of a grin remained, surfacing past that all-business exterior. Then she brought her gaze up.

A full-on smile curved her pretty, ruby lips, followed by soft laughter floating and touching Hawk like a thousand wisps of delicate fingertips.

The air in his chest stilled, leaving no room for his heart to momentarily beat. Ash's light nudge with his knee pulled Hawk's steady stare from the rearview mirror to his cousin's twisted smirk. Noah's expression matched Ash's. Only then did Hawk realize he himself had been beaming like a cock-eyed teen.

He sat back, putting himself in check. Though she continued to send short glimpses his way, her silence held through the stretch of highway and side streets, then the car came to a stop in front of the hotel's entrance.

They exited before Reyna could assist with the rear door. Two hotel attendants came forward, one rolling a shiny brass luggage cart, but were waved off.

With their bags in hand, Ash and Noah thanked their driver for the ride.

Reyna's erect spine, her tall heels firmly rooted, hands linked behind her, severed any connection they might have formed, but Hawk dismissed caution. "I'd like to get to know you. When you get off, maybe we could grab a drink. A coffee perhaps?"

"I don't date clients."

"How about making an exception?" He managed to pull another cute smirk from her that seemed to carry with it a long breath of contemplation. "It's one date. We don't have to call it a date. A meet and greet. I like to think I'm good company."

"It seems you would be. But no. Your departure is tomorrow at noon?"

"Yes."

"Is eleven for pickup okay?"

"It is."

Her head turned, then rotated back to him. "I'm afraid I have a call coming in. Enjoy your evening. Happy holidays." She tapped her earpiece and strutted off.

A hand landed and gripped Hawk's shoulder. Startled, he hadn't noticed his cousin's close proximity to him.

"That was painful to witness. You were so close." Ash tsked and shook his head as they strode inside. "You're like Icarus."

They'd been best friends from the cradle, born within days of each other. More like brothers than cousins. But they were gravely competitive in all things. Both had their share of beautiful women. Except, unlike his cousin, Hawk had grown tired of the chase and wanted to settle down.

He gave Ash a side look, knowing better than to encourage him, and yet . . . "I'm sure you're eager to share how that is."

"It's simple. You flew too close to the sun . . . or in this case, 'Star.'" Ash fell into robust laughter, and Noah joined in as they situated themselves in the long check-in line. "My point," Ash added, sobering. "Reyna Star has access to the rich and famous. Hawk, my man, you're not in her lane. Neither am I for that matter, but what do they say? 'Shoot for the moon, and if you miss, at least you'll be among the stars . . . Star.'" Ash laughed more at his own ridiculous wit.

"Yeah, bro," Noah chimed in. "You saw her. She's a sophisticated lady, used to the finer things in life. You . . . well, you're an ogre." He jerked out of the way of the large, open palm aimed at the back of his head.

"But, no fear, my friend. Reyna Star was a mere blip on your timeline," Ash continued.

Hawk gave a nod. "Already forgotten." If only that were true. There was something about her that pulled at his senses. He knew he'd shot high with Reyna and indeed got burned down to the bone. As he licked his wound, he tried to steer himself back to the objective for being there. "We're here to have a good time."

"We're here to indulge in the opposite sex," Ash proclaimed.

"That we are." Hawk agreed. "And when it comes to an ample supply of beautiful women, our buddy, Mason, never disappoints. There is sure to be plenty at the party tonight for—"

"Excuse me?"

Hawk swung around to the sultry lilt that had easily imprinted on his brain. His chest constricted, air trapping in his airway. It felt almost as though he'd conjured her from a dream to reality.

"Reyna."

Her stare was sharp and steady, shifting from him to Ash, over to Noah, then pressed upon Hawk. "Didn't mean to interrupt. One of you left your phone in my car. I always double-check the cabin just in case."

Hawk took the device he knew to be his. "Thank you."

She inclined her head, her eyes unwavering, her stare about as frigid as her voice was gentle. "Enjoy your party. Sounds like it will be a memorable one."

An awkward shared silence hung for a moment. "If I might put in context—" he started.

"Gentlemen, have a good evening."

"How much of that do you think she heard?" Ash asked as she strode off, aiming her unhurried steps toward the exit.

Hawk clenched his molars, quite certain she'd gotten an earful.

*Just great.*

# *Chapter Two*

MEN LIKE SWAN were all the same. It never took them long to show their true colors.

Reyna wanted to kick herself. She felt foolish to even believe Swan was the decent sort. She'd encountered many like him so often in her line of work. The wealthy ones were the worse, thinking every woman was available to them. *Well, not this one.* It was the very reason North Star functioned with a steadfast rule—never get involved romantically with clients. She'd come close to breaking the very creed she'd implemented. *Damn him for that.*

Her irritation, mainly with herself for the near lapse in judgment, was still turned up as she pulled into Ace's garage hangar to the sound of Nsync's spin on "All I Want Is You This Christmas" echoing into the exposed steel rafters. Bright-white twinkling tube lights were wrapped around the casings of the high industrial windows. Thick ropes of silver garland adorned the otherwise dull utility-gray support beams. Reyna squinted at the tall, overly decorated artificial Christmas tree erected in the corner. There were so many lights twined within the branches, it was difficult to stare directly at it for fear of damaging her corneas. Though the combination of it all was near blinding, the holiday décor was just what she needed to return the festive warmth to her veins.

It was their busiest time of year, so no surprise the hangar was empty, except for the lone Rolls Royce jacked up off the floor with its hood raised. The synchronized clanking coming from Rico, stretched out beneath it, working his tools, clashed with the holiday harmony.

Reyna went to the vending machine and bought a bag of chips and a soda.

"Rico, you think you used enough lights?" she teased while opening the bag on her amble over to him.

He rolled from underneath the car and got up, looking around at his handiwork. "Maeve said to do it up right." The rag he took from the back pocket of his oil-stained jeans and used to wipe his hands before accepting his snack was well past the date to discard for good. "What do you think?" he asked, while munching on the wad of chips he'd stuffed into his mouth. "Looks good, right?"

"For one thing, I'm sure astronauts can spot that tree from space." Reyna laughed, and he joined her. "How many strings of lights did you use?"

"Twelve." He rocked proudly on his heels, admiring his décor.

Reyna's eyes widened, then squinted again. She drew her focus away from the brilliance of the tree, which appeared to lean heavily to the right, and angled her chin at the car under repair. "How bad is it?"

"Nothing I can't fix. I will say it's high time Frank put this one out of its misery. The patchwork he has me doing is only good until something else breaks." Rico turned up the chip bag, caught the bottom crumbs, then finished off the drink before giving a nod in the direction of Reyna's vehicle. The radiance of its glossy black surface glimmered in the holiday spectrum of lights. "That right there is where it's at. Frank needs to up his game around here."

"No, he doesn't. I'll have competition. Frank is fine in his lane. Pun intended," Reyna countered with a grin.

"Rey, I know you have an all-women driving crew vibe going in your company, but I don't mind being like, you know, the token male." A wide white smile set off his tan-brown complexion. "Especially if I get to drive one of those."

North Star had a total of three vehicles, which included the one on order. If business continued upward, a fourth custom Bentley would be in the works by this time next year. Reyna would need another driver when car number three rolled in next spring, one who would maintain the stellar service her premier clientele had come to expect, and her drivers adhered to. A reputation North Star had built in a short span of two years.

"What about the work you do for Ace? And I don't mean the overabundant use of Christmas light decorations," she joked, then set a stern tone. "Rico, I don't want a conflict with Frank. I won't poach you from him."

"I'm freelance, remember? Frank calls me in when he needs me to fix one of the cars or help around the garage. Beyond that, my time's my own."

"You could drive for Frank."

"I already asked. He said he's not taking on any new drivers."

"My new vehicle won't be ready for another three to four

months."

"I can wait." He didn't bat a lash.

It'd been Reyna's objective to only hire women. But, aside from the obvious, Rico checked all the boxes she expected in her staff. "I'll think about it."

"That's all I can ask for. I'll have my black suit, shirt, and tie on the ready, just in case." He grinned.

Their heads turned to the Bentley pulling into the garage and parked. The driver's side door opened.

"Speaking of worth the wait." His wide smile gleaming about as bright as that tree, Rico stood up straight, chest out, and hastily tucked his grease-stained T-shirt into the waistband of his overworked denims. "What's up, Danielle? You're looking nice this evening. If you're in for the night, I'll give your car a wash."

"Go ahead." Danielle got out and tossed Rico the key fob. Red, green, and gold dangling ornament earrings offered a hint of color to the black hip-hugging dress beneath her black leather jacket as she strutted over, tall and measured in her spiked heels. Her smooth, brown complexion was glammed up by a hint of rosy blush, and her signature holiday red lipstick. "What the…?" She stopped short and brought her hand up to block the blinding light beaming from the corner. "Geez. That has to be a fire hazard."

Reyna pointed at Rico.

"What are you trying to do, catch a satellite signal?"

"I'll unplug it." Rico jogged off.

"Yes, do that." Danielle turned to Reyna. "I thought you were off this evening."

"Frank needed a pickup. Another car stalled." Reyna

aimed a thumb at the Rolls behind her. "I'm headed home after I chat with him. You should come by. I'll be trimming my Christmas tree. With Lily away, I've been slow in getting the place decorated. It's not as much fun without her."

"She's happy to spend the holiday with Daddy for sure."

"Thrilled. She's thirteen, but still leaps into his arms whenever she sees him." Reyna grinned, remembering how excited her baby was when her father arrived, eager to spend her entire winter break with him. There was a smidgen of envy that Lily labeled him the fun parent. "He spoils her rotten."

"As he and all dads should with their little girls."

They moved out of Rico's way as he situated himself back underneath the car.

"Say you'll come." Reyna headed toward the door that led to the back offices, propping the heavy steel open with the pointed toe of her stiletto. "It'll be fun. I'll pick up a charcuterie tray from Peppers."

Danielle brushed her ponytail back over her shoulder, her bottle-dyed chestnut strands catching on the colorful, round ornaments swaying at her lobe. "Now you're speaking my language." She continued her stroll out of the hangar, aiming her heels in the direction of her red Camaro parked outside, a short distance away.

"So you'll come?" Reyna hollered over the rev of Danielle's V8 engine.

"You mentioned food. I'll be there," came the yell out the window as Danielle punched the gas pedal and sped away.

"Evening, Maeve," Reyna greeted on her way past the

reservationist's office. She paused and pivoted, returning to where the elderly woman stood on a small wobbly stool, generous hips swaying somewhat off-balance as she tried to tape Christmas lights along the high windowsill above her shelf. Reyna rushed in. "You shouldn't be up there." She took Maeve's hand and guided her carefully from her unstable perch. "Have Rico do that."

Puffing in and out and straightening her blouse, Maeve regulated her breathing before she was able to reply. "I can do it." Her words were still slightly choppy. "I love decorating for the holidays." She pulled a tangled bundle of multicolored lights from the small box on the desk. "Did you see the wonderful job Rico did in the garage?"

"It was hard to miss." Reyna chuckled.

"By tomorrow, this entire place will be a merry wonderland." Her jolly smile brightened her flushed face, which gleamed almost as luminous as those twinkling lights above her head. "Have you done any decorating yet?"

"After I chat with Frank, I'm headed home to get started."

"I wondered why he was still here past five."

"He's waiting for me. I better go."

At the end of the hall, Reyna rapped on the closed door before opening it. "Evening, Frank." His gaze rose above his bifocals, which rested on the bridge of his nose, and his brow puckered, exaggerating the natural grooves in his weathered pink skin.

"These damn devices are a blessing and a curse, I tell you. My son sent new pictures of my granddaughter's first visit with Santa. I saved the pictures, but I'm not able to find them."

"Let me try." Reyna took the cell phone and made a few taps. "Here you go. You somehow moved them to your photo delete folder."

His head tilted, brow raised. "There's a delete folder? Not sure how I managed to do that. Look." He held out the phone. "Isn't she about the prettiest little angel you've ever seen?" A warm smile slid all the way up into the outer crinkles of his cheerful blue eyes. "She turned eight weeks old yesterday."

"She's adorable." Lily at that age felt so long ago now. At only sixteen and with a newborn to care for, Reyna had been scared out of her mind.

"Thanks for helping out with the fare. I didn't get a call, so I assume Mr. Swan took no issue with the sudden change in his reservation from Ace to North Star?"

Julian Swan—Hawk. *Or more like Hulk.* He was easy on the eyes. Dark, wavy hair just about touched his bulky shoulders. His mustache-and-beard combo neatly tapered close. His pupils a sea storm of pale gray. A navy-blue crewneck sweater stretched taut over a muscular chest, thick biceps, and flat abs—

Reyna blinked, drawn back to the here and now by the call of her name. "Sorry, what was that?"

"I asked if there were any issues with the client."

"Right. No." Swan should be the last person occupying space in her head. "What did you want to talk about?" She took a seat in the chair before the desk, its low profile back making it difficult to relax. Purpose by design—Frank's way of getting you in and out of his office. No time to get comfortable. His drivers understood that.

"I'm going to retire."

"Yes, I know." He'd been saying that since the day they met. Reyna helped herself to a peppermint from the filled bowl on the desk, working the wrapper free. "You and Ethel are going to grab your tackle boxes, set your fishing lines, and put your feet up." She popped the candy into her mouth while settling in to listen to him chat about the best fishing spots he and his wife frequented. He'd only returned to work a few days ago following a two-week, deep-sea sailfish excursion. Apparently, such excursions were a thing.

"The fish must have really been biting for you and Ethel, if it's got you talking about retiring again."

Frank leaned forward, linking his sun-spotted hands atop the desk. The grave expression his eyes took on made Reyna tense up. "You're serious?"

"Ethel had a biopsy done on her left breast. It was positive—" At Reyna's gasp, he brought up a hand. "She's okay now. They did surgery and believe they got it all. But the scare of what might have been . . ." A potent, visible fear took the reins through his short pause. "As for Ace, it's all settled. Well, not completely, but the sale is in the works."

His monotone voice contrasted with the seriousness in his direct stare. Reyna leaned forward and rested a hand atop his. "It's good Ethel is doing okay. But how are you? It must have been difficult."

"Yes. The entire situation made us realize it is time for me to hang up my hat and relax these old bones. Ethel and I want to do some traveling, spend time with our first grandbaby."

"You weren't on a fishing trip those two weeks you were away, were you?"

"I was seeing to Ethel."

He didn't say more, and Reyna didn't need him to. Frank cherished his wife. The mere thought of losing her undoubtedly must have kept him in a constant state of worry.

"I've been in talks with Cecil over at Elite Car. If I'm able to iron out the particulars, it'll be a done deal by year's end."

Reyna's eyes widened. "That soon! And my lease with Ace? I renew in January."

"That falls into the *particulars* part I've been trying to work out. Cecil isn't interested in renewing North Star's lease. They are strictly commercial and don't see a benefit in having a partnership with a private service."

Reyna slowly sat back. January would start her third year of business, and North Star had finally turned a financial corner. The hard work and sacrifices were beginning to pay off. It had been close to impossible to find affordable lease space until she met Frank. Owners tried to gouge her, didn't have available square footage, or, like Elite Car, simply didn't wish to do business. Many unreasonably saw her as competition. Cecil White, owner of Elite, certainly did—that and the fact that she'd bruised his ego with the words *not interested* in going out with him.

North Star was growing, yes, but with current overhead and the need to bring on an additional driver, the amount it would cost Reyna to have her own garage hangar simply wasn't in the budget for at least another year or so.

"Rey, I'd appreciate it if you kept this between us. I don't want to upturn the staff. It's the holidays, the worse time to spring this on everyone. Change in ownership brings uncertainty."

Reyna read his genuine concern. He'd been fair and kind to her these past years. She came to her feet on a heavy sigh. "I'm going to head home."

"Rey, I'm really sorry. But I must do this, you understand."

At the door, she turned, offering a small smile to soothe his glum gaze. "You have nothing to be sorry about. Give Ethel a hug for me."

# Chapter Three

"THIS WAS FUN. So glad you came, and thanks for helping me trim the tree." Reyna walked with Danielle to the door.

"Who knew paper-mache was so versatile? Girl, for a moment there, I thought I might have to steal decorations from that supernova I came upon earlier tonight. What was Rico thinking?" Danielle laughed.

Reyna joined her. "The light coming off the tree practically pulsed. You risked losing vision to look at the poor thing straight on." They laughed more. A lover of all things Christmas, her friend had been surprised and disappointed when she'd discovered Reyna's ornaments were made from recycled paper and corrugated cardboard. It was a way of making Christmas less about shiny things and more about its true meaning. Not to mention, Lily's dad always went overboard. She received enough bright and shiny gifts.

"But seriously, your tree turned out beautifully." Danielle pulled out her phone and snapped a picture of the twinkling evergreen across the room.

"Yes, Lily and I really enjoy making the ornaments. She's been gone hardly two days, and I miss my baby already."

"Of course you do." A comforting hand touched Reyna's

shoulder with a light pressure. "That matter with the hangar—you'll figure it out. You always do. Just know I'm with you all the way." They hugged close. "I better get going. Sending you positive energy, girlfriend. And don't forget your Christmas list," Danielle called on her way down the walkway.

"Sure." Reyna smirked and closed the door. Like she really believed in asking Santa for the perfect man was going to work. As for the hangar dilemma, a free spirit, Dani didn't let much get under her skin. But the confidence boost, and the fact that her friend wouldn't desert her, lifted a smidgen of weight from Reyna's weary shoulders. She clung to that nugget of solace as she tidied the kitchen in between wide yawns, exhaustion setting in.

The doorbell rang. An immediate second chime followed by a trail of knocks. Had Dani returned? Reyna looked around to see if any belongings had been left behind.

"I'm coming," she yelled on her jog to the door and pulled it open as the bell rang yet again. The sight of her ex-husband, Blake, and Lily standing there sent a swift surge of energizing oxygen to her brain. "Wh—?"

Features twisted in an all-too-familiar scowl, Lily marched inside and went straight to her room. The bedroom door met the frame with a resounding *boom*. Reyna swung her head back to Blake, who had a secure grip on the handle of Lily's hot-pink floral hard suitcase. The strap of the matching duffel bag was anchored on his thickly muscled shoulder.

"What's going on?" Reyna widened the door to let him in. He set down Lily's luggage, then gave Reyna a kiss on the cheek. Over the years, they had gotten back to a comfortable place of genuine friendship. But his inability to communicate when he knew the outcome would result in her blowing up was something he had yet to improve upon. "You two are supposed to be in Mexico by way of your home in Texas. You show up at my door, no call or text, and you've put our daughter back on a plane in less than forty-eight hours of picking her up."

"You make it sound as though I sent her home alone." He followed Reyna into the kitchen. "Trust me, she would've preferred it. Wouldn't speak to me the entire trip." Blake eyed the charcuterie tray and empty wineglasses on the counter. "Did I interrupt something?"

Reyna stuck the food in the fridge and the glasses in the dishwasher, then folded her arms at her chest on a turn to face him. "Blake, what's all this about?"

"I was going to call but—"

"But instead, you decided no communication was best to avoid an argument until you absolutely can't avoid one."

He jerked a look in the direction of the hallway and then back to Reyna, questioning surprise lifting his hazel eyes. "Is there . . . are you . . . is someone here?" He kept an even tone, maintaining their rule to never argue within earshot of their daughter.

"What?" Reyna frowned, then quickly realized the tunnel he was headed down. "No. Danielle left not too long ago. We decorated the Christmas tree."

With a look at the twinkling lights over in the living room, the tension left his shoulders.

"But I could've been with someone." Not hardly. She

couldn't recall the last time a man shared her bed. "You're not supposed to be here."

They'd made a pact to never bring a man or a woman around Lily until there was a strong indication the relationship was becoming serious and to let the other know first. Since their divorce ten years ago, neither had yet done so. "Why are you back?"

Blake rested against the counter, strong arms crossing his wide chest. He kept his six-three bulky frame in top shape. His black hair, once worn in a curly, stylishly untamed Afro or kept neatly braided beneath a bandana, he now trimmed close. His tapered beard was replaced by smooth-shaven, tan-brown skin. The new look suited him and matured his distinguish look of youthfulness. "I've been called to Alaska. There's a pipeline malfunction. I'm flying out straight from here to meet up with my team there."

A chemical engineer, if Blake was ever called in to help fix a problem, it meant the situation was bordering on critical. But Lily came first. "You'll just have to tell them you can't go. They can find someone else."

"If I could get out of it, you know I would."

Yes, Reyna knew it. Blake was a terrific father. But there had been some shortfalls along the way to get there. First loves, they'd gotten married, ready to conquer the world together as young parents—Reyna, barely sixteen, and Blake, months shy of eighteen. Blake's parents, Mr. and Mrs. Star, were old-school, upstanding Catholics, and not wanting their grandchild born out of wedlock, they were all for it. So much so, they insisted Reyna and Blake live with them. Their little family would start out on stable footing, according to Mr.

and Mrs. Star.

Reyna's parents saw her predicament as a blessing. A new flower to blossom upon the earth. Hence, Reyna's mother had given Lily her name.

Modern-day nomads, Reyna had grown up living out of an RV, homeschooled as they moved from state to state. *The only way to really appreciate the world is to explore it unencumbered,* her parents often said. Those years spent with Mom and Dad highlighting a random point on the map to show where they were headed next—the excitement, the adventure—were the happiest of moments.

But then Lily was born. A child needed structure.

"Blake, Lily's been looking forward to spending her winter break with you. The trip to Mexico, waterskiing, deep-sea diving, hiking . . . it's all she's been talking about."

"I hate that I won't get to enjoy the holiday with my baby girl. I also hate that I live so far away from her. You could move back to Austin. Then this wouldn't be an issue. I could see her every day."

"So, I'm the one who must compromise . . . again?" Reyna said low. Tightly. "You forget how that turned out for me the last time. You got to revel in your fraternity parties, doing who knows what, and I was home trying to take online classes with a screaming infant in my arms." An unfair statement on an old, reconciled argument, but the point of contention always triggered bad memories.

Blake's parents had urged their son not to turn down his college acceptance to Northwestern University. Reyna had agreed. It'd been decided he would finish college first and then she would do the same. Young and naive, they hadn't expected within those four years they'd grow to want different things.

"You forget, my parents offered you the opportunity to go to school while they took care of Lily," he remarked.

"You choose to forget, they wanted to *take* Lily. I knew it, and you did too." It was why Reyna left the Stars' home and tried to make it on her own. "And move back to Texas? Should I simply toss away my business while I'm at it?"

"Of course not. I only meant—"

Both turned at the squeak of the bedroom door. Lily entered the living room and plopped down on the sofa, drawing her legs up to her chest, her thumbs working the pad of her cell phone. She'd changed out of her hoodie and jeans into cotton pjs—a simple pink, long-sleeved T-shirt and pastel-printed pants. Sandy-brown curls formed an unruly mass at the crown of her head. Eyes the color of her father's glanced toward the kitchen, and neither of her parents escaped her heated look of annoyance before she returned her attention to her social media. Blake crossed the distance and sat on the coffee table in front of her.

"Sweet pea, don't be upset. I'm really sorry that I have to cancel our fun." He tried to tickle her bare feet, but she jerked them away.

Lily was stubborn. Like father, like daughter.

Reyna grabbed her phone from the kitchen counter and went to her bedroom, allowing Blake space to smooth things over. She could see he had a long road ahead of him.

Should she put her phone beneath her pillow, as, in a moment of silliness, she and Dani had sworn it would convince Santa to grant their dating wish? Nah. If conjuring a good, decent man were that easy, women would have St. Nick on speed dial. Besides, having done the baby-, marriage-, and divorce business already, the powers that be likely were exhausted with her. On that dismal truth, she placed the device on the nightstand, then crossed to the bathroom, stripped, and stepped into the shower, doing her best to wash the weight of the day away. But her mind was in overdrive. Where would she find parking space? There were locations over on the south side. Rent was dirt cheap.

The Bentleys wouldn't last a night.

*Ugh.*

Skin patted dry and well moisturize, she donned her robe atop a simple white tank top and shorts pajamas, then padded out of the room and down the hall, but slowed, picking up Blake and Lily's conversation. She turned around and started toward her bedroom to give them privacy, then pivoted. Teeth clenched. Then twirled back again. It was wrong to listen in on daddy-daughter time, but she found herself pinning her body against the wall, ears perked.

"I promise to make it up to you," Blake said. "You've wanted your own ATV. What if I told you that's what I got you for Christmas?"

Reyna bit the inside of her jaw to prevent from storming in there to protest such a purchase, already picturing broken bones. Blake was an adventurer and was turning his daughter into his mirror image.

"Really!" Excitement easily cracked Lily's upset. "Daddy, why not tell your job you're on vacation?"

"I can't, sweet pea. I'm part of a team. If I don't go and help, oil could spill into the ocean. You want to be a marine biologist. Science, chemistry—they're your area of focus at school, right? You know what would happen if the pipes burst?"

"It would kill sea life and also harm the ecosystem."

"That's right. I must go to make certain that doesn't happen. Look on the bright side—you'll get to hang out with your mom this holiday."

A resounding huff. "The only friend I have at my new school is gone for the holidays. Everyone will have stories to share about all the fun they had over winter break. I'll be stuck here. All Mom does is work." Another hard huff. "She's no fun, not like you. She would've never let me zip-line over that creek. And when my belt snapped—"

"I had you, along with the backup safety harness. You weren't going anywhere."

"I know. I wasn't scared. But Mom would've freaked out. 'Lily, that's it! Never again!'" she mocked in a stern voice that Reyna understood to be her own.

"Don't be so tough on your mother. Everything she does is with your safety and well-being in mind. She only wants what's best for you."

Backup safety harness or not, a cold streak of fear rushed down Reyna's spine, chasing the gnaw of guilt. *All Mom does is work. She's no fun, not like you.* When had she lost touch with Lily? Also, when had Reyna become such a stick in the mud? There was a time she was as adventurous as Blake. Well, maybe not as daring. But she knew how to have fun. Relax. Throw caution aside. In what ways? Reyna mulled over the thought. If the answer was that much of a struggle, her child might be right. But then it came to her.

It was the worst possible time to take off work. But given the news Frank had sprung on her, she needed to think on what to do next. A short break might be mentally beneficial to clear her head and come up with a plan.

The money she'd saved in the vacation fund for next year's family spring break trip to Yellowstone could go toward a winter getaway instead. Sure, Mom and Dad would be disappointed at not getting to see their granddaughter, but they would treat it pretty much how they did everything that fell short—the stars simply didn't align.

Reyna padded lightly back to her bedroom and eased the door shut. She dialed Frank. The line connected surprisingly after only a short ring.

"Rey, how goes it this late hour?"

She knew he was a night owl like her, but still. "I hope I didn't disturb Ethel."

"Not at all. I'm enjoying my pipe out on the porch. She never lets me smoke in the house. What is it? I know what I told you this evening was a hefty pill to swallow."

"It was, but it's not why I'm calling. Has anyone reserved the Rolls?"

"No, unfortunately. Ace don't often draw that level of clientele. It was a waste when I bought the car at auction."

"Would you be opposed to me using it? I'd split the profits."

"Go ahead. Rico has it running again. Only for it to sit in the garage, gathering dust. And no need for any split. Consider it my Christmas gift to you. Hold a moment. I'm on the phone," he said. "I better go see to Ethel. Have a good night."

"You too." Reyna closed the line and dialed Rico. With the vehicle sitting unused, money was flowing down the drain. Why hadn't she thought of it before?

"Rey, what's up?" he answered on hardly a ring, more of a chirp.

"Evening, Rico. Do you have a minute?"

"Sure."

"Would you be interested in driving for North Star temporarily? Through the holiday rush."

"Absolutely! You know I've wanted—"

"You'll drive the Rolls Royce." Reyna could almost hear the air in his balloon of excitement deflating.

"Ace's car?"

"Frank's letting me use it since it's unreserved. I'm taking a trip and will be driving the Bentley."

"Oh. Okay. Yes, I can do that." More upbeat. "I got you. You can count on me."

"Great." That was what Reyna wanted to hear. "I'll be in touch with the details."

"Cool."

Finally, she called Danielle.

"Rey, good timing. I'm walking in the door. Traffic was outrageous."

"I know you're exhausted. We can talk in the morning."

"No, I'm fine. What is it?"

"I need a big favor."

"Name it."

Reyna moved to the nightstand and scrolled on her electronic pad. "Would you mind picking up my eleven o'clock tomorrow? The schedule has you on break at that time.

Their flight out of MIA is at noon. I know it's short notice. Lily's home. I need to see to her."

"No problem, but I thought Lily wasn't returning until after New Year's."

"Short explanation—Blake was called in to work. I'll send you the client's info. Pickup is downtown."

"On it."

"Thanks."

She cut the call and left the room, closing the door behind her with a deliberate thud. With heavy footfalls to make her presence known, she went into the living room. Lily sat curled up against her father's shoulder, the pair laughing with their heads hovering over her cell phone. Both looked up.

"Mom, you have to see this video. There's a dog who can dribble."

Reyna took a seat on the coffee table in front of them and gave a look. "Pretty cool. He's actually good." She chuckled and sat back. "How would you like to take a trip this holiday? Maybe somewhere snowy? We could go skiing."

Lily's eyes lit bright. Then her head took on a quizzical tilt. "Really? You're not going to work?"

"Nope." Reyna shook her head. "I've already made arrangements."

"I've never skied before. I don't know how."

"Neither do I." Reyna grinned. "We can learn together. You know how to surf. Can't be any harder than that, right?"

"So, like an actual trip outside of the state of Florida?" Lily asked, still looking unconvinced. "Where would we go?"

That part she hadn't worked out. The level of skepticism

was not lost on Reyna as her mind shuffled through ideas, not sure exactly where they'd go that would be impressive enough. But then, she remembered something her client, Noah Swan, said. "The Berkshires. I hear the slopes are already covered. We'll make it a road trip. I'll have it all planned. Tomorrow, shopping for warmer clothes, and Monday at dawn, we'll head out."

"That sounds pretty cool to me," Blake said with an encouraging look at Lily.

"Now off to bed," Reyna told her daughter, happy to see the glowing smile plumping her cheeks.

"Awesome!" Lily jumped up and flung her arms around Reyna's neck, hugging tight before zipping off to her room.

Smiling, Reyna took a seat on the sofa and folded her arms at her chest, feeling triumphant. "See, I can plan fun things too."

"You heard that, huh?" Blake regarded her. "She didn't mean it. Lily was only sulking. She knows you work hard."

"No, I do need to spend more time with her. She's growing up so fast. Soon there will be boys—"

"Never!" Blake scowled. "I have a license to carry."

Reyna laughed. "My point is, I want to bond with my daughter. What better way than a holiday road trip?"

"How about you take the word 'plan' out of your plans? Try winging it as you go," he suggested with a smirk.

"I am. Although, if you recall, the last time I threw caution to the wind, nine months later, Lily was born." She hadn't been reckless since.

Blake hissed low, scratching his chin, grinning. "You have a point."

They both chuckled.

But perhaps Reyna had also wound herself a bit too tightly. It was time to loosen up a little.

# Chapter Four

Will Danielle remember to update the reservation availability dates on the website? Did Rico meet his pickup on time? Did he remember to tidy the rear cabin and restock the drawers with libations and clean glasses after every client vacated? Both tasks were essential. North Star hadn't achieved its five-star stellar-service reputation by slacking off on the minutia. One screwup could demolish it. Word of mouth was everything.

"Mom, how much farther?"

Her mind full of myriad thoughts, Reyna filled the gas tank and finished up at the pump. She turned to see Lily poking her head out of the passenger-side window, a strawberry-flavored Twizzler dangling between her lips. Her baby wore a full-face grin; she'd been in good spirits the entire drive.

When Lily wasn't stretched out in the comfort of the rear cabin, bingeing on the mountain of snacks they'd brought along, they sang songs, became very competitive at license-plate "I spy," and enjoyed a host of other road games. They were having a good time. That alone made the trip worth it. The fullness felt in Reyna's chest matched Lily's mood. Certainly, she'd needed this excursion just as much.

"Mom?"

Reyna brought her sunglasses up on her head and gave a look at her watch. "About an hour to go. We should arrive a little after five." She accepted the wet wipes Lily held out the window, then got back in the car and pressed her hands against the warmth of the air vent. A mix of sun and low clouds promised a biting evening chill. With every mile north, the temperature seemed to drop a degree. "That's, of course, if there are no traffic issues."

Back on the highway, while Lily napped, Reyna weighed if a direct phone call to Cecil White at Elite Car would help to sway him on brokering a lease with North Star? Perhaps she'd accept his offer to dinner. Could she stomach it? Only if she wanted to inhale the nauseating scent of chewing tobacco all evening while trying to avoid his consistently moist wandering hands. The mere idea of spending an evening with Cecil brought about an acute, hard swallow to combat the bile.

About an hour later, Lily stirred and came out of her slouch against the door just as the welcome arch for Haven Creek greeted them up ahead.

"There's snow!" Lily perked up, head snapping toward the passenger window to see blankets of pillowy white fluff covering the vast, hilly landscape. Off in the distance, snowy treetops gleamed from the angle of the setting sun, creating a wintery portrait.

*Beautiful.*

Reyna crossed a short wooden bridge over an icy lake, then drove a small stretch of road and followed the navigation that took her onto Main Street. Or, as the bright red sign below it read, Reindeer Lane. As a matter of fact, she noticed as they coasted along the wall of traffic, most of the signs had festive alternate identifiers, names like Jack Frost Avenue and Candy Cane Boulevard. She chuckled. *Who put in that laborious effort?*

Only a dusting of white powder coated the red-brick sidewalks and merchants' storefronts, where people bustled to and fro with shopping bags aplenty.

"Who are you waving at?" Reyna asked Lily, whose hand fanned back and forth past the window.

"Her." Lily pointed. "That family with the little girl waved at me." She shrugged. "Seemed rude not to do it too. What's with all the mistletoe?"

Reyna looked around. Enthralled by the twinkling white lights strung overhead, she'd dismissed the thick clusters of greenery that hung above every storefront entrance. The leafy sprigs were also on street signs and wrapped around light poles—literally everywhere.

"Mom, look . . . there's a Mistletoe Ball on Christmas Eve." Lily directed Reyna's attention to the large banner arcing from one side of the street to the other up ahead. It depicted a man pressing his lips against a smiling woman's rosy cheek, who returned a mischievous side-eye back at him. Both wore Santa hats.

"Hmm, that's a new one. Does everyone shell out kisses?" Reyna puckered up, smacking her lips. It drew a snicker from Lily. Though making light of it, she was truly curious what went on at such a gala. If an individual went solo, what then? Was it a free for all kiss fests?

"Can we go?" Lily eyed her eagerly. "Sounds cool to me."

"Let me find out more about it." Reyna wasn't making any promises without investigating first. Throwing caution to the wind didn't mean subjecting her and Lily to some sort of wild smooching debauchery.

Traffic broke. They made their way to Harbor Mist Inn, where she'd reserved their stay, still counting her luck to have landed a room after nearly an hour of searching within a five-mile radius of the area.

She parked alongside a row of other vehicles right in front.

"We're not staying at a hotel?" Lily got out and looked up at the white-brick, three-story Victorian dwelling, scrunching her nose.

Reyna retrieved their luggage from the trunk. "Here." She handed Lily her bags. "It'll be fine. You'll see."

They took the six steps up to a gloriously wide wraparound porch. Both zeroed in on the clump of greenery hanging above the entry door and chuckled.

"When in Rome." Smiling, Reyna gave Lily a kiss on the cheek. "Now your turn." She angled her face and twitched her lips. "Come on."

"Mom, you're so being extra right now." Lily rolled her eyes, but grinned and delivered a peck.

"See, that didn't kill you." Reyna got a light, playful shove.

They entered the establishment to a stream of activity. People congregated in the reception area, not a vacant sofa or chair available. On the far side of the room, an ornately carved, high-gloss wooden mantel went all the way up the wall to the ceiling, a good twenty feet at least. The fire burning within warmed the rather spacious square footage. To the right, positioned within a curved window wall, stood a well-decorated Christmas tree with ornaments that complemented the ivory-leather furnishings and teal accent pieces throughout the space.

"Isn't it lovely?"

Reyna and Lily spun to the smiling woman standing but a foot behind them, her cornflower-blue eyes bright and cheerful, her Santa hat slightly tilted atop her blond head.

"I beg your pardon?"

Ms. St. Nick's teal turtleneck and cream-colored slim trousers matched the room's decor. "You were admiring the mantel, weren't you? Everyone who walks through that door for the first time does the same. A local merchant made it. Took him a while, the perfectionist he is. It was carved from reclaimed oak. It turned out beautifully." She extended her hand. "I'm Geraldine, the manager, but everyone calls me Geri."

"I'm Reyna Star, and this is my daughter, Lily. We're checking in."

"Yes, from Florida. We spoke on the phone. Welcome."

"I was relieved you had a room available. I was beginning to worry I wouldn't find one."

"That's only because the couple who reserved it canceled. We were fully booked by September. My dear, you called at the right time. I'd say it was meant to be." She smiled warmly, then shifted her gaze. "Lily, a good friend of mine has a daughter about your age. I look after her while her mother's working. She—" They turned their heads at the entry door opening. A horde of boisterous teens filed in, each talking louder than the next. All carried ice skates draped over their shoulders by the tied shoestrings. "There she is now. Kate?" Geri called. The girl removed her red winter knit hat, her rich auburn hair falling in long waves. She broke away from the group and came over. "I want you to meet Ms. Reyna Star and her daughter, Lily. They've just arrived and will be staying here."

"Hi." Kate offered a smile, blue eyes as amiable as Geri's.

"Hi." Lily returned the same.

"Now, let's get you your room. You'll want to get settled before the ice sculpture unveiling kicks off." Geri circled the counter.

Reyna turned away from the girls, who fell into an easy chat. "The what?"

"Aunt Geri, we're gonna hang out in the game room." Kate beckoned Lily to follow her.

Lily looked eagerly at Reyna. "Mom?"

"It's just through those double doors." Geri pointed where the other teens were already trotting toward.

Reyna's head rotated from one to the other, trying to keep up. "Uh, okay. Sure."

"She'll be fine. Kate's a good girl. She keeps that rowdy bunch of hers under control." Geri studied her computer screen. "As I mentioned when you phoned, the room has only one king-sized bed. That side of the inn was an add-on last year. It's one of the larger suites, with a parlor that has a pullout sofa bed. It also faces east and gets the most beautiful sunrises."

"One bed is fine. What was that you said about an ice sculpture unveiling?"

"Yes, Ring of Ice. It's the first event of many that will take place throughout the month leading to the Mistletoe Ball. You'll find more information in here." Geri slid over a trifold brochure. "I'll have Dicky bring up your luggage when he returns from an errand." After a few clicks on the keyboard, she handed Reyna her room key. "You're up the stairs, turn left, and at the end of the hall."

"Thanks. And no need for assistance. I can manage." Reyna started to gather up her luggage, but Geri hurriedly rounded the counter and seized hold of her belongings.

"Nonsense. Dicky will see to it. He should be back any minute. When he returns, he'll bring your things up straight away."

"Appreciate it." Reyna strode upstairs, deciding not to argue. It was pointless. The woman had confiscated and held her and Lily's suitcases hostage behind the counter.

The chill in the suite met her at the door. She tugged her coat tighter about her and glanced around the generous living space.

The digital thermostat on the wall to her right read fifty-nine degrees, and she felt every bite of it. After raising the temperature, she found the remote to the gas fireplace and performed a series of clicks, but it didn't turn on.

She took closer stock of the place, giving a good look around. Upholstery done in colors of soft sage and cream. A floral-pattern area rug covered a large area of pine hardwood floor.

A wall-mounted TV hung above the hearth, angled over at the sofa and high-back chairs. A small square table for two was situated before a lovely floor-to-ceiling bowed window that overlooked a beautiful blanket of snow-covered ground and mature evergreens off in the distance. Straight ahead, a set of pocket doors opened wide. She went into the adjoining room. The same curved window and café table were positioned to the left of a large, four-poster mahogany bed centering the room. She sat on the edge of the bed and laid back, eyes closed, her body sinking into the pillowy softness. The nippiness in the air made it tempting to crawl beneath the thick duvet. Maybe turn on that small flat screen mounted on the wall over in the corner and watch a movie, something she rarely had time to do.

A knock at the door sent Reyna springing upright and out of the room to the main door. An eye to the peephole found a young man with a black winter cap pulled down to his thick, honey-blond eyebrows. "Yes?"

"I'm Dicky. I have your luggage."

Reyna opened the door. Her and Lily's duffel bags hung in balance from both shoulders, and he had a suitcase clasped in each gloved hand.

"Where would you like me to put them?"

"Right here is fine. Thanks." She pulled a ten-dollar bill from her back pocket and handed it to him. "The fireplace isn't working. And the thermostat hasn't budged. It's freezing in here."

He walked over and fiddled with the unit on the wall, then came back. "May I?"

She gave him the remote. After a few tries confirming what she already knew, he handed it back. "Sorry about that. I'll let Geri know. She'll get it taken care of."

"Thanks." Reyna closed the door.

After putting her and Lily's things away in the tall, twin armoires, she checked her phone. The Find Friends app verified that her daughter was still on the premises.

Reyna left the room in search of warmth. But for an elderly couple, the reception area was devoid of guests. Geri looked up from her computer and hurried over.

"Ms. Star, Dicky told me about the heating and fireplace. I have someone on the way. So sorry for the inconvenience."

"Thanks, and please call me Reyna."

The group of teens filed out of the game room as boisterous as they had been going in.

Lily jogged over, her smile reaching all the way to the outer corners of her eyes. "Mom, everyone's headed to the ice sculpture party. Can I go? There's ice-skating after."

Reyna was hoping to rest up following their long drive and get a fresh start on the festivities around town tomorrow. She checked her watch: 6:47. "Sweetheart, you don't have skates. And we haven't had dinner. How about we res—?"

"There are skates to rent there. But she can borrow a pair of mine. I asked my mom to bring them." Kate came up behind Lily, looping her arms about her neck, pressing her cheek to Lily's. The two evidently had formed a comfortable familiarity. "We're both size seven. Oh, there she is. Mom, over here." Kate waved.

"All right, everyone, that's enough. Take it outside before I arrest you for disorderly conduct," said the woman outfitted in a police uniform and carrying a pair of ice skates. Though her stern order to the teens carried with it a playful wink, instantly, the group's loud chatter dropped to a reasonable tenor and the roughhousing ceased, not taking any chances with her dictate.

"Mom, this is my new friend, Lily, and her mom, Ms. Star."

"It's Reyna. Nice to meet you." They shook hands.

"I'm Tess. Aside from my duties as mom and delivery woman, apparently"—she held out the skates to Lily—"I'm the sheriff, if you haven't already guessed it." With a grin, she tapped a blunt nail at the badge on her chest.

"Kate, we'll catch up with you on the ice," one of the boys called out from the group as they started out the door.

"Lily, will you be there?"

Reyna's head snapped around and centered on the rather tall boy who'd posed the question. His summer wheat-brown eyes in that tawny-tan face were focused on her daughter. Curly brown locks hung from beneath a black winter knit cap at the forehead and nape. Reyna turned back to find Lily blushing.

"They're a good bunch," Tess remarked. "Obviously excited about tonight. The unveiling kicks off the town's holiday festivities. There's food and music. You'll enjoy it."

Reyna put a pin in her surprise at the boy's show of interest in Lily and addressed Tess. "I'd heard this area is a great place to ski. It's why we came."

"Oh, the slopes are a draw here for certain. But the regulars come because Haven Creek has holiday events planned just about every day leading up to the ball on Christmas Eve. This year's theme is mistletoe. It's a lot of fun." She laughed. "I must sound like an advertisement."

"Tess, you all should probably get going if you want to

grab a good spot," Geri said from behind the counter.

"You're right. Kate, I guess we better head out."

"Mom, we're going, right?" Lily asked low. She had clearly conformed already to the town's festive energy around her.

Reyna, on the other hand, was still trying to get her bearings and needed a good night's sleep to rejuvenate. But given that the objective was to try to take the word *plan* out of her plans, she answered, "Sure."

TEN TONS OF ice had been transformed into what the mayor called "Haven Creek's holiday storybook." Perfectly sculpted ice figures such as Rudolph, Santa's sleigh, nutcrackers, Frosty the Snowman, and many others circled the ice rink. One by one, the ceremony unveiled each carving under a spectacular display of lights. Master sculptors, talents from as far away as Greenland, participated in the event.

Reyna couldn't recall the last time she'd skated or the last time she'd had so much fun, though her backside would be sore tomorrow after landing solidly on the cold ice several times. She stroked the area that took the most blows as she and Lily made their way upstairs.

"Mom, how many times did you fall?" Lily smirked.

Reyna cut her a humorous side-eye. "Four, if you don't count that one poor soul I crashed into on the way down."

Laughter bubbled up between them. "Not everyone's a natural like yo—" Reyna paused. The door to their suite set slightly ajar, barely touching against the frame. She planted a hand on the hardwood and pushed it opened.

Her eyes widened. Julian . . . Hawk Swan stood but a few steps away. He'd stopped short on his stride from the direction of the bedroom, mirroring her reaction. "How . . .? What . . .?" Reyna's throat locked up.

"You . . ." He blinked, then blinked again, managing to come out of his surprise and continue forward. "This is your room? You're staying here? In Haven Creek?"

"Mom, who's he?"

Reyna jerked a look at Lily behind her. "He's, uh . . ." Lily's cell phone ring broke the awkward struggle to explain their association.

"It's Dad!" Eyes alight, Lily opened the line on her way into the bedroom. "Hi, Dad. Guess what? I went ice-skating . . ."

Reyna slid the bedroom's pocket doors closed, then drew Hawk forward by walking toward the main door. She turned to face him, still working through her own shock. "What are you doing here and in my room? How did you know I'd be here?"

"That's your daughter?" His dark eyebrows lifted, then his regard slid into typical inscrutability. Reyna had observed such a reaction numerous times before. "Really?"

"We've established that she's my daughter." It came out harsher than intended. Fatigue and the throb in her right hip shortened her tolerance. Over the past thirteen years, if she'd received a dollar every time someone looked surprised to learn Lily was her child and not her sister, she'd be a wealthy woman. "And no, she's not adopted." That one too.

"I didn't mean—"

"It doesn't matter." Reyna exhaled low through her nostrils, too exhausted to try to discern any more from it.

He crouched his big body before the gas fireplace and adjusted the slats on the vents, then came to his feet. Only then did she realize the cozy, warm blaze coming from the hearth.

A distressed black, long-sleeved T-shirt hugged the bulk of his torso and thick biceps, tapering over a flat abdomen. Her gaze roamed lower still to his faded denims fitting appreciatively along a sleek lower body.

Long fingers on both hands combed back the dark, wavy tresses that nearly reached his massive shoulders. The gesture was so surprisingly sexy, her body's sudden response stoked a wild current to pulsing and almost had her asking that he do it again. She swallowed hard to tamp down the urge. "You work here? Wait . . ." She frowned, perplexed. "The private plane . . . the Citation . . .?"

"The individual who held the party I attended—it's his plane. He flew us out to Miami."

"So you lied to me." His silence was answer enough. "Wow." Reyna didn't know which annoyed her more—his dishonesty or her weakness to him. That face and body had been stamped into her memory from the moment they'd met in Miami. How could she still find him so incredibly sexy after learning the kind of man he was?

"How was the party? If I recall, there would be beautiful women aplenty for you to sink your teeth in." Okay, she'd embellished that last part. Her scowl betrayed her attempt to simply ridicule.

"I wouldn't know. I didn't hang around long enough to

find out. What I can say, the steak I had delivered to my hotel room was perfectly cooked, and *Die Hard* on the TV never gets old."

Reyna didn't know what to make of that. He'd flown to Miami specifically to attend his friend's holiday party, apparently with the expectation of meeting a harem of women, yet he'd skipped out, opting for room service and a modern-day Christmas classic. "You're maintenance here?"

"I suppose, tonight, I am. The profession is disagreeable to your opulent palate, I take it." His smile was clearly mocking and his gray eyes frigid. "In any case, actual maintenance wasn't available until the morning. I was asked to take a look at the heating and the fireplace. Both are working now."

He pointed at the thermostat on the wall behind her, then retrieved his heavy jacket from the spine of the chair. "It's set to seventy. Adjust as you see fit."

Their attention rotated to the bedroom doors sliding open. Lily looked between them. "Mom, Dad wants to talk to you before he goes to bed." She held out her phone.

Reyna turned back to Hawk, who'd already crossed the threshold. "Thanks for taking care of the repairs. It's definitely a lot colder here than Miami."

"Glad I could help. Have a good night." His tone mechanical, he went on his way.

Reyna hurried to the door, wanting to call him back as she watched his leisurely, even stride down the hallway. Her question about his profession hadn't meant to insult, yet had done just that. But he hadn't been truthful about owning the private plane. Nor had he indulged in party depravities her active imagination had worked up.

Apologies needed to be had on both sides.

She went to the fireplace and held her palms out, letting the flames soothe the chill, enjoying the warmth of Hawk's labor. Spontaneity wasn't one of her strong suits. *Take the word,* plan, *out of your plans.* This wasn't Miami, and he was no longer a client—

"Mom?"

She turned to find her daughter with an impatient look and the phone extended. "Right."

# Chapter Five

"Reyna Star? Here? In Haven Creek? How is that possible?"

"Plane, train, or automobile." Hawk shot Ash a sardonic side-eye as they separated the donations for the clothing- and food drive.

"Are you sure it's her?"

"Of course I'm sure."

"You spent, what, short of an hour around her, most of which was staring at the back of her head from the back seat. You could be mistaken, is all."

"Geri needed a favor. She called me in to fix the heat in Reyna's suite. Tom is down with food poisoning and had given Geri an ETA on availability for the morning."

"More like food overconsumption." Ash kept pace with Hawk into the storefront. They each picked up garbage bags filled with donated coats that had been dropped off and carried them in back. "The man shoves it in like he's about to take his final walk to the chair."

"Reyna has a daughter," Hawk remarked as they dumped the contents on the long table and commenced sorting by size.

Ash shrugged. "Most women have kids at our age. Do

what I do—give the little tyke a doll, maybe a coloring book, something that'll occupy her for about an hour or so while you're with her mother."

"She's not a toddler. I'd guess she's around Kate's age."

Ash's eyes widened. "Sixteen?"

"Dude, really?" Hawk shook his head. "Kate will be fourteen next March. She's your cousin. You should know that."

Ash shrugged again. He tossed the last coat in his pile into the box. "Reyna has a child that old? She didn't look to be more than twenty-five at most. That would mean she was—"

"Doesn't matter, because I think she might also be married. If not, she's entangled because of the kid. In fact, the husband—father—called while I was there." Hawk stacked a large, stuffed box atop another, lifted, and maneuvered around Ash within the tight confines of the small storage room to exit.

"Have you heard back about the space next door?" Ash followed, cradling two boxes, as well, out to Hawk's black Ram 1500 truck parked just out front, and placed the donations on the rear bench seat.

"Not yet." The store was bursting at the seams and needed more square footage. Hawk had been itching to bust out the wall between his shop and the vacant space next door, but the owner refused to budge. Yet, he'd let the place sit collecting dust. The location was once a thriving craft store run by the owner's wife, who passed away three years ago. There was a sentimental attachment, so the widower didn't want to part with it.

"Bro, let me find you another piece of real estate. It's

what I do. Something that won't break the bank, like the space you're going after. You and I could even do any repairs ourselves."

"For one, I told you I don't want to relocate. My shop sits in a prime spot on Main Street. And two, I'm not paying you commission."

"Yeah, yeah. So, you're not going to pursue Reyna? She's in your town. Literally staying a good workout jog away from here. I thought you said you wanted to be shackled by Christmas." Ash shuddered his displeasure.

"I said I want to settle down." Hawk closed the truck door and pivoted. He couldn't contain his grimace at the clump of mistletoe dangling above the entrance to his shop. The mayor thought it whimsical for the theme of this year's holiday gala to be displayed at every storefront in a show of support. For Hawk, it was a constant reminder of his lacking love life. There were women, surely, but none he could see himself with long-term.

He flipped the sign to *Open* on the door, then circled behind the counter to prepare the register. The shop didn't officially open for another fifteen minutes, but the streets were already starting to crowd with holiday shoppers.

"The point is, you want to be entrenched in a relationship," Ash continued.

"Precisely." Hawk came from behind the counter and fanned a hand out at the array of painstakingly hand-carved, meticulously sculpted, sanded, varnished—some painted—wood pieces, his passion displayed upon every shelf. "This is what I do. As you said, I'm not in Reyna Star's lane." Hard air quotes. "And I'm not so vain that I can't accept that." It had been somewhat bruising that Reyna would consider him beneath her.

"It's not like you have a shortage of women who'd want that number one seat. Of course, these women obviously have questionable taste, seeing as they're into Sasquatches." Ash threw his head back in laughter. "Oof!" He groaned between chuckles from the quick double punch Hawk connected with his rib cage. "Dude, you don't know your own strength. But seriously, Hawk, you have options," he said with sobering clarity.

"Damn right I have options." Hawk lifted his mentally slumped shoulders.

"That's what I'm talking about." Ash slapped the counter. "It's her loss. Frankly, the impression I got of Reyna, she's likely high maintenance. You undoubtedly dodged a bullet with that one."

Hawk didn't quite agree, but nodded, appreciating the show of support, as warped as Ash might be at times.

The bell over the door chimed. Patrons began filing in, easily crowding the small square footage.

Hawk's cell phone rang. He pulled it from his jean pocket and let go a low curse. "It's Tony. I need to take this. Handle the register for me, will you? And if Noah gets here, tell him he's fired. He asks for a job, then doesn't show. Typical," he grumbled on his way to his office.

"Got it." Ash moved behind the counter.

Short minutes later, as Hawk was working out the issue on a shipment with his furniture vendor, the door to his office opened.

"Hawk?" Ash whispered. "Hawk?"

"Excuse me for a moment." He placed the call on mute and turned around. "I'm going to need another ten minutes. Can you hang around? The table I shipped to Tony last week arrived damaged. I have to deal with this."

"She's here!" Ash's eyes were wide.

"Who's here?"

"Reyna Star! She just walked in. I don't think she saw me. There were several people in front of her."

Though Hawk's heart one-two punched against his ribs, then jumped again, he feigned composure. "I could really use you out front."

"Right, forget her." Ash nodded. He raised a fist in the air before closing the door.

As Hawk listened and jotted down the areas of the table that would require repairs, anxiousness knotted his nerves. He wanted to see her again. Felt near desperate to see her. And he was fully aware their interactions always seemed to end up contrary to one another. She was out of his league. Right then, it didn't matter.

Tony was always so long-winded. "Shoot me a text with pictures of the damage. Depending on what I see, I might be able to drive up and make the repairs on-site," Hawk cut in when talk veered away from the table's malady.

He stuck the phone back into his pocket, started for the door, but pivoted and combed his fingers through his hair. Of all days to shorten his shower this morning by skipping a shampoo. With the leather band kept on his wrist, he pulled his hair into a ponytail, then looked down at himself. His plain white T-shirt beneath the unbuttoned red-navy plaid shirt could use a run of the iron. At least his jeans weren't the worse for wear. The pair he'd worn when he'd fixed the heating in Reyna's room had seen better days. He'd come straight from working on a rocking chair in his garage.

On a lung-cleansing breath, he headed out front. Noah was behind the counter, tending to a customer.

"I see you found your way here. Where's Ash?" Hawk asked.

"Don't know. Can I borrow your truck this weekend? Mine is still in repair."

"You and I are going to have a talk later." Hawk ignored the perplexed frown. He moved through the shop, cutting around customers. Ash's loud laughter guided Hawk to the rear shelves to find his cousin yuking it up with Reyna. Seeing the two together, an unreasonable sense of possession kinked his better judgement.

Her eyes shifted, and she paused mid-sentence. A smile touched her lips. Hawk reciprocated with a tentative one of his own.

Ash turned around, wearing a ridiculously wide grin. "Hawk, I was just saying to Reyna how wonderful it is to see her here. She'll be in town for the Christmas holiday."

"Good morning, Mr. Swan."

"Good morning. And it's Hawk." His rigid tone hadn't been intentional, but he was still feeling the residual from the earlier conversation with Ash, where he'd been reminded of her rebuff.

"Right. *Hawk*, I was telling Ash, my daughter—"

"Her name is Lily," Ash supplied, still smiling.

"Yes, Lily ditched me to hang out with her new friends, so I thought I'd check out the town this morning. I'm looking for an ornament to place on the Christmas tree at the inn, which I'm told gets donated to a needy family. I think that's wonderful."

"It was Hawk's idea. He's big into giving back," Ash remarked, hands in his front pockets, rocking on his booted heels.

*Grinning idiot.*

Hawk pinned his cousin with a hard look, then said to Reyna, "Did you find what you needed?"

"I wanted something different from the traditional ornament."

"You came to the right place. Hawk made everything you see here."

"Ash." Hawk shot him another chiding glare.

"You made these!" The ribbon of a red-lacquered train car, a white polar bear on ice skates and wearing a red candy-striped scarf, several gold-gilded angels, and a host of other wood-carved ornaments dangled from the bend of her gloved index finger. First a look of surprise heightened her pretty, brown eyes, then suspicion—or was that disapproval?—showed itself in the pinch of her brow. She looked around at the wood pieces of furniture and wall décor. "This is what you do?"

"We can't all be rock stars." Hawk leaped on the defense. "It serves me well."

"I didn't mean—" She let go a soft breath. "Look, I think we may have gotten off on the wrong foot." Wearing a smile, she removed her glove and stuck out her hand. "Hi, I'm Reyna. My friends call me Rey."

He studied her a moment, wanting to latch on like a survivor's tether. "Julian. Hawk to those who know me well and know not to call me Julian." He cut a slight grin and accepted the olive branch, delicate and warm within his large hand.

"Well, Hawk, it's a pleasure to meet you." She gave another look around. "Not only can you fix heat pumps and gas fireplaces, but you also create beautiful pieces. Such a remarkable skill. How amazing. I think I will get all of these. And maybe this one for Lily." She picked up a ballerina perched atop a small music box.

"Excuse me?"

Hawk turned to the customers seeking his assistance, recognizing the couple who'd been in the shop the day before. He addressed their inquiry about the mini armoire stationed against the wall, but all the while, his mind was on Reyna's show of admiration for his work. He'd been prepared for her snub again and knew how to handle it. But her genuine praise was as surprising as it was unexpected, and it revved a renewed spark of attraction.

Who was he kidding? As if her allure had ever left him.

On the couple's pivot to inspect the piece of furniture, Reyna came up on her booted toes, leaned in near his ear, and whispered, "I wonder what other talents you possess, Mr. Swan?" Hawk's spine went arrow-stiff. He spun and watched her saunter off, blending in with the early morning shoppers moving about.

*I'll be damned.*

"Sir, the armoire," the man said with a slight lilt of impatience.

Ash's light elbow at Hawk's side catapulted him back to the couple before him. He did his best not to rush them and answered question after question, down to the type of screws used. By the time they were satisfied and decided to make the purchase, he hurried toward the front, hoping to catch Reyna. But she was gone.

As he pulled up the furniture piece on his computer and typed in the couple's information, he asked Ash, who was standing on the other side of the counter, "What was that about? You with all the pumping up." It was intentionally cryptic given that there were patrons near, but his cousin caught the meaning and responded with a shrug.

"She's not as stuck-up as I thought. In fact, the contrary. A total one-eighty from how she'd been in Miami."

"The lady had a job to do. She's a professional."

"True that." Ash rounded the counter, shoving Noah out of the way, and leaned back, resting against it, arms folded. "I have to say I enjoyed talking to her. She has wit. I like a lady who can give a good rejoinder."

Hawk had yet to witness that side of Reyna. There was a hint of envy felt.

"Hawk, your truck? Can I borrow it? Please," Noah asked again. "Emily's going back to Jersey on Sunday."

The printer beeped, then spit out the contract for the armoire. Ignoring his brother, Hawk handed the papers to the couple to sign, finalizing the sale.

"I know where she'll be this afternoon," Ash whispered cheekily and ambled off toward the back office.

"She told you? Why would she tell you?" Once again, possessiveness took on a vise-like grip. Hawk stalked after him.

"Hawk, man, come on," Noah pleaded.

"Yes, now do your job." Hawk caught Ash by the arm, his fingers unintentionally tight, and let go when Ash tried to flex beneath his palm. "Why did she share her itinerary with you?"

Ash brought a hand up. "Relax. I can assure you it was completely innocent. Then again, she smells really nice." Laughing, he jumped back, dodging Hawk's hard shove, chuckling. "I'm just messing with you. Cool your heels. At any rate, I don't go back on a flip. You know that. And I can see there's a vibe happening between you two.

"On her way out, Reyna mentioned she had to finish her shopping because she signed herself and her daughter up for some gingerbread house-making thing later. Sharing her plans seemed to be simply her looking forward to spending time with her daughter, no more to it."

"Where is it?"

"How would I know?"

"Well, you seem to know every other thing about her," Hawk groused. He went back to the counter and snagged a brochure from a stack the city administrator had dropped off to all the shops about a week ago. He flipped opened the trifold and scanned through a long list of holiday events. His head came up; he smiled.

"Found it."

🎄

"Uncle Hawk, do we have to? It's so lame." Kate pouted over in the passenger seat while scrolling through her social media.

"It'll be fun. You'll see." Hawk cut the ignition. "We never get to spend time together." They got out and started across Haven Valley Country Club's parking lot.

"Can't we go skiing instead? Making gingerbread houses is dumb. You can't even eat them. They're sprayed with stuff to make them hard as a rock."

"I've already purchased tickets. Give it a chance."

"It's—" Kate halted her sloth-like drag along the pavement. "Lily's here! That's her mom's car." Her steps picked up into a sprint to the entrance.

Hawk put in wide strides to catch up to her. "Lily?" He pretended not to know the girl's name, but he was surprised to learn his niece knew Reyna's daughter.

"She's this girl I met. She and her mom are staying at the Mist. They're from Miami."

"The license plate gave it away." Hawk grinned, though he, too, felt a pulsing flutter at seeing the shiny black Bentley parked a short distance away. "I remember now. I did run into them while doing repairs," he prevaricated evenly.

They entered the building and made their way to the clubhouse out back. Kate jumped in front of the door, blocking their way forward.

"Lily's supercool. Uncle Hawk, please don't embarrass me." She wore a pleading look.

Hawk drew on a feign of insult. "How would I embarrass you? I'm down." Smiling, he delivered the peace sign.

She cringed. "That's how. For starters, don't say and do stuff like that." Kate's shoulders lifted. "Seriously, Uncle Hawk, I really want Lily to like me, okay? Harper's trying to get Lily to be best friends with her. She invited Lily to her house because I told her I was planning to do it. Harper can be such a tool."

"Language," Hawk chided. Yet, the teenage drama was real in his niece's small world. He could see how much friendship with Lily meant to Kate. "How about I get to know Lily's mother, show her what a great family we have?" His actions were purely selfish, but it brought a smile to Kate's face.

"Would you? That's a great idea! Be extra nice, okay?" Kate opened the door to a room of mingled voices that practically drowned out Nat King Cole's harmonic melody, "The Christmas Song," coming from the in-wall speakers.

Participants sat on benches along several rows of tables. Atop each were all the fixings and utensils needed to construct their very own gingerbread house. Coordinators carried trays of candy, adding to the pile of sugary embellishments.

"Look, there they are at the end there. Lily?" Kate waved and hurried over.

Hawk followed and noted how Lily asked the person next to her to scooch to make room for Kate. The appreciative smile that spread up into his niece's blue eyes made him smile. He came forward and caught Kate's subtle head tilt toward Reyna.

"Is there room for one more?"

Reyna's gaze rose, holding his. "This is a nice surprise." She scooted, giving Hawk the corner end. A slow smile crested her cheeks, stalling the air in his chest. She was stunning. Absolutely mesmerizing. And Ash was right. She smelled nice—a subtle, fresh floral scent that made him want to explore where on her body it began and ended.

As things kicked off, the host stood at the front of the room and made a short announcement, offering thanks and information that the gingerbread houses would go on display at the Mistletoe Ball, with proceeds going to support the women's shelter, Calvary House.

Everyone began selecting what they needed to start their construction, and seeing Kate and Lily, their heads together, the pair laughing, enjoying each other's company, Hawk angled his head toward Reyna, whispering, "Is it really a nice surprise?"

"Yes." Her eyes fluttered up, meeting his. "Very nice."

They spoke in low tones, with subtle glances at the girls and those around them.

"You're Kate's father?"

"Uncle."

"That would mean Tess is your sister."

"It's usually how that works." He grinned.

"She's a lovely woman. And your parents?"

"Both passed away within a year of each other when I was a teenager. First my mother—cancer. Then my father suffered a heart attack. We believe it was from the stress of my mother's illness."

"That's terrible. I'm so sorry."

"Thanks. Tess has been there, stepping into both roles. And you? Are you married?" Hawk saw no need to mince words as he firmly held the roof of his house in place, allowing the seams to set. "When I was in your suite . . ."

Her gaze flashed to his. "We're divorced, but my ex and I are good friends, of sorts."

He wasn't quite sure what that meant. Was it ex-husband with benefits? Best to table the subject for another time.

They focused for a long while on their houses, in between teasing the other about whose construction should be demolished. Ash was right again—Reyna was enjoyable company, easy to talk to. Even funny at times. Open, unpretentious, and the air about her unencumbered. Hawk soaked her in, every miniscule ounce, but he couldn't get enough. The heady feeling was strange, her pull on him unexpected.

About three hours later, everyone's masterpieces were done. As they headed out, with the girls walking ahead, allowing them a wide gap, Hawk whispered to Reyna beside him, "You said something to me before you left my store this morning."

"I don't recall," she murmured with a glance at the girls, who had whispered giggles of their own.

"I think you do remember." He surely couldn't forget it. The coy expression she wore was sexy as hell. "I'm curious what you meant."

They came to a stop a short distance away from her vehicle. Kate and Lily had perched themselves on the back bumper. "Maybe you can expand on it over dinner." There was just enough hesitation to know what her response would be.

"I can't."

"Coffee then."

"I promised Lily I'd take her to buy a pair of ice skates. Apparently, it's now her new favorite activity. Me, not so much. I'm on my butt more than my feet." She laughed a bit awkwardly. "Later, she and I have other things planned. Lily's been a social bee since we got here. I want to bask in the quality time with her today while I can."

"Of course. I understand. Well, you two enjoy the rest of your day."

"You as well."

She started forward, but paused and reversed her steps while pulling her cell phone from her coat pocket. "Put in your number."

Hawk took the device and quickly sent himself a text, so he'd have her number as well, feeling all of sixteen, already setting his mental clock to call her later tonight.

"Take care," she said and continued on her way.

"You do the same." He walked with Kate back to his truck. As he backed out of the parking spot and passed Reyna going the opposite direction, she honked the horn, and he waved.

"You were right, Uncle Hawk. This was so much fun," Kate told him.

"Mm-hmm."

*I want her.*

That was the fact of it. But her daughter, Lily, took priority. As she should. Was there a way to get Reyna to break off a small piece of herself for him? Would she even want to? He mulled over that as he listened to Kate talk about her group of friends, who was doing what, who liked who, and who was being a total dweeb. Harper currently seemed to hold the honors in that last regard. He offered advice where he could, having little to no experience where kids were concerned. So could he handle the role of step—?

*Far too soon to even consider.*

As he came into the long gravel driveway of his sister's home, he spotted Tess through the glass storm door, running the vacuum.

"Thanks, Uncle Hawk." Kate gave him a warm hug, then hopped out.

"Had fun?" Tess opened the door for Kate, who nodded and delivered a kiss on her cheek before bouncing inside. With her coat in hand from the wall hook kept just inside the door, Tess came down the front steps and over to the driver's side door. "It was nice of you to spend time with her. You know she adores you."

"She's a great kid. And it allowed me to get brought up to speed on all the gossip." He fluttered his lashes. "Harper is being a total dweeb. And Brooke is OMG, so like into Tyler, but won't admit it." Hawk mimicked his niece's high voice while fiddling with the ends of his hair.

Tess laughed. "Oh, I know. Has she told you about her new friend, Lily Star? She's this teen who's in town with her mother for the Christmas holiday. They're staying over at Harbor Mist. 'Mom, Lily's like totally everything.'" They shared a laugh. "I spoke with Lily's mother, Reyna Star. Nice lady. The two seem like good people. I know Kate thinks so."

"I've met them." Hawk filled in the details from his first encounter with Reyna in Miami to fixing the heating, being careful to skate around his interest in the woman. It didn't stop Tess's radar.

"What are the odds that she would end up here? You

should ask her out."

"Tess, don't start playing matchmaker again." The last thing he needed was his sister getting involved in his love life. He had to take it slow with Reyna if he stood even half of a chance with her. "You saw what happened with Francesca when you meddled."

"Phish." She fanned a dismissing hand. "Frannie's looking for a wealthy man to make all her monetary dreams come true."

"Then why would you think she'd be interested in me?"

"You can be charming when you want to be. And let's face it, you're closing in on the other side of thirty-five. Don't you want a family, kids, before you hit forty and can't swing a bat or sail a Frisbee with your son or daughter without throwing out your back? If Keith were still here, we'd have a small army. He always wanted lots of children." Tess sighed, her amber eyes taking on a faraway daze for a moment.

Tess's husband, Keith, a firefighter, had died seven years ago doing what he loved. Hawk rested a hand upon her forearm that was braced on the truck's door, his tone supportive but firm. "Sis, Keith was a good man. I know he'd want you to be happy sharing your life with someone."

Another full sigh as she came out of her lean, spine erect. "Between my job as sheriff and raising Kate, I have enough on my plate. Besides, I'm too set in my ways." A small smile. "You, on the other hand . . . Reyna Star has pretty brown eyes and flawless brown skin. If I had a figure like that—"

"Time for me to go." Hawk put the truck in reverse and started rolling backward.

"Just consider it," Tess called, her words bouncing off the brisk breeze.

He had more than considered it. He'd lost sleep thinking how to win Reyna.

After dropping off the boxed donations at the veterans' center, he spent the rest of the day at the store tending to customers. Noah was on his best behavior, taking orders and doing his part to get the patrons out the door with their purchases.

As the afternoon met the evening, and now in bed, Hawk flipped through late-night talk shows in between studying his phone, in particular, Reyna's number. He'd typed out a dozen text messages to her, only to hit delete. It was a true test of fortitude not to call her. He'd put himself out there, laid the foundation of what he wanted by asking her out, but she'd declined. For good reason. Her daughter came first. He'd give her space and allow her to make the next move, in a way that didn't crowd her. It would also solidify they were on the same page, that she wanted the same thing.

*I wonder what other talents you possess . . .*

It was one comment. Hardly even a tease, yet it stirred up a chaos of desires.

He tossed the phone over to the cold, empty side of the bed, pushing back against temptation, and turned off the TV. His eyelids heavy, mental exhaustion settled over him, dragging him off to sleep.

# Chapter Six

GLARING RAYS OF sunbeams danced across Reyna's face. She squinted at the large bay window, with its heavy damask pink-floral drapes drawn open wide, exposing the start of bright-blue skies. Geri was right about the room having a spectacular sunrise view.

Reyna turned her head on the soft pillow to the empty rumpled sheets beside her, then to the closed bathroom door. The shower shut off. Back home, it would've taken a foghorn to get Lily out of bed this early on a Saturday.

Lily had complained about how difficult it was to make friends at her new school. A private academy, the teens already had their friend groups formed since kindergarten. Even the moms had their cliques. Reyna hadn't bothered to try to fit within their circle. Most didn't work outside of the home, and she saw nothing in common with them. In contrast, here, Lily made friends the moment they'd arrived. To that, her daughter had become the center of attention. There was even a boy who had Lily in his sights. They'd have a little talk about that. And when Blake found out . . . Reyna chuckled on that thought as she grabbed her cell phone from the nightstand. It'd been placed on mute to not disturb Lily during the night.

Her anticipation deflated. No missed calls, voicemails, or text messages from Hawk.

She was rusty when it came to dating. Heck, anything outside of a firm handshake with a man was about as far as she'd gone in the past ten years. Raising Lily was her priority and getting her business on its feet took second chair. There simply hadn't been time to pursue a relationship.

When a woman gave a man her number, was that not a sign for him to call?

Across the room, the bathroom door opened, freeing a gust of steam. Lily emerged wearing a large bath towel and brushing her damp hair up into a ponytail. She'd added just enough hair gel to keep the unruly curls in place. Thanks to Blake, their daughter had never been the frilly, dainty sort. Even if she fell and drew blood, she dusted herself off and kept going.

Reyna glanced at the clock on the nightstand: 8:20. It only made her want to snuggle deeper under the warm downy blanket. Hours waiting up for the call that never came left her in much need of more shut-eye.

"You're up early."

"Miss Geri said there will be homemade cinnamon rolls served at breakfast," Lily answered as she put on a bra and panties, followed by jeans, a long-sleeved, plain red T-shirt, and a black, front-zipped hoodie.

"Ah, your favorite. The breakfast of champions." Reyna grinned around a yawn and sat up. "Hand me that flyer. I see you've been productive this morning." She noted the opened textbooks next to it. Lily retrieved the trifold brochure from the café table.

"I emailed my lit paper."

"That's great, sweetheart." Reyna reviewed the list of events. "There's something to do here practically every single day until Christmas. We missed the twenty-five themed Festival of Trees decorating event. Bummer. It occurred the day after Thanksgiving. We've done the gingerbread house. There's a horse-drawn carriage ride through the Field of Lights. Come enjoy the illumination," she read. "Goodness, it's over half a mile!"

She scanned further. "Ooh, wreath decorating! Dried flowers, grapevines, evergreen birch branches, and pinecones straight from the woods and Haven Creek's very own organic and botanical garden." Reyna looked up excitedly; it was right up her alley. "How wonderful is that?" Lily frowned— better keep reading. Reyna skimmed past skiing, snowboarding, and snow-sled riding, instantly picturing broken bones, mainly her own. They'd get around to doing all the snowy activities. She needed to mentally build herself up to it.

"There's cookie decorating. Ornament making. We could attend the reading of *'Twas the Night Before Christmas* at twilight while sipping eggnog and likely enjoy some of those cookies. You'd like that, right?" She set the brochure on the bed. "So, which is it? All sounds fun. How about breakfast with Santa? It starts in about an hour."

"Santa?" Lily rolled her eyes upward. "Mom, really? I'm not a baby." She plopped down on the foot of the bed to don her socks. "I want breakfast downstairs, which will be cold if you don't get up now." She dove, belly flopping across the bed and bouncing Reyna about to catch her buzzing cell phone on the opposite nightstand. "Mom,

Kate's downstairs!" Her thumbs rapidly tapped away.

Reyna reluctantly threw back the covers and got up. "So, what will it be?"

Lily took the flyer and studied it. "Hmm, four-lane snow tubing..." Her eyes flashed up. "Ice bumper cars! Awesome! Let's do that."

A professional driver, this was right up Reyna's alley. "Okay. Sounds fun."

"Can Kate and Brooke come with us... and uh, maybe Jacob?"

"Would Jacob be the curly-headed boy?" Getting a shy look and a nod, Reyna bit back a grin, deciding to put aside the boy discussion for later when she had more time to get into the details of this new realm her daughter was embarking upon. "Sure. If their parents are okay with it. I see you and Kate have become BFFs," she said while shuffling through her limited wardrobe in the armoire, settling on black leggings and a fitted cream-colored turtleneck.

"Mom, no one says BFF anymore." Still stretched out across the bed on her stomach, legs up and crossed at the ankles, Lily texted away.

"I only meant you two have become fast friends."

"Kate is supercool." Lily rolled over and sat up. "She's nothing like those snooty girls at my school."

"Her uncle seems nice." Reyna gave a look over her shoulder on her way to the bathroom and regarded Lily's shrug in response, her attention centered on her phone. "I mean, it was nice of him to spend the afternoon with his niece, don't you think?"

"Yeah, I guess." Lily looked up. "I'm hungry. Can I go

down?"

That was about as much as Reyna knew she'd get. "Yes. But do not leave the inn."

As Lily hurriedly put on her boots and sprinted out of the room, Reyna headed to the shower, then dressed and blew out and flat-ironed her curls to smooth, straight strands. Unlike Miami, her thick tresses loved the low humidity.

With her computer, she sat at the round table by the window and began reviewing North Star's logs. Her eyes shifted to the beauty of the pristine white snow blanketing the open field. In the distance, snow rested atop tall evergreens, covering limbs in a feathery winter-white coat. Wind drifts blew and swirled the white powder about like an aggressively shaken snow globe. Sunbeams cut through rolling clouds and struck treetops, adding to the picturesque landscape.

*Gorgeous.*

She pulled her gaze away from the lovely scenery and checked Lily's location. Her peace of mind satisfied, she returned her attention to her work. Rico was meeting his pickup and drop-offs on time. Danielle seemed to be keeping things in order. So far, no fires.

Reyna's phone rang. Speaking of . . .

"Hi, Danielle. I was reviewing your recent report. Everything looks good."

"Yes, all wheels are turning. Rico has been sharp. He also cleans up nice. He wears the black suit well. Will you keep him on after the holiday rush?"

"I'm still thinking about it."

"How's Lily doing? Having fun, I hope."

"She is. There's a girl her age here. They've been hanging out a lot, having a great time." Wow. Reyna managed to deliver that like it was no big deal. But, of course, it was a big deal. She'd whisked herself away from her business at the peak of the holidays, of all times, solely to bond with her daughter. But did Lily recognize that? No.

How could her child making friends turn into such a frustration?

"Glad she's enjoying herself. Well, I'll let you get back to freezing your buns off."

"It's much colder than I'm used to. Call if you need anything." Reyna started to disconnect but paused. "Dani?"

"Yes?"

"Um, when you give a man your number, it presents the signal you want him to call you. That's still a thing, right?"

"For sure. Why? Did you meet someone?"

"Sort of. Do you remember the fare I picked up for Frank when the Rolls broke down?"

"Yes. I did the drop-off for you. Three hot guys, hard to forget. I will say two had me worried I'd have to hose out the back cabin seats. Both looked smashed to the wind. They could hardly stand. The third one with the dreamy gray eyes and a head of dark hair that makes me jealous—a mane like that is wasted on a male—he came off stuck up, as though he couldn't be bothered with me. I saved him the trouble by raising the privacy glass and placed the intercom on mute." Danielle huffed. "Tell me you're not referring to one of them, especially the last one?"

Reyna bit her bottom lip. "Well, see, it turns out the

man with the hair, um, I ran into him here. Actually, he lives in Haven Creek."

"Wait, did you know that before you went there?"

"No. When Frank sent over the reservation info, I saw no need to review it; the fare had been fully paid. I happened to overhear one of the men mention the Berkshires as a good ski location."

"Oh. Rey, I know you don't date much, but I can say with confidence and experience, he's not the one. Be thankful he didn't call. I'll bet Mr. Stick Up His Butt didn't meet one bullet point on your list."

Reyna gave a quick look at said list. "He's attractive. Great physique." Honest, trustworthy, forthright, thoughtful, altruistic—those attributes on her list had yet to be determined. But he misled her to believe the private jet was his. Well, technically, Ash had framed the untruth, but Hawk didn't dispute it. He did spend the day with his niece making gingerbread houses. That must count for something. Thoughtful, maybe?

"Rey, I can throw a stone in any direction in Miami and hit an attractive man with a great chest and rear end. Take advice from someone who has dated a lot of men—you can do better. With that said, I guess we're allowed to hook up with clients now?" A sassy laugh. "On second thought, if you're just looking to have some fun while on vacation, get a little cuffing in, I say go for it."

"Cuffing?"

"You know, that temporary relationship one gets to hold them through the chilly months and during the holidays. And by the way, these days, we women sometimes make the first call. Hashtag empowerment."

Reyna thought on that. "It's still a flat 'no' on dating clients," she made clear. "And Mr. Swan isn't a client. Doesn't matter because he didn't call, so the discussion about him is moot." She kept levity, not allowing dismay to show in her tone. "I better go check on Lily."

"Give her a hug for me."

For long minutes after the line disconnected, Reyna gave into the disappointment while trying to pinpoint where she'd gone wrong during the exchange with Hawk. He'd asked her to dinner. Coffee as well. Twice if she'd count Miami.

*And you turned him down each time.*

Ugh.

# Chapter Seven

REYNA PARKED AT the curb across the street from Hawk's Custom Woodworks. She'd waited an entire day, but Hawk hadn't called or texted. Whether she should approach him had weighed heavily on her mind during the short twenty-minute drive. What would she say? When it came to dating, she was beyond rusty. Blake was the last serious relationship she'd been in. It sounded pathetic even in her head. But true, nonetheless.

The tap on the passenger window startled her. It took Reyna a second to release the breath caught in her throat. She pressed the button, lowering the glass. Tess leaned in, resting a forearm on the door's edge, the glint of her badge reflecting in the side mirror. Two fingers on her other hand were hooked over her shoulder, holding the curved wire of a hanger sticking out of a black garment bag.

"Afternoon, Reyna. Didn't mean to scare you. I saw you parked and wanted to say thanks for inviting Kate to ice bumper cars yesterday. She couldn't stop talking about all the fun she had." Tess eyed the Bentley. "Especially getting to ride in this. It's really nice."

"It's my company car. I'm a driver. That is, I own a private car service."

Tess nodded. "I heard you had a carful. You poor soul." She laughed.

"Yes, it ended up being five of them. They behaved for the most part. Lily has been having a lot of fun. She really adores Kate."

"The same with Kate. Lily's all she talks about. That, and boys lately." Tess rolled her eyes heavenward. "I tell you, I'm not ready."

"Me either. And on that note, I got dumped again today by my daughter, so she could hang with the cool kids." Reyna smirked. "I thought I'd visit some of the shops."

"My brother, Hawk, mentioned to me when he dropped Kate off that you two met briefly in Miami. You should check out his store. He makes everything himself." Tess straightened and stepped back. "I'm headed there now."

She stood there waiting in that authoritative way cops did. Reyna brought the window up and got out. "Yes, we met in Miami, and I've been to his store before," she said as they crossed the street and entered a bustle of patron activity. "It's even busier than when I came the last time."

"Hawk wants to expand into the vacant space next door, but the owner is being difficult." Tess gave a wave to the young ladies working the register as they continued toward the closed door to the right of the counter, which fed into a short hallway and to another door. She pushed it open, amplifying the sound of Hawk's raised voice.

With his back to them, he was standing in front of his desk, cell phone to his ear, giving someone a severe verbal lashing. "I don't give a—"

"Hawk!" Tess called.

He spun around, wearing a menacing look that quickly transformed into surprise when his eyes shifted to Reyna standing just over the threshold. She gave a slight wave and said a low, tentative, "Hi."

"Hi." His voice was barely above a whisper, posture stock-still, staring back at her. He returned the phone to his ear. "I'll call you back."

"Here." Tess handed him the garment bag. "I was over at the cleaners. Mr. Bennett said your tux was ready. I thought I'd save you the trip."

"Thanks." He moved past Reyna, closed the door, and hung the bag on the hook behind it. When he turned to her, his face was back to all smooth angles. "This is a surprise."

"Evidently," Tess muttered. "Who's got you spitting fire at them?"

"That knucklehead brother of ours. I let him borrow my truck to visit his girlfriend. Not only is he not back as we agreed, he let it get towed. I promised the center I'd have these donations delivered today. They're counting on this stuff. My storage is overflowing with more of the same, and I anticipate just as much coming in throughout the week."

"Hawk has been collecting for the veterans' center and women's shelter for several years now," Tess explained.

Reyna looked around at the stacked boxes taking up the small, windowless office, then back at Hawk. His thick eyebrows knitted, nearly forming a unibrow. His jaw was tight. A hand anchored on his hip. The other stroked the back of his neck.

"Does Noah know which lot your truck was taken to?" Tess asked.

"He said he'd only discovered minutes before he called me that it wasn't parked where he'd left it."

"Text me his location. I'll reach out to some of my contacts, have them run your plates. We'll track down your truck. As for the donations, I'd help you out, but I got to get back to work. I'm down two deputies today. Hawk, I know how you are about keeping your word, but I'm sure Nick will understand."

"I can help with the boxes," Reyna said, while mentally putting a checkmark next to *altruistic*, right above *menacingly handsome* on her list.

"I can't ask you to do that," Hawk returned.

"I don't mind. I want to help. Lily is at the inn with her friends playing video games, so I have the time. Like you said, they're counting on the donations." Was it wrong of her to seize on the opportunity to spend time with him? Maybe.

"That's a terrific idea. Right, Hawk?" Tess grinned. "Reyna, I know Geri is keeping an eye on the teens, but I'll swing by the inn again."

"Thanks."

Still smiling, Tess moved to the door, but turned back. "Reyna, will you still be in town for the Mistletoe Ball? I think I mentioned it's on Christmas Eve."

"Yes, we leave the day after Christmas."

"You'll need a gown. Lily too. It's a snazzy affair. Hawk's tuxedo is for the event."

"A gown?" Reyna gaped.

"I'll send you the names of several stores to consider." She pulled open the door. "Hawk, I'll be in touch. In the meantime . . ." She shot him a wink on her way out.

Reyna looked up at Hawk as butterflies fluttered wildly in her stomach. She swallowed and released a quiet breath while unzipping her parka, suddenly feeling rather warm. Unlike her objective to be in his company, he appeared completely focused on the task, securing and taping down boxes. This was important to him. She got in gear. "So, all of these items need to get transported?" She went to lift a box, but the sheer weight prevented it. "Goodness, what do you have in there?"

"Here, let me." He stacked the box atop another and squatted deep, faded denims hugging across a perfect rear end. The long sleeves of his gray T-shirt stretched and flexed under the bulk of muscles as he lifted, then turned.

*What a body. He most certainly gets a checkmark for that.*

Hawk tilted his head at the closed door, thick waves of dark hair falling forward. "Would you mind?"

Reyna blinked. "Oh. Yes, of course." She pulled opened the door and noted the soft grin cut across his shadowy bearded face as he moved past her. She followed. It was safe to say he'd picked up on her admiring his wonderfully sculpted physique.

"Grab the blanket from the storage room there, if you wouldn't mind."

Directed to the adjacent door, she pushed it opened, but could barely extend it all the way. Boxes upon boxes, large garbage bags filled to near bursting, and worn suitcases stacked against the wall—it all swallowed up the small room. Luckily, the blanket was staged a foot inside the door—no need to hunt for it.

She met Hawk outside at the curb, still holding the boxes as though they were filled with feathers. When the street was clear to pass, she hurried across while taking the key fob from her jean pocket, clicked, and the trunk slid up. "Several can sit on the back seats," she said amid slipping on her gloves.

"That's what the blanket is for. I wouldn't want to damage the leather." He grinned over his shoulder on a stride back to his store.

Reyna took a moment to appreciate his casual swagger, as though nothing was too serious to have to rush to it. Her sudden surge of want took her by surprise.

*Stop it. You're here to assist him. Which does not include picturing him naked.*

*But man-oh-man, he's hot. Reyna, girl, get a grip.*

She gave herself a mental slap and focused on spreading the blanket along the bench seat, then jogged across the street and caught the door just as Hawk was heading toward it from within, carrying two more boxes and a couple of blankets draped over his shoulder. He now wore a parka but unzipped.

"I was coming to see what I could grab." She took the blankets, and again, followed him to her car.

"No need. There are only two more and they're packed solid." She covered the bucket seats, and he situated the boxes.

After the last two were loaded, she slid into the driver's seat with Hawk's big body settled beside her. "What's the address? I'll map it."

"This isn't Miami. More like Mayberry." His easy grin and playful attitude brought about that fluttering in her belly and carried with it a flood of desire that had been dormant for quite some time. Neither spoke for short seconds, their gazes locked. "A few turns will get us there." The tenor of his voice was low, but rich and smooth, like a perfectly aged Bordeaux. It was hard to tell who came in closer first, their stares holding, their even breathing mingling.

"Then I suppose that would make Tess Sheriff Andy," Reyna all but whispered, leaning in ever closer as her eyes dipped to his kissable lips.

The laugh that sprang from him, a loud, head-thrown-back, thick chest-rumbling sound, startled her. Seconds before, he'd seemed . . . they'd both appeared prepared to . . .

Reyna sat up straight and gave herself another hard mental shake. Wondering what his lips and tongue would feel like dueling with hers and imagining how his large hands would fondle her body wasn't particularly something she should be thinking about while parked on a busy street in the late afternoon. Not to mention, they were about to transport donations to the needy. *Priorities, Reyna. Get it together.*

"I think Tess would find that relatable," Hawk teased at his sister's expense, still chuckling. "I see you're old school. I like the classics myself."

Out of nowhere came the pleasant images of Lily sleeping peacefully in her bed while Reyna and Hawk sat curled together on the sofa beneath a cozy blanket, glasses of wine on the table before them as they enjoyed a late-night black-and-white movie. "I was twelve when my parents finally purchased a television. The oldies were the only shows I was allowed to watch." Reyna maneuvered into the flow of traffic that was suddenly moving at a crawl.

"Twelve? You're saying you'd never watched TV before the age of twelve? Take a right at the light," Hawk directed.

"There were occasions when we'd visit family, but for the most part, no. We lived out of an RV and moved around a lot. After my father had a health scare, he and my mother decided they would experience all that life could offer. We didn't stay more than six months anywhere we landed. Dad would take odd jobs here and there."

"What about school?"

"Homeschooled." Reyna took another right turn at Hawk's guidance. "I was fourteen when we finally settled in Galveston, Texas. I begged to go to regular school so I could be like normal kids. It's where I met my ex-husband. Almost two years later, Lily was born." She glanced over. A soft nod was his only reaction.

"Another two blocks take a left. So, you two married at sixteen?"

"I was turning sixteen. Blake"—she gave another glimpse at him—"my ex, he was two months shy of eighteen. We divorced when Lily was three. With Blake completing undergrad and grad school back-to-back, I was pretty much on my own raising Lily during that time. It was tough going, but I got through it. I took online classes, finally received my BA, then started my business, which turns three in January." Reyna chanced another look over. His stare was intense, steady, as though if he blinked, he might miss something.

"The building is up ahead on the right." He pointed. "Where that man's sprinkling salt on the walkway. You can park there at the curb."

"The sign says 'No Parking.'"

"It's fine. We won't be here long."

"If I get a ticket, or worse, towed . . ." Reyna failed to maintain her stern expression. His gorgeous white smile was contagious.

"You won't. Trust me."

His voice dropped into that now-familiar low, deep tenor, rich and velvety, sliding across her senses like smooth satin. Trust him? That was the problem. He was making it too easy to trust him. No man was this perfect and not already snagged by some fortunate woman.

She pulled over and cut the engine. The red-brick building appeared to have once been a firehouse. Veterans Day Center, an unassuming plaque read above the hunter-green double-entry doors.

As they got out of the car, the man wearing a New York Giants knit winter hat looked up and greeted them with a warm smile. For some strange reason, Reyna had expected an elderly man, even a cleric or the like to run the center, not someone with the same height, massive build, and wealth of good looks as Hawk.

"Nick, sorry I'm late. I'm without my truck." Hawk looked over his shoulder. His large palm spread at the small of Reyna's back, drawing her forward. "This is my friend, Reyna Star. She was kind enough to help me out."

"Reyna Star." His British tongue gave to her name a regal air. Nick shifted the sack of sand-salt like an unruly toddler in the curl of an arm and extended his hand. A slow smile curved his lips as a flare of intrigue lit his smoldering brown eyes. The gesture only added to a handsome face the shade of decadently rich chocolate. "A beautiful name for the beauty who owns it. It's a pleasure to meet you." That hand, marred by about a dozen scars, took Reyna's fingers, and pressed a warm kiss to the back of her knuckles, his eyes steady with hers. "Hawk, I thought we were friends. You've been holding out on me. Reyna, where has he been hiding you?"

"Hawk and I only recently met."

"Ah, you're not dating?" His eyes twinkled mischievously bright as his fingertips added a warming caress across her palm. "Good to know."

"He and I—" Reyna started.

"We should get the boxes brought in. I've taken up enough of the lady's day." The gruffness in Hawk's voice was matched by his harsh stare directed at Nick, who merely grinned back at him.

Reyna reclaimed her hand and clicked the key fob inside her coat pocket, popping open the trunk. Nick sat the bag of sand on the pavement, and he and Hawk grabbed a box.

"You just missed David, but Ty and Amelia are in back sorting what he dropped off," Nick remarked, his gait moving a bit off-balance, as if he had an annoying stone stuck in the heel of his boot.

They entered to a roar of activity. Adults, young and old, congregated, lounging on a couple of worn sofas and chairs spread about, watching *Family Feud* on the wall-mounted television screen. A game of chess was underway between two men while several stood by, intently observing. At another table, four men were in a laughing debate over a pair of kings flipped face up.

"Hawk, what's up? Good to see you," said one of the players in the chess battle. In fact, Reyna witnessed several greet him with much deference as they crossed the main rec room to a door that fed into a wide hallway of six rooms, three on either side, ending at a set of steel doors.

As Reyna half-listened to Hawk and Nick chatting in front of her, both moving at a measured pace, she caught glimpses inside opened doors. One space was outfitted like an actual classroom with chalkboards and desk. The rest were converted into sleeping quarters, about six cots each.

In the back cafeteria, donations were being sorted upon long tables. Hawk and Nick added their boxes to the many others cluttering the floor.

"Hey, Ty . . . Hawk could use a hand."

A young man left the pile of clothing he'd been sorting and jogged over. "Watcha got?"

"A few more boxes." Hawk started off with Ty, but turned back to Reyna. "This shouldn't take long."

"Here." Reyna handed him the key fob, then went over to the table where Nick stood talking with several volunteers. "There's so much stuff."

"Which is a good problem to have."

"Mind if I ask how you got started with all of this?"

"When I couldn't return to active duty"—he lifted his right pant leg, revealing a prosthetic—"I felt I'd lost more than my shin. Felt I was drowning. It was Hawk's idea. I now help and support my brethren in a different way."

"Hawk served?"

"Army. We met in Kandahar. Hawk's a good chap.

Grateful to call him friend." Nick angled his head, studying her. "My turn to ask how you two met?"

"Nick, go pester someone else."

Reyna turned around to find Hawk coming toward her. He and Ty set their boxes on the floor. Hawk handed her back the key fob. "Thanks."

"I was merely curious." Nick grinned a bit wolfishly at Reyna. "He can be so touchy about his privacy."

Hawk shot his friend a glared warning that was easily dismissed. "That's everything. We can head out."

"You're not sticking around? I need to win back my twenty," a woman said from the other side of the table behind a mound of clothes she'd been sorting—a woman who'd been watching Reyna from the moment she entered the room.

"Hi, Amelia." Hawk smiled, and Reyna detected a sort of fondness there. "I'll try to swing by later. And I'm sure you meant 'lose another twenty.'"

"We'll see." Amelia's eyes shifted. "Are you going to introduce me to your friend?"

Reyna was wondering the same with a hint of hostility over the woman's deep scrutiny projecting back at her. Before Hawk could do so, she stuck out her hand. "I'm Reyna."

"Good to meet you, Reyna. Resident or visitor?"

"I'm visiting from Miami."

"Cool. Having snow on the ground for Christmas will surely be a change.

"My grandparents recently moved to Clearwater. They grew tired of the cold winters here."

The inquisitive expression in her attractive, tawny-vanilla face seemed to warm around the hint of a grin, and Reyna let go of her unwarranted aggression.

A touch on her elbow, she turned her head and got another head tilt toward the exit from Hawk. She turned back to Amelia. "It was nice meeting you."

"You as well."

They said a few words to Nick on the way out but didn't speak the entire short walk to the car.

Dusk had all but erased the sun, bringing with it an arctic chill. She blasted the heat and allowed the car a moment to warm up before she pulled away from the curb.

"What's the rush? I was getting to know your friends. Amelia seems nice. What's her story?"

"Her brother died in Afghanistan about three years ago. As for she and I, it was brief."

"I meant in relation to the center. Beyond that, what you do and with whom is really none of my business." Not that she hadn't already picked up on the connection.

He shifted within the confines of the seat belt to face her and used his fingers to comb back his wavy locks. "Reyna, I don't want there to be any misunderstanding getting in the way with us. I won't let it happen this time. I'm interested in getting to know you."

"Why me?" She looked over at him, wanting to gauge his expression more than his words. "Have you ever dated a Black woman before?"

"Does it matter?"

"Yes, it matters. I don't want to be some fetish of yours. Or your holiday cuff for the season."

He frowned. "My what?"

"Cuff, cuffing, your temporary fling." She shook her head, not completely sure of the meaning herself.

"You should've turned left. Make the next right at the light, then a left at the intersection."

"I'm twenty-nine with a teenage daughter, which is a commitment in itself. I'm not just some woman vacationing, looking for a holiday hookup."

"Don't turn—you were supposed to turn left."

Distracted, Reyna realized the mistake a second too late. A short distance away, the gondola lights flickered on, illuminating all the way to the ski hilltop. "I really don't have space in my life for problems and complexities a relationship tends to bring with it."

"Are you searching for a reason to reject me? Look at me, Reyna."

She met and held his intense gaze through several rapid heartbeats, then returned her attention to the road ahead. "I'm trying to figure out what's wrong with you."

His brow furrowed once more. "Pardon?"

"Look at you. You're gorgeous. You help people in need. You spend time with your niece, making gingerbread houses. Yet, you claim you're not involved with anyone. There must be something I'm missing."

"Why can't it be that I haven't met the right woman yet?"

"Oh, let us not forget you allowed your brother to borrow your vehicle simply so he could see his girlfriend when you needed it to transport items to the veterans' center. It wouldn't be much of a surprise if you sing to the elderly at nursing homes too."

"I do."

Reyna's head swiveled.

"I'm joking." He sported a grin. "Make a left at the intersection. Have you gone skiing yet?"

"No. I don't know how. I've been putting it off. Lily will want to do it soon, I'm sure."

"I'll teach you. We can go now if you like."

"I can't tonight. How about tomorrow? Same time? I'm taking Lily snow tubing in the afternoon, then she has already said the kids are coming by the inn to hang out, play video games. I'll be free then. I can pick you up at your store if you're still without your truck."

"That'll work. I should be back from the nursing home by then."

Reyna tried but couldn't suppress her grin. His was simply contagious. Her heart was treading on dangerous ground. He was wrong for her in so many ways.

Though she had yet to determine what they were.

# Chapter Eight

A RAP ON the office door before it opened. "Hawk, look who I ran into." Ash stepped aside.

Seated behind his desk, Hawk shifted his attention from his computer. His stomach lurched, jolting him to his feet in tense surprise. Fiery waves of red hair. Green eyes like glimmering gems. Jennifer. Their relationship had been recent and short and passionately intense. But there was nothing else to offer . . . on both sides.

He circled over to her. "Jen."

"Good morning, Hawk."

"Jen was at the Christmas party I attended last night. I told her you had planned to show but must have gotten busy here at the shop. I'll let you two catch up." Beaming as though he'd found and delivered the one missing piece that revealed the entire picture to a puzzle, Ash dashed out the room, closing the door behind him before Hawk could signal that he stayed put.

Reyna was expected to come by later. The way his luck ran, she'd stroll into his office any second. His pulse jumped. He took a step back.

Jen took a step closer, too close, sporting that seductive crooked twist of her lips he remembered well, and tugged on the tail of his untucked flannel shirt. "You look good, Hawk. I was hoping to see you last night."

"Jen, I'm not sure what you might have been told, but—"

"Ash said you'd be happy to see me. Was he wrong?"

"I'm involved with someone. It's serious." At least on Hawk's end. Reyna discovering the two of them behind a closed door alone was a complication he didn't need.

Her brow rose, then smoothed. "Oh. I see. You were always one to get to the point of things. It's what I enjoyed about you." There was a double entendre woven into those words. "I hope she knows how lucky she is."

"I'm the lucky one." Hawk moved around her and pulled open the door, relieved Reyna wasn't standing on the other side.

"Ah, right." Jen nodded, needing no further hint.

He walked her through the storefront to the exit, passing Noah and Ash at the counter.

On his way back to his office, he caught Ash by the bicep, squeezing. "I need a word." He tugged, then flung his cousin inside the room, slamming the door behind them. "What were you thinking, suggesting Jennifer come here? You know I'm seeing Reyna. What if she'd walked in on us?" It took all he had not to deliver a solid fist to the man's empty cranium.

"Jen asked about you. I thought you'd want to see her. You once said she was a lot of fun."

"Once. And don't ambush me like that again! Got it?"

"Okay, okay, I overstepped. But, bro, an ex and a teen. You're sure you want to take on Reyna's baggage?"

"I don't see Reyna having an ex-husband and a teenage daughter as baggage. Many women who are divorced have children."

"That may be. Hawk, man, Reyna's an attractive woman, but you have women at your disposal who are far less weighed down. Hence, Jen. Why, when you don't have to, is my point."

His cousin's shallowness was nothing new, but it now was starting to pinch a nerve. It went without saying Reyna's beauty was what had initially attracted Hawk, but the depth of her inner strength mesmerized him so much more. He'd sensed it on first meeting her back in Miami and felt drawn to her. Now, knowing what all she'd accomplished as a single mother, he was in awe of her.

Most of all, Reyna wasn't just stunningly captivating. Whenever he was near her, she made the air around him blissful, too, regardless of his mood. And the moment when they finally came together as one, the taste of her, the scent of her, the heated friction their bodies would ignite, her soft flesh pressed against his—without a doubt, it would be explosive.

"Reyna lives in Miami. Another problem for you," Ash said. "And what do you plan to do to win over the kid? Good luck." He snorted.

"Did you know there are airplanes that can fly nowadays?" Hawk shot back and took a seat back behind his desk. "As for Lily, how hard can it be? I'll treat her like I do Kate—show interest in what she likes, listen to her talk about her friends, school, boys."

"That's if she's willing to share." Another snort.

"Stop trying to find obstacles. Lily will have to get to know me; I'm aware of that. I'm great with kids. Dude, enough with the negative vibes. I got this."

Ash brought up a hand. "Fine. I hear you."

"Good."

# Chapter Nine

"**A**RE YOU READY?"

"Ready as I'll ever be," Reyna answered as Hawk buckled himself in over in the passenger seat. She followed his navigation for several blocks and onto a stretch of road that took them up an incline. Beneath twilight's cloudless sky sat a massively impressive resort nestled by tall mountain peaks.

Hawk's phone rang as he exited the car. Reyna listened to his side of the conversation and could make out that he'd canceled on someone tonight.

"If you have somewhere else to be, we can do this another time," she offered when he ended the call.

"It's just Ash, asking if I'll come by to watch the game."

"Sunday Night Football. You should go."

"I'm where I want to be. I need a break from him anyway."

There was a clench in the hard angle of his square jaw. "Everything okay with you two?"

"Nothing that won't pass. Now, let's get you on skis."

A family matter. She wouldn't push. "I don't have ski gear." Reyna followed him inside, amid texting to check on Lily. *Having fun?*

The response flashed just as fast. *So much fun. We're playing Twister.*

*Nice. See you later.* She added a trail of kissy-face emojis.

"I'll get what you need, and we can rent skis."

"I figured as much." Reyna kept pace with his determined strides to the apparel and grabbed several items in quick succession. Within short minutes, he had the cashier ringing everything up. Then they headed to the changing rooms.

When she emerged, Hawk was there waiting with her ski helmet. He'd chosen them matching outfits in royal blue with bright reflective yellow stripes along the outside seams. She'd observed several couples dressed in twin suits, as though it was a thing or something, identifying who belonged to whom.

Hawk merely stood there staring at her, smiling. "What?" Reyna glanced down at herself. "I look ridiculous, don't I?"

"I found you breathtakingly beautiful from the first moment I set eyes on you." He came forward and placed the helmet upon her head, adjusted the strap, and tenderly brushed wisps of her hair back over her shoulders, then tipped her chin up with a light touch of his index finger. "Let me make something clear. I want you, Reyna Star. Understand that."

His whispered words left no room for misinterpretation. Though her heart slammed against her breastbone, Reyna kept her reply impassive. "We better do this before I change my mind."

"Do you have the key to the locker where you stored

your things?"

She removed the helmet and patted the zipped pocket of her jacket. "Right here."

"Okay. Then let's do this."

They exited through a set of automatic doors at the rear that took them to a small booth. Hawk rented skis. Then, remaining on flat ground, he started his version of *Ski Lessons for Dummies*. Reyna became skilled at snapping her boot into the ski. Balancing and using the poles to propel forward. Positioning her body so as not to strain her back. When she felt comfortable that she'd mastered the basics, they headed to the lift and let the gondola carry them up.

As the chair moved slowly along the wire cable, she attempted to distract herself from the growing altitude. "Lily's father likes to do adventurous things with her. She goes on and on about how much fun she has with him. I'm considered the boring parent."

"Is that why you're trying to ski?"

"Yes," she said plainly. "It's a way I might bond with my daughter. She's growing up so fast. Do you know a boy named Jacob? brown curly hair. Looks too old to be scoping out my baby."

"Jacob Gagneaux. I think he's about fifteen. Good kid. His father is a commercial airline pilot, mostly international. He's not home much. His mother teaches at the high school. I think math."

"He's a tall fifteen."

Hawk laughed. "His father's around six-five. The boy was destined."

The conveyor stopped, hovering them high up over

snow-covered bushes. Reyna looked around, anxiety swiftly shifting to panic. "What's happening?" They hadn't gone very far, and it was the beginner's chairlift, but it was too high up to consider getting off without suffering many broken limbs.

"Try to relax. It's normal. It'll start moving again any second."

Several quick pulse beats punched Reyna's chest, and the seat hadn't budged. "What if it doesn't move? I've seen online videos where people have had to be rescued off these things. Some have had to jump into nets." She looked behind them. The chair was empty, as was the one in front of them.

"The town looks beautiful from up here." Hawk took her gloved hand in his. "Reyna, look at me," he voiced softly.

She turned her head, locking onto his gray gaze, and felt an instant calm settle over her, like a soothing, warm flame.

It was indeed a lovely, elevated bird's-eye view of Haven Creek. Main Street could be seen twinkling in the distance. The stars illuminated the clear night sky above. "It's really beautiful."

"You see those bushes there?" Hawk pointed at the thick foliage blanketed in snow. "Those are mistletoe. We're seated above it. That still counts, wouldn't you agree?" He winked.

Reyna wasn't so certain about the bushes, but he'd supplied a reasonable justification for what she was sure he wanted to do. For what she wanted to let him do. "It counts." Her heart was jackhammering now for an entirely different reason.

His warm breath feathered across her mouth before making contact. He took his time, tasting her slowly, dipping his tongue within and withdrawing, tauntingly. She parted her lips, giving him full access, wanting much more. Both slanted their mouths, left then right, as the kiss grew deeper, hungrier, an endless joining of tongues.

A rush of desire threaded beneath her thick clothing. She wanted him, wanted to strip them both down to bare skin and explore the hard terrain of his exceptional physique.

"I want you too," he murmured between breathless kisses.

Had she voiced it aloud? Must have. Her mind was trapped in a sensual haze.

The chairlift started moving again, forcing them to break apart, their gazes heavy with passion, their breathing hurried.

"Remember to turn in the way I taught you when exiting the lift," he said, still exhibiting that hot, telling gleam in his eyes.

Reyna got her head back into the game, prepared herself, and made a small hop off the lift, turning her skis appropriately.

Hawk moved to her. "Perfect. You're a quick study. This beginner's landscape is mostly flat."

"Then let's get going." Adrenaline fueling her, she kicked into gear the skills she'd learned. Hawk stayed at a smooth pace beside her. In no time, they made it down the slight slope and back onto the lift, reversing the way they came. They unsnapped themselves from the skis. Hawk returned the rentals, and they changed back into their clothing.

Now at the car, Reyna, revving with confidence, rested a hand on the hard plane of his chest, and his eyes moved there before his gloved hand came to rest atop hers at his calm, beating heart. "This was fun. Thanks for the crash course. What do I owe you for the ski outfit?"

He curled an arm around her waist, drawing her ever closer. "You don't owe me anything."

Curiosity was getting the better of her as she fiddled with the zipper on his parka. "In Miami, why didn't you stay at your friend's party? I heard you say there would be women *aplenty*"—her lip rolled upward at the bitter taste of discontent—"and it was the main reason you'd flown out there."

"Yes, I admit to saying that. But it was pointless to hang around when all I did was compare every woman to that fascinating driver I'd met earlier." He tipped her chin up with the edge of a finger. A smoldering glint lit his eyes. "On second thought, in payment for the ski apparel, maybe another kiss would suffice." His mouth took possession of hers, a hand capturing the back of her nape, holding steady. She willingly surrendered to the demand of his smooth lips devouring hers and hooked her arms around his neck, riding the rapid patter of her pulse.

"Would you mind driving?" she asked around their dueling tongues, her senses caught in a spiral of sensations. "It would be much faster getting to your place if you do." He drew back, blinking rapidly. Her intent bloomed in his eyes as he pulled open the passenger door for her and got into the driver's seat. Short of thirty minutes, they parked into the long driveway of his home. Headlights shone on a darling craftsman, modern farmhouse-style, two-story dwelling. A lovely glass-enclosed wraparound porch hugged the left side of the home. Beyond it was a covered boat situated in front of a triple-wide detached garage. Snow rested on bare branches of aged oak trees and dusted tall evergreens flanking the property. Undoubtedly, in summer, thick foliage offered privacy and blocked out the neighboring homes that were already a good distance away on the quiet road.

They entered the mudroom through the side door of the glass enclosure. Fishing rods leaned against the wall in the corner. A carved bench stretched along the far wall, the wood's character beautifully shown in its lacquered finish. It was the perfect accoutrement for sitting to remove wet boots. Hawk walked over, took a seat, and began doing just that.

"Did you make it? The bench. It's lovely." She took off her parka and hung it on the hook by the door.

"Yes." He removed his coat and patted the space beside him. "I don't bite."

Her bold words had brought them here. Reyna crossed the short distance and sat down. He moved to his knees in front of her and began unlacing and removing her boots, strong, formidable fingers kneading her calf as he did so. Taking her hand, he came to his socked feet and guided her into a well-appointed, modern, eat-in kitchen of stainless-steel appliances, soft-gray walls, white, subway-tiled backsplash, and wide wooden-planked floors. The color scheme carried through to the living room in the open-concept layout. Large windows would bring in an abundance of natural light. A host of gifts lay beneath the brilliantly twinkling Christmas tree positioned before it. A deep-cushioned gray sofa and two black leather recliners were properly arranged around rich mahogany tables and stationed in front of an enormous fireplace mantel. Its intricate detail was a well-crafted piece of art and took up the entire wall.

Reyna twirled and nearly bumped into Hawk. "You made the mantel at Harbor Mist." It was a statement of certainty. The two were very similar.

"The owner of the Mist is a family friend. He saw mine and asked if I'd create one for his property." Hawk crouched to set a log and quickly got a fire going, adding instant warmth.

Reyna studied the grand balustrade staircase that curved up to the second level and offered an opened view of the area below. "What type of wood is that? It's so beautiful." The natural reddish-brown hues in the grain resembled bold paint strokes, its lustrous shine practically gleaming in the firelight. Such exceptional talent. How did he have time for complex projects while running his busy store, and forever performing acts of altruism along with it? All that and charming. He was simply too good to be true.

"Tigerwood. And, yes, I made it also," he said as he came to his feet and pushed his wavy tresses out of his face with a comb of fingers. Such an ultra-sexy gesture.

"Are you still trying to figure out what is wrong with me?" His arm hooked her waist and drew her against his body. A small smirk twisted his pretty lips that she now could confirm were wonderfully soft.

"I am, yes."

The arm cradling her waist jerked her tighter against his big frame. His other hand cupped the back of her neck, anchoring her as his mouth claimed hers.

He was such a good kisser, the way he didn't rush his

deliciously thorough exploration. Reyna ran her hands over the hard planes of his chest and broad back, familiarizing herself with his body. He was wearing too many clothes. They both were. She broke away from his deliciously fervent kiss and began unbuttoning his navy-plaid flannel shirt, dragging the material off his bulky shoulders. He shrugged out of it, followed by his T-shirt, then tugged up her sweater, drawing it over her head. Static made her hair stand out as though she'd stuck her finger into a live socket.

He chuckled while smoothing the strands. "You look adorable."

"Like I've been electrocuted? You find that adorable?"

"Your hair out of place, standing here in your lace bra, you look wildly sexy."

Before she could utter a rebuttal, his lips met hers once more while his hands moved along the curves of her body, cupping her breasts, and squeezing her bottom.

A musical ringtone came faintly from a distance, one Reyna easily recognized. She pushed at Hawk's shoulders, breaking away from his devouring mouth. "That's my phone. It's Lily's ring." She rushed to her coat and grabbed the device from the pocket, answering, "Hi, sweetheart," around trying to reclaim her breath.

"Mom, where are you? I'm not feeling well. Miss Geri had me go to bed."

Reyna sat on the bench and grabbed her boots, tugging them on. "I'm on my way. I'll be there very soon." She disconnected and tied the laces. Hawk came forward with her sweater. His flannel shirt hung upon his torso unbuttoned, his tanned, muscular pecs exposed.

"Is she okay?"

"I don't know. She's in bed." Reyna put on her sweater and hurried into her coat. "It's so late. I should've been there." Guilt gripped her in a suffocating hold.

"It's only ten after eight."

She moved past him and out the door. As she got in the car and brought down the window, he jogged after her in unlaced boots and that opened shirt. "Hawk, you shouldn't be out here dressed like that. You could catch a cold."

"Let me know how she is."

Reyna nodded as she set the GPS and backed out.

The entire drive to Harbor Mist was filled with thoughts of regret.

*You're a mother with responsibilities to your child, for goodness' sake.*

The primary purpose of the trip was meant to spend quality time with Lily for the Christmas holiday, not in the arms of some strange man. Well, Hawk wasn't a stranger. They were acquainted. After tonight's kissing and groping session, they were even more so. Tabling the thought, Reyna parked and rushed inside the inn.

"Reyna?"

She turned in her race toward the stairs at Geri's call.

"Thank you for seeing to Lily. I'm sorry I wasn't here."

"No, don't be. I put her straight to bed with a cup of tea. Oh, and a light snack, in case she felt better later and wanted a nibble of something."

"I appreciate it."

"I'm sure it's nothing serious. Lily, Kate, and the others were having a good time in the game room, so much so that

I had to tell them to keep it down. I checked on the bunch several times. Lily seemed fine. Tess stopped by with pizza and wings. She hung around a bit and played Twister with them. Before Tess left, she let Lily know you were with Hawk, helping with donations." What appeared to be a naughty smile crept into the woman's pink cheeks. Geri took a small step closer, blue eyes twinkling. "Were you two able to accomplish what you set out to do?" she asked in almost a whisper.

Reyna's face warmed all the way to her hairline. Goodness, was her desire for Hawk stamped on the center of her forehead? "W-we delivered items to the veterans' center, yes. There was quite a lot of stuff. Hawk has his hands full with all he does. I better go check on Lily." It was wrong to play on that fib. Reyna turned for the stairs, happy to be out of the woman's grinning inquiry.

Then she pivoted again. "Geri, how long after Tess told Lily where I was, did Lily become ill?"

"Um." Geri looked skyward, thinking. "Not long, come to think of it. She had eaten quite a lot of pizza and wings by then. They all had. She probably just needs to sleep it off."

"Right."

Reyna headed upstairs and entered the room to the soft glow of the TV flooding out from the bedroom. She left her saturated boots by the door, peeled off her heavy parka, and clicked the fireplace remote to curtail the slight draft filtering in from the hallway, then crossed to Lily's side of the bed, taking a seat on the edge. A partially filled mug of tea and a hearty piece of untouched butter cake on a plate sat on the nightstand.

A light palm to Lily's forehead—cool to the touch. Eyes heavy from sleep fluttered opened. "How's my baby?" Reyna asked softly. "I heard Kate's mom brought pizza and wings, two of your favs. Did you eat too much?"

Lily rolled onto her back and rubbed her eyes. "I guess. Miss Tess said you were with her brother, helping deliver donations to the homeless."

"I was, yes."

"But when Miss Tess left, Kate said she heard her mom tell Miss Geri that her uncle Hawk likes you."

Hazel eyes studied Reyna's. Hard. Unblinking. Reyna reared back with a feigned look of confusion. "Why would she say that? That's ridiculous. I was helping Kate's uncle deliver items to the veterans' center." Goodness, she was now lying to her child. "As a matter of fact, I think tomorrow, we will go there to help." Then it wouldn't be a total untruth. The perfect penance. "They could use as many hands as possible. You'll see for yourself. Maybe after, you and I can go skiing." That seemed to erase the disapproving look at the mere mention of Hawk's name. *Ugh.*

Lily's cell phone on the nightstand rang. Reyna came to her feet and handed the device over. "It's your dad."

"Daddy!" Lily answered, springing upright. "Yes, tons." Legs crossed, she grabbed the plate and balanced it within the well of her thighs, pinching off a piece of the dessert, tummy ache evidently no more. "The kids here are really cool . . . oh, okay. Mom, Dad wants me to put the phone on speaker."

Reyna turned from the armoire. "Hi, Blake."

"Hey, I only have a few minutes, so I wanted to catch

you both. We're working late to get this leak under control. How have things been there so far?"

"Really good, actually."

"Dad, today Mom took me and my friend, Kate, and my other friends snow tubing. Then we all hung out and played games. Well, Mom went with Mr. Hawk to—"

"Mr. Who?"

"Kate's uncle Hawk."

"I was helping deliver clothes to the veterans' shelter," Reyna interjected around the inward cringe knotting her stomach. She didn't want Blake to think she'd broken their agreement. Had she betrayed their pact as it was?

"Yes, Mom said we're going there tomorrow to help out. Then we're going skiing." Lily bounced happily, still munching on the cake. "I can't wait."

"Cool. Have fun. Well, I gotta run. Sweet pea, I'll call you tomorrow. Blowing you a kiss. Love you."

"Love you too."

"Good night, Rey."

"Good night."

Reyna took the phone and the plate, placing both on the nightstand. "You should get some sleep." It hadn't been lost on her that Lily didn't mention her malady to her father when she was happily spilling tea about Reyna. "I'm going to take a shower, then get a little work done."

The jetted tub called to her instead. Head back, eyes closed, she let the bubbles caress and soothe like a multitude of working fingers. Hawk's fingers. Reyna let her mind wander back to what it felt like to have him touching her, kissing her—

She jumped at the low buzz of her cell phone stationed on the closed toilet lid, jolting her out of her musing. *Hawk.* The mere sight of his name sent a warm current rushing through her with a giddy headiness. On a full inhalation and release, she opened the line. "Hawk."

"I hope I'm not disturbing you and Lily."

"I'm in a bath. Hold on." She got out, toweled off, and put on her robe. Phone in hand, she left the bathroom and gave a look at the bed. Lily lay on her side, long lashes fanning soft shadows upon her tawny-brown cheeks. Snoring breaths pushed past her slightly parted lips. Reyna turned off the TV and padded out of the room, sliding the doors closed behind her. She curled up in the chair before the warm glow of the fire.

"Hawk?"

"Yes. How's Lily doing?"

"She's fine. Just had a little too much to eat. Thanks for checking." Reyna weighed whether to share her suspicions of what really brought on her daughter's illness, which seemed to miraculously dissipate when skiing was suggested. "Hawk, Kate shared with Lily that she'd heard her mother tell Geri that you like me."

"I do like you. Very much. I find your caramel-brown eyes enthralling, your smile drunkenly contagious, kissing you so irresistible that I can't get enough, and your body so tantalizing that I want to explore every inch of you."

Reyna chewed her bottom lip. It had been a long time since a man had voiced such beautiful sentiment to her, so it was dismaying for her to say, "I haven't dated much following my divorce. As far as Lily knows, not at all. To explain, my ex-husband and I have this arrangement that—"

"That you two would get back together."

There was a discerning drop in timbre, like a rough grate against a chalkboard. "No, not at all. We agreed we wouldn't bring a man or woman around our child until the relationship became serious. Lily has never been introduced to anyone, man or woman."

"You and your ex? In all of the ten years?"

"That's right. So you see, the concept that a man might *like* me is new to her. For thirteen years, she's had both her parents all to herself."

Hawk's pause—a pregnant silence that pulsed through long ticking seconds—worried Reyna. He would walk away. Few men would want to be bothered with such a burden.

"I'm taking Lily to help at the center tomorrow. Then we're going skiing. It'll be her first time." Reyna felt it was a reasonable subject change to break the awkwardness.

"If she's anything like her mother, she'll do great."

"She's a daredevil. Her father takes her skydiving, parasailing, ATV riding over steep hills, and who knows what else. I cringe, simply thinking about it. Blake has always been an adventurer, and he's shaping his daughter in his image." Reyna chuckled. "All in all, he's a terrific father. There isn't a day that goes by he and Lily don't talk. He and I have a great relationship. We—"

"I have a call coming in I need to take. Good night, Reyna."

Reyna blinked. "Oh. Okay. Good ni—" He was gone. The abruptness stung. Foregoing work, she went back into the bedroom, dressed in her comfy cotton pjs, then slid beneath the covers.

The time was closing in on ten thirty. Whoever had called Hawk took priority. Was there really an important call? Practical reasoning would say yes, and that his quick disconnect had nothing to do with her rambling on about her ex. What was she thinking? A man who asserted his interest in a woman didn't want to hear about an ex-husband. Her purpose had only been to show Blake was highly involved in Lily's life. *That is precisely all that needed to be said.*

Rusty at the whole dating thing was putting it mildly.

# *Chapter Ten*

"WELL, HELLO, YOU two. A late start to the day, I see. I'm afraid you've missed the breakfast buffet, but I can have the kitchen whip up something. I usually prefer to stick to the schedule to keep things running smoothly, but for my two favorite guests, it's perfectly fine."

Reyna, with Lily beside her, came to the foot of the stairs. "Hi, Geri." Did the subtle wink and the special consideration have anything to do with Tess making known where Hawk's romantic interest lay? After last night's phone call, Reyna was pretty sure she was nowhere close to the top tier on his list. "Thanks, but we want to try brunch at a little café house we spotted in town."

"There was a picture in the window of pumpkin pancakes," Lily added.

Geri looked at Lily. She touched her forehead with the back of her hand like a concerned mother. "You're feeling better, then?"

"Yes, ma'am. Thank you for the tea and cake."

"Geri, thanks again for seeing to her last night."

"It was no trouble at all. It was nice of you to help at the center. I'm sure Hawk appreciated it. As a matter of fact, he stopped by for breakfast. With all that he does for me whenever I can't get maintenance here fast enough, offering him an open invitation to grab a meal is the least I can do. But he usually politely declines, always too busy. Until now." Another twinkling grin.

Could the woman be more transparent? "We should get going before the café switches to its lunch menu."

"Yes, of course. Oh, have you gotten your dresses for the ball? Tess said Hawk has his tux."

Reyna stalled her hand on the door handle and turned. "No. I guess I need to get on that."

"There were six hundred in attendance last year. I'm hearing that number has doubled. It's such a lovely holiday event. You wouldn't want to miss out."

"I'm looking forward to it." Reyna returned a smile, sealing her commitment and exited.

THE CENTER WAS packed with volunteers, even many seated on the floor with their piles to sort. The truck that arrived that morning had brought in about twenty large boxes of donations from neighboring towns, a good percentage coming from local businesses.

The door to the cafeteria opened again, and Reyna glanced up from the task in front of her. She checked her watch to see that it was a quarter past one.

Hawk knew where she'd be today, yet he hadn't showed. The fact that he came by the inn this morning, but didn't bother to call or text, gave ground to Reyna's speculation. Someone else took up space on his radar.

She'd spoken with Danielle that morning, and her friend advised she keep talk about Blake to a minimum. Her pragmatic friend also said that if Hawk was that insecure, he wasn't worth the effort. All that might be true, but logic didn't make Reyna feel better.

Lily was working at the next table with another young volunteer, chatting and laughing while doing a great job of separating a huge mound of unopened toys.

The sudden tummy ache had returned following brunch. It was Lily's way to try to get out of going to the center, of course. But when she understood she'd have to stay in bed and skip their planned ski outing, once again, the malady was no more.

Reyna brought her attention back to the pile in front of her but was soon distracted by the squeak of the heavy metal door. In walked Hawk. Beside him was Amelia. His usual casual dress and heavy parka had been replaced with a gray suit, white button-down, and smart blue-stripe tie beneath a sharp-looking charcoal-gray wool coat. His dark hair was pulled into a ponytail, his facial hair neatly groomed and tapered close. Black leather gloves covered his big, strong hands. Amelia strutted in her heels while shrugging out of her coat, revealing a lovely royal-blue dress that complemented her subtle curves nicely. She found a place among the horde of items ready to be sorted.

"Mom, we need more boxes. Mom?"

Reyna blinked and cut her gaze from Hawk, whose eyes had just met hers from across the room. "Okay, sweetheart." She circled from behind the table and made her way to Nick, doing her best not to look at Hawk beside him. She'd foolishly lowered her barrier and let him in and now only had herself to blame if her heart got bruised. A small smile and a nod were all she gave so as not to convey the raw emotions she'd been trying to keep in check the entire day.

"Nick, where can I get more boxes?"

"Through that door, then take a right. First room on the right," Nick replied, and was quickly summoned by another volunteer.

"Thanks."

"Reyna?"

She didn't bother acknowledging Hawk's low call on her way out. She entered the storage room, flipped on the light, and took a deep breath with a slow release, trying to unconstrict the pressure surrounding her heart. So easily he'd imprinted himself there. And she'd allowed it because she liked him. Really liked him. His kisses—forceful, then soft, greedy and hot. His scent—crisp, clean, earthy, and completely male. The pale-gray hue of his eyes. The solid weight of his body. Even the rough glide of his hands on her skin. Reyna shook her head, letting practicality rise above feelings as she looked around, not finding a ladder to reach the folded boxes on the top shelves. She came up on the balls of her feet; the tips of her fingers grazed the corner of corrugated cardboard, stretching upward to catch just enough . . .

"Let me get that."

The smooth, familiar voice came from behind her, so close, the heat of his chest seared through her thick sweater. An arm circled her waist, drawing her against him as he reached and effortlessly grabbed a stack of boxes. She withdrew from the warm comfort of his embrace, too easily sucked into the need, the yearning, and turned to face him.

"I almost had it. I didn't need your help." His head tilted at her abrasiveness, his eyes steady, studying.

"What's wrong?"

"Nothing." She tried to take the boxes from him, but he pulled them back. "Hawk, I need those."

"Tell me what's bothering you."

She pursed her lips, then paused, prepared to walk out without what she came for. "You—"

"I—"

Both spoke in concert.

"Go on." Reyna braced herself, in dread and a resigned expectation of what he'd say. To date a woman her age with a teenager meant compromise that extended beyond the two of them.

"No, you first."

She sighed, hating how frustratingly vulnerable she felt in that moment. "I was going to say, you don't have kids. I don't expect you to understand how important it is for divorced parents to work together."

"And I was going to say, I'll have to find a way to get Lily to approve of me. Maybe then she'll be okay with me seeing her mother."

Reyna's heart fluttered, that breathless tightness returning in her chest. "Last night when you hung up in a hurry, I thought you . . . well, it must have been important. But if it really was because of the things I said about my ex, I only meant he's closely involved in Lily's life."

"I can assure you, it had nothing to do with that."

Anxiety dissipating, she nodded. "I also heard you

stopped by the Mist this morning for breakfast. The food there is really good." Once more, her emotions felt so exposed.

"I stopped by, hoping to get a glimpse of you." He took her hand. "I'm sorry for my rudeness last night. Amelia called. I'd been waiting all day for a meeting confirmation. Her uncle owns the vacant space I've been trying to purchase. He's been adamant about not selling because it belonged to his late wife. Amelia managed to get him to meet today to try to help convince him to sell it to me. As I explained in my text to you, I—"

"What text? You didn't text me."

"I most certainly did. The moment I opened my eyes this morning, I sent a message to you apologizing for cutting our call short."

"You might have texted someone, but it wasn't me." Reyna pulled her phone from her back pocket, prepared to disprove his claim. "See. No text from you."

"I beg to differ." He brought out his phone, scrolled, and tapped. "There's my text to you, but no reply."

Reyna frowned. "That's odd. Maybe the inn experienced a Wi-Fi outage that prevented the message from getting through."

"That's one possibility." A dark eyebrow rose.

She held his stare, reading the doubt behind his cool gaze, not wanting to believe what she was certain rolled around his suspicions. "She wouldn't . . ." Was her daughter the culprit? Lily knew the phone's password was her birthday. And once again, Lily was up bright and early, her day starting well before Reyna woke. Reyna clenched her teeth.

"Wait until I—"

"Don't do anything. Please," Hawk said. "She'll know I confirmed the missing text message. This way, she'll think I treated your lack of response as not a big deal."

"Hawk, I can't allow her to get away with this. I'm trying to raise an honest, respectable young lady. She needs to be disciplined for this act."

"Alleged," he said.

Reyna all but rolled her eyes. "Who else would have deleted the text? She knows the password to my phone." She made a mental note to remedy that issue.

"Reyna, if you could, let this one slide. For me. I'm trying to gain points with your daughter. You reprimanding her over this won't help with that."

*Goodness!* To even fathom her child would do such a thing said how deep Lily's disapproval of Hawk lay buried. And how heavy the punishment would be if the charge against her turned out to be true.

Hawk took her hand, a winsome grin returning, adding to his good looks and easily tugging on Reyna's affections. "Can you let this one go and also forgive me for my rudeness last night, madam?"

She sighed. "Fine . . . this time." Oh, but there would surely be a reprimand at some point.

"Thank you."

He set the boxes on the floor, leaning them against the closed door. Reyna found herself being scooped about the waist and jerked to his chest. His head dipped and his mouth descended on hers, conquering, feeding on her lips, his tongue probing within. "I've thought about kissing you again from the moment I woke this morning."

His breathy whisper between brushes of his lips compelled Reyna to hook her arms around his neck, settle into his hungry mouth, and take what she'd yearned as well. She slipped her hands inside his suit jacket over his shirted chest and shoulders, seeking warm, hard flesh, loving the feel of his beautifully built frame.

But she couldn't get caught groping him in the storage room. Reluctantly, she broke away. "Hawk, I'm a mother of a teenager who can be ornery on a good day. It's a package deal with me."

"I'm aware. If you're trying to scare me away, it's not working. What else you got?" A soft chuckle accompanied his words.

"What about the fact that I live in Miami and you live here?"

"I'm aware of that as well. We'll work it out."

Reyna wasn't completely cajoled, given the not-so-mysterious disappearing text message was still an issue, but let the matter rest for the time being. "I better get these boxes out there." She turned and grabbed the stack, but pivoted, eyeing him from head to his buffed black shoes. "You look nice, by the way. Were you able to get the space?"

"I think so. But I won't celebrate until the papers are signed. He could still change his mind. It wouldn't be the first time."

"I hope he doesn't."

"Me too."

She took hold of the doorknob. Hawk's hand came up and planted firmly on the solid wood, halting her departure.

The hard contours of his body pressed against her from behind. His fingers stroked her hair, the gesture so provokingly gentle, before he brushed the strands aside and his warm breath feathered the side of her neck. He took in a deep inhalation.

"I love your scent. Like new jasmine," he whispered and tasted her skin, a silky soft glide of his lips along the curve of her neck as he cupped a breast. "You have no idea how much I want you, Reyna." His voice was low, soft, and severely raw. On another long breath in and slow exhale, he released her and pulled opened the door. "But I'm a patient man."

Her pulse jackhammering, Reyna stepped out of the room and looked up, meeting the smoldering heat of his gaze. She had a pretty good idea of the level of his desire because she felt those same flames.

The energy of activity in the cafeteria was ample cover to not notice them entering only a few paces apart. Lily, the social butterfly she'd become, was too busy chatting with a small group of teens to care.

As she got back into the groove of sorting and boxing, Reyna couldn't help watching Hawk at Amelia's table, the two holding an animated conversation. He'd glance over in Reyna's direction every now and then, but respectfully, didn't show any outward affection in front of Lily. Reyna was starting to regret that rule.

By late afternoon, with most of the items packed and loaded on the truck to be shipped to the many families in need, and after saying a few words to Amelia, Reyna and Lily headed out. Hawk and Nick stood at his truck. Both sent her a wave. Reyna returned them a slight nod before getting into her car.

She, Hawk, and Lily would help at the center, then they would ride home together. Grab dinner and share their day. After, maybe they'd play a family board game or watch TV. And when the house was quiet for the night, Reyna and Hawk would lay tangled together beneath the covers. She'd curl herself within his powerful strength, his security, and blissfully drift off to sleep with—

"Mom?"

Startled, Reyna jerked out of her fantasy to Lily staring at her from the passenger seat.

"Are you okay?" Lily directed her attention out the window over to Nick and Hawk, and where Reyna had been staring.

"I'm fine." Reyna smiled a bit awkwardly as she pulled out of the parking lot and noted from the rearview mirror Hawk was still looking her way. She sighed, longing to have that which might be out of reach to her. But as her mom would say—dreams are free, so throw in everything you wish.

They returned to the inn, changed, then Reyna drove herself and Lily out to Rushing Peak. She rented skis and now was attempting to show Lily how to properly snap her boot into the ski. In such an eager rush to get going, she continued to jab her foot into the slotted opening like one trying to stomp out a fire.

"It's not going in." Lily stabbed her boot again and again.

"You're being too forceful." Reyna bent to try to help.

"Mind if I assist?"

Reyna looked over her shoulder. Hawk stood with Noah beside him, the low sun gleaming behind them like a beaconing halo. Both wore ski gear, but Hawk wasn't wearing the matching set he'd purchased with her.

"Reyna, hey! What a coincidence to find you here," Noah said, his deep voice high-pitched, carrying far too much emphasis. Evidently, Hawk had schooled him on his and Reyna's involvement. "And who is this pretty little lady?"

"This is my daughter, Lily. Lily, this is Mr. Hawk's brother, Noah."

"Hi." Lily gave a mere glance up at Hawk as she shook Noah's gloved hand.

"Let's see what you got here." Hawk crouched at her ski. "First, always remove any packed snow off the bottom of your boot. That'll make setting fully in the ski easier." He used the point of his balancing pole to clear the sole. "Now, nock the toe into the binding first. Good. Align the heel with the back bind and push down." He smiled as he came to his feet. "You got it. Try the other one." Lily positioned and locked her boot in place with ease.

"Perfect. You're a natural."

Noah came forward. "Let me show you how to balance your weight and use your poles." As he got into the fundamentals, Hawk stepped out of the way.

Reyna pretended to struggle with her boot in the ski. "I can't quite nock it. It's harder than it looks."

"Here, let me help." Hawk bent to his knees and took hold of her calf, his fingers offering up a gentle stroking as he guided the toe of her boot into the binding.

Reyna placed her hand at the angle of his neck and

shoulders to steady herself. "I'm surprised to see you," she said. Her thumb subtly caressed the side of his neck, and she felt him lean into her palm. He looked up. "I'm glad you came," she voiced silently.

"I missed you," he whispered.

"I missed you too."

"I think this little lady is ready to kick up some white stuff," Noah announced, smiling, as was Lily.

"Can we go on the higher slopes?" Lily asked.

"Absolutely not!" Reyna stated without debate. "You barely know how to stand up in those things. Spend some time learning on the smaller hills first."

"Mr. Hawk said I'm a natural." Her focus landed on Hawk for support.

"A little time on the green . . . *beginner* slope is a good way to really hone your skills and learn how to navigate," he said, and Reyna read that frigid look of objection her daughter shot at him for not championing her appeal. It didn't get any better from there. On the chair lift, along the flats and slight inclines, and then back at the ski lodge, as the pink dusky sky gave way to a starlit night, Lily hardly said a word to Hawk. In contrast, she chatted and took Noah's ski tutelage without rancor the entire time.

"Did you have fun?" Hawk asked Lily and received the universal teen nod and wordless, "Mm-hmm."

As Lily walked alongside Noah up ahead, the two teasing one another, he easily finding common ground with her, Reyna was disappointed that Hawk was unable to do the same.

"She'll come around. It's one outing," Hawk assured.

If only Reyna shared that same confidence. "I think Lily still has it in her head that you like me. I'm certain it's where her animosity sits."

"She would be right. It's taking everything I have not to throw you down in the snow and ravish you," he laughingly whispered and playfully reached for her.

Reyna jerked out of the way, although she did smirk. "It's not funny." It was good to see he wasn't put off by Lily's less-than-gracious behavior.

"Hey, how about we get some dinner?" Hawk suggested as they approached their vehicles. "There's this terrific Italian bistro."

"That's sounds perfect. I'm starved," Reyna said with a look at Lily. "We'll go back to the inn to shower and change."

"I'll pick you up." Hawk checked his watch. "It's approaching six thirty. I can swing by around eight."

"Noah, you're coming with us, right?" Lily asked.

"Sure, I'm down."

"Awesome!"

Reyna exchanged a look with Hawk, who gave a subtle shrug. Lily was like her father—stubborn to a fault. When she dug her heels in on something she felt strongly about or opposed, no one could convince her otherwise. And when that happened, her mood could be unpredictable. The missing text message still a quietly floating bone of contention, Reyna knew Lily's position all too well where Hawk was concerned, and her daughter was the most important priority. Hawk was just a man she'd met. There would be another . . . one day.

She groaned inwardly, unable to even accept those words in her head. Where did it leave her and Hawk?

---

"Thanks for dinner, Mr. Hawk."

"How about you call me Hawk?" he told Lily as he stood at the door of their suite with Reyna.

Lily nodded. "Good night."

"Get ready for bed." When the door closed, Reyna and Hawk moved short steps away. "Dinner was delicious. Thank you for trying to get to know Lily and for having to listen to her talk about her dad all evening. She thinks the world of him."

"Yes, he skydives, rock climbs, parasails—the man's one footstep shy of walking on water." A pinch of envy seeped through Hawk's common sense. He wasn't in competition with the child's father. "Sorry, I shouldn't have said that."

"It's okay. I feel the same way sometimes. Having her so young, I had to grow up quickly. One of the reasons we took this trip was for me to show her I can be just as much of a free spirit as her dad. Anyway"—Reyna palmed his face in both hands, her eyes holding his, instantly cooling his insecurity—"I appreciate your efforts."

Hawk let her guide his lips to hers, a sweet assault of his mouth as he took her into his arms, pressing close, attempting to meld his body with hers through their heavy coats. Slender fingers slipped into his hair as her kisses grew in intensity. A hot, greedy stroking of tongue on tongue sent his blood rushing in an intoxicating current of need.

He wasn't ready to break the contact but let go when she gave a light push at his shoulders just as the door opened to the suite. Lily stood there in her pink long-sleeved cotton T-shirt and pink-and-white plaid pants.

"Mom, Dad wants to talk to you."

Reyna took the phone. Hawk gave a thumb gesture over his shoulder, signaling his exit. She nodded and headed inside.

A thirteen-year-old girl—how difficult could it be to win her over? Easy as pie, he'd told himself on first thought, but now, he wasn't so sure.

No doubt Lily had deleted the text message, cementing her crusade against him.

To top it off, the child's father and Reyna were more than co-parents. There was a bond not only rooted together through the child they shared, but Hawk sensed something much more intimate, at least on Reyna's end. How could a relationship exist between him and Reyna when she hadn't fully severed the familiar ties with her ex? How could Hawk get over that hurtle?

How could any man compete with that?

*This isn't a competition.* From the looks of things, if it were, he'd likely come out on the losing end, for the battle was not with Blake but with Reyna.

Hawk never backed away from a challenge, but this was a new, peculiar beast to conquer. Lily was sure to test him. That was abundantly clear. As for Reyna, she made his heart pound and his body pulse in ways he'd never felt before. But was a relationship with her worth the near unsurmountable mountain he'd have to climb?

# Chapter Eleven

"I DON'T FOLLOW. What do you mean, she's 'close' with her ex-husband?"

"Precisely what I said." Hawk carried the box from the storage room, nudging Ash out of the way of the door, and went into the storefront. "The man calls her every night." He restacked shelves with the birdcages he'd recently made, albizzia wood lightly sanded, giving it a distressed white appearance. "I keep telling myself it's no big deal, but I don't know."

"Like I said, baggage. Is he calling Reyna directly?"

Hawk shrugged, hating that Ash might be right. "I've been present twice when he called, and twice he wanted to talk to Reyna. It seems abnormal to be that chummy with your ex."

"They do have a child together. There's history. A familiarity. You said Reyna doesn't want her daughter to know she's seeing you because of some arrangement she made with her ex. That's a new kind of weirdness. Maybe they're divorced-with-benefits or something."

"Thanks for the image." Hawk shot his cousin a murderous look, now unable to erase the thought from his head of Reyna in bed with a faceless superman, if he was to go by

Lily's praise of her father.

"What?" Ash followed Hawk back to his office. "It's not impossible. Listen, Reyna's nice and all. And Hawk, I know you're on the hunt for 'The One.' Maybe Reyna's not it. I mean, are you really ready to take on the role of daddy to somebody else's kid? A teenager at that. If the child was, say, a toddler, you could discipline her in a way that suits you. A thirteen-year-old, well, you're simply an irritation. I'll say it again—why put yourself through that when you don't have to?"

Lily's behavior yesterday gave truth to Ash's words. Hawk stretched and rolled his tense shoulders amid a wide yawn. A jumble of complex feelings for Reyna had kept him up most of the night. Ironically, it was also her steadfast determination to succeed as a good mother and her drive as a successful businesswoman that attracted him. Add to it how she could fill that lonely half of him, how her kisses crumbled his will to resist to dust, and he was sure hours spent exploring every inch of her would be so magnificent, he wouldn't ever want them to leave his bed. But her involvement with her ex might outweigh all of that.

He grabbed the stack of paid invoices from the desk and began filing them away as he said, "Maybe you're right about her not being the one."

"Better to discover it now than—"

A soft knock, then the door opened. "Hawk, glad you're here. Thought you might be at the center this time of day."

Hawk turned to his sister, out of uniform. He went back to filing. "Off today?"

"Yep." Tess gave Ash a kiss on the cheek. "We did some

shopping for the ball. Hey, Rey, I'm in here," she called over her shoulder.

Hawk's heartbeat punched and punched again before it steadied at the sight of Reyna entering while drying her hands on a paper towel.

The straight tresses she usually wore were replaced by voluminous curls that broke over her shoulders from beneath a dark-purple wool hat. A matching scarf circled her slender neck. The unzipped gray jacket allowed Hawk a peek at her figure in that fitted cream-colored cardigan. Simple black leggings covered shapely legs and tucked inside knee-high black boots. He couldn't look away, let alone take an even breath. If her mere presence could make him lose all speech, what did it say for his fortitude to end it and walk away?

He drew on what little strength of will he had, keeping his tone neutral so that he didn't come off like a puppy bouncing about in front of her for attention, continuing to file the papers. "Afternoon, Reyna."

"Hi, Hawk."

She came forward to reach the waste can and tossed the crumbled wad in her hand, the subtle floral tease of her perfume scenting the air. He quietly inhaled, closing the cabinet drawer and leaning a shoulder against it. Those lovely, unblinking brown eyes bore into his. "Tess said you all did some shopping."

"Yes, for the ball. I was glad to find something for myself and Lily at this late date."

"Wait until you see her gown." Tess gaped with a wide smile. "It's this slippery, clingy satin material. And it's backless"—she gave a hand gesture across her breasts—"with a low-cut scoop across the front and—"

"Where are you all headed next?" Hawk cut in. He didn't need the visual.

"After forcing Kate and Lily to trudge about with us all afternoon, we promised them mani-pedis," Tess answered.

Just then, Kate and Lily rushed in, giggling and chattering a mile a minute about who knew what.

"Mom, can Lily come to our house?"

"That's up to Lily's mom. Reyna, it's fine with me. I'm off until tomorrow afternoon."

Hesitation weighed in Reyna's seconds of silence.

"Lily couldn't be in more protective hands," Ash tried to assure her.

"Okay . . . sure."

The girls squealed happily.

Tess gave Hawk a look, and a small smile touched her lips. He could almost see her meddling wheels turning before she twirled her attention back to Reyna and the girls. "Oh, I have an idea. How about a sleepover? And we can invite some of your other friends over to watch Christmas movies. It'll be fun. I'll make fresh popcorn and bake some cookies."

"When did you take up baking?" Ash asked. "Ow," he groaned from the hard elbow jab Tess delivered to his side.

"Reyna, Lily's welcome to stay the night," Tess continued.

"Mom, can I?" Lily tugged on Reyna's hand.

"Sweetheart . . ." Reyna hesitated.

Hawk busied himself around his office, trying to convey an indifferent air. Simply seeing her made him break a sweat like some pimply faced teen in the presence of his crush.

What was happening to him?

"Mom, please?" Lily pleaded.

"You can stay the night."

More squeals between the girls.

Tess checked her watch. "Well, we better get going if we want to make our spa appointment." She hugged Ash, then did the same to Hawk. "You're welcome," she murmured at his ear and sauntered away, grinning on her way out.

Ash closed the door behind them. "You—" he began, only to be nudged forward when it reopened.

Reyna poked her head inside. "Oh, sorry, Ash. Hawk, it appears I'll be dining alone tonight. Would you like to join me?"

"I—"

"Bro, we have that event to go to." Ash eyed him. "You remember."

Hawk's emotions were fragmented, warring between setting a cautious distance—he didn't need the complication—and the fulfilling, eager desire to share an evening with her. "Right." He looked at Reyna. "Maybe another time."

Her smile faded, disappointment clearly coloring her expression. "I see. Well, they're waiting for me at the car. Enjoy your evening."

Before the door even met the frame, Hawk leaped and caught the knob. "Reyna?" She turned, and he realized how stupid it was of him to try to resist her. All his compressed feelings twined and knotted in his gut. How could he erect a wall between them when he mourned her over the very thought? "I can do dinner."

"I wouldn't want to interfere with your *event*." She angled her head and gave Ash a light wave of fingers. But her tone was sour.

"Reyna, I'd love to have dinner with you tonight."

"The man makes a mean eggplant Parm," Ash put in.

Hawk delivered him a murderous look while at the same time wanting to kick himself for his feeble attempt to push her away. He took her gloved hand in his. "I can pick you up around seven."

"I'd prefer to try your *mean eggplant Parm*." Her smile extended to her eyes and nestled into his soul. "Does seven still work?"

"Yes."

"Okay, then I'll be at your place at seven." Accepting his nod, she left.

Hawk stepped back into his office and closed the door. He turned hard eyes on Ash. "Man, what the hell? First you tell me I should cut things off with Reyna. Now you're suggesting I cook her dinner—which, by the way, I've only made eggplant Parmigiana once. It wasn't anything to brag about." He could grill a steak, and he knew enough that he wouldn't burn the house down, but to cook to try to impress a woman? That was a stretch. He snatched his phone from the desk and started searching for the recipe. "You couldn't suggest something simple?"

"I would hold to my words about cutting short your involvement with Reyna, but you're so deep in the abyss in love—"

Hawk's head snapped up from the YouTube how-to video. "What are you talking about?" A sudden rush of anxiety started to wind him up into a constricting coil. "Who said anything about love? I'm still getting to know her."

"Okay, maybe not love. But from that look on your face when Reyna walked in, I thought I'd have to get you some oxygen." Ash laughed as he pulled open the door. "Call it whatever is palatable to you. From where I stand, you've been bitten by something, my friend." He swatted the air. "I better go in case it's contagious." His lean frame took on a full-bodied shudder on the way out.

Reyna's sultry voice was the sexiest melody. He simply couldn't stop thinking about her—yes, his attraction was on a level of lustful intoxication.

But did it encompass love?

He really needed to flesh out what was really going on with her ex before he handed over to her the full reins to his heart.

# Chapter Twelve

THE DOORBELL RANG. Hawk tugged up his charcoal-gray slacks and shrugged his arms into a freshly pressed, pale-gray button-down, tucking in the waistband with marathon speed, and buckled his belt.

The clock's bright-blue digital numbers read 6:42. Reyna was early. He should've anticipated her timeliness.

He ran a comb through his damp hair, then slipped on black loafers, foregoing socks.

The bell rang again.

He sprinted downstairs and gave a glance at the kitchen, still in disarray from his less-than-stellar culinary talent on his way to the door.

No matter how many times he told himself to relax, that tonight was like countless others he'd spent entertaining a woman, the pounding going on in his chest said otherwise. Whatever he might feel about her must be dialed back. There was still uncertainty where her ex fitted into the picture. Where he himself resided as well.

He pulled open the door. The brisk evening breeze carried the familiar, pleasant scent of her perfume to his nose. "Hey. I'm early. I hope it's okay."

"Yes, of course." He stepped aside, and breathed her in as

she moved past him. Her fragrance, an intoxicatingly light floral, whirled around him like a pheromone. It would explain the hard stab of yearning that struck him whenever he saw her.

He assisted her out of her coat and hung it in the closet. She strutted with a sexy sway of her hips farther into the living room and tossed her purse on the recliner before moving over by the hearth, extending her hands before the fire. Her hair was once again straight tresses parted down the center of her crown. She brushed back the silky mane over both shoulders, then turned. The way she did a deliberate study of him up and down, steadily, brought on a heightened state of awareness. Was he misreading the smoldering heat in her gaze?

"Something smells good."

"I suggest you reserve praise until after you've tasted it. I still have to prepare the salad."

She crossed to the kitchen, where pots and pans cluttered the sink. He took a moment to admire the V-shaped bodice of her red cashmere sweater dress. Clingy fabric stretched over her breasts and imprinted along her lean body, exposing a hint of trim thighs. Black leather stiletto boots gave that superhero vibe she easily pulled off.

"Sorry for the mess. I thought I'd have time to straighten up."

"Don't be. You weren't expecting me for another twenty minutes. But I was hungry."

"Ah, so you're really only here for sustenance." His grin matched hers.

"And I was eager." She winked.

"Eager. Is that so?"

"Very much." Her eyes never left his as she stepped in close enough that their bodies brushed. To Hawk's stunned surprise, her mouth took full possession of his, sucking in his breath until she struggled with her own.

Her hands moved impatiently over his chest and shoulders as if searching for something, then delicate palms settled against his cheeks.

Her teeth toyed with his earlobe and along the side of his neck, a slow glide up and down, before her lips found his once more—hard, then excruciatingly tender, sending a web of sensation throughout every humming nerve ending.

This uninhibited side of her was a welcome surprise, and he reveled in it, fully giving her what she desired. His hands moved over her soft curves, exploring every angle of her beautiful body, their caresses trekking in tandem, stroking their passions raw, their kisses unending. When they finally drew back, only far enough to meet the other's fiery gaze, nearly breathless, she smiled. "That was nice, Mr. Swan."

"Very nice." One bout of impromptu, mind-numbing kisses didn't mean she was professing some profound devotion to him and only him. He had to get a grip. "We should probably eat." Yet neither broke their embrace, continuing their warm caresses up and down the other's back.

"Yes, we probably should." With a light peck on his lips, she finally stepped away, washed her hands at the sink, then took the baked eggplant Parmigiana from the warming oven and set it on the dining table between the two place settings he'd arranged earlier.

"Is red wine okay?" he asked.

"Sure." She went to the fridge and loaded her arms with all the fixings for the salad, moving about his kitchen with an easy comfort, as though tonight was another typical evening they shared. He liked the contented feeling it brought to him.

As she chopped and diced, Hawk came up behind her and enveloped his arms around her, loving the way their bodies fit together. He simply couldn't keep his hands off her. "You don't have to do that. I'm supposed to be cooking for you, remember?"

"I don't mind. Besides, it's my fault our dinner was delayed." She looked up, wearing a cheeky grin. "You looked so yummy, I couldn't resist." A light chuckle bubbled up from her.

"I propose all of our dinners start out like that." Still smiling like a crushing schoolboy, he grabbed a resting bottle of Cabernet Sauvignon from the slotted wine shelf and filled their glasses at the table. Reyna carried over the Caesar salad.

Throughout the meal, Hawk talked more about his plans to expand his store and learned how Reyna got started in her business. She told him that she was looking for a new hangar for her vehicles. They shared favorite movies and songs. Mostly, the evening was filled with continuous laughter, something he hadn't experienced on a date in a long time. It felt good. Really good.

"You're kidding. You fish?" Hawk gaped, grinning. "No way."

Reyna chuckled. "Why so shocked? You forget, I grew up living out of an RV. Camping, roughing it was normal homelife for me."

"I can't picture you baiting worms on a hook."

"I prefer to use live shrimp. Redfish and speckle trout love it."

Hawk's head fell back in an uncontained loud bout of laughter, as did Reyna's. She leaned in. "Now if you're into catfish, which I'm not, bait with worms."

Still chuckling, he shook his head and sat back, staring at her lovely face in utter amazement. She wore a smirk while sipping her wine, clearly proud of herself.

"She's beautiful, funny, smart, and can catch us dinner if the need arises." He laughed, and she once again joined him.

"Let's see." Reyna tapped her chin. "You're an expert wood craftsman, you help the needy, you create gingerbread houses with your teenage niece, and now I discover you're a terrific cook. Next, I'll learn you can communicate with sea life." Elbows on the table, she rested her chin atop her linked fingers with an adorable quirk to her lips.

"Well, I have a confession. I do try to spend time with Kate, although not as much as I'd like. In any case, I'd found out you were going to be at the gingerbread house event. That's the true reason I was there." Dark lashes fluttered as she reached for her wineglass again, but Hawk caught her hand, never taking his eyes off her, and pressed a kiss across her knuckles. "Like I said, I've wanted you from the first moment I saw you." He released her and watched as she leaned back in her chair and expelled a shaky breath, then clutched her glass like a lifeline and took in deep swallows.

"So, how did you get the nickname, 'Hawk'?" She got up and began clearing the table.

An abrupt shift in topic from the apparently uncomfortable emotional waters. He took the hint. Together, they loaded the dishwasher and tidied up. "I saved a baby hawk from getting run over."

"Wow!" She straightened, gaping at him.

"I'm kidding." He laughed and received a playful shove to the shoulder, their relaxed ambiance returning. "It's really not all that fascinating. Sort of a play on my last name—I'm not delicate like a swan, but more savage like a hawk. I'm not sure who was the first to say it, but I believe it was my maternal grandmother. From what I was told, she said I ate anything put before me. The name just stuck."

Reyna's cell phone rang. She crossed the room and retrieved the device from her purse. "It's my driver, Danielle, checking in. She's the woman who picked you up for your departure," she said while typing out a text.

"Because you had a more important fare to tend to." A small niggling still hung over the slight.

"My ex-husband returned with Lily. It was his turn to have her this Christmas, but he was called to work."

That cleared up one matter. "Your ex gets Lily every other year?" Hawk asked casually, piecing together the depths of their involvement.

"Yes, and opposite summers. Blake would prefer I move back to Texas so he could see Lily all the time. They're very close," she said as she continued to tap on her phone.

"I see."

"By the way, I got you something." She fished in her purse again and returned to the kitchen with a small white box tied off with a red ribbon.

"Should I open it or wait until Christmas?"

"Open it."

"In that case, I have something for you as well."

Her eyes widened. "You didn't have to get me anything." Though the excited gleam in her expression said differently as she followed him into the living room and over to the Christmas tree. "Really, it wasn't necessary."

"Of course I did." Hawk crouched low, shuffled aside gifts for his family to find the small package buried beneath, then stood and handed it to her. "I saw this and thought of you. Go ahead, open it."

"You first."

He untied the ribbon and removed the lid. A whimsical hawk lay on white tissue paper. The bird's profile was cut from heavy cardstock and drawn with carefully feathered lines of black-, gray-, and a touch of brown markers. The wing shimmered in fine white glitter. Its red beak was shaped to a perfect point and its red tail fanned wide. A small hole punched through the neck secured a thin gold ribbon tie.

"It's a hawk ornament I made. See?" Smiling, she flipped it over. "That's my initials and today's date. I had some time, so I popped into the craft store. It's something I like to do." The glee fell from her face, mistaking his ticking silence for disappointment.

To the contrary, Hawk was in awe. He couldn't recall a woman ever giving him a gift, especially one made with her own tender hands, and without expecting something in return.

"You don't like it. It's okay."

She tried to take it, but he held it back. "I love it. More

than love it." He tipped her chin up and kissed her lips, so soft and warm, then moved to the tree and hung the bird, giving it a high perch to be seen at all angles. "Now, your turn." The not-so-elegant wrapping tore away easily.

"*One Hundred Love Sonnets* by Pablo Neruda," she read after staring at the book's cover for a long moment, then flipped to the page where Hawk had thought he'd successfully smoothened out the dog-eared corner and began reading quietly. On her quick intake of breath, he snatched the book and snapped it shut. "I was skimming through it," he rushed out with awkward reasoning. In that moment, Ash's words struck home with wrecking ball-like force. Feelings for her had manifested into an intense squall, a quiet storm, catching him unaware.

Reyna took the book back, found the passage again, and continued to read in silence the rest of the sonnet that spoke of endless, starving desires. When she finished, her gaze lifted from the page, delving into his, a small flicker catching in their depths from the flames of the firelight.

She stood there, simply staring at him. Hawk was quite certain she'd run out of there. Instead, a warm, delicate hand clasped his.

"Make love to me," she voiced softly, giving his fingers twined with hers a light squeeze. She placed the book on the center table, grabbed her phone, then led the way to the stairs.

🌿

HAWK AWOKE TO the low, musical chime of Reyna's cell

phone. He slid up an eyelid—the clock registered ten after ten. They'd only slept about an hour.

His arm lay across Reyna's middle. A leg draped her thigh. He stayed perfectly still as she reached for her phone on the nightstand and answered sleepily, "Hi, Blake."

"Hey. Sounds like I woke you." The deep cadence of his voice rose above some sort of loud pounding sound in the background.

*You did,* Hawk inwardly growled.

"I was asleep, but it's fine. What is it?" Reyna asked.

"I texted and called Lily, but she didn't respond. That's not like her. Is everything okay?"

"Lily is at a sleepover with her friend, Kate. But she should've answered. I'll check on her and get back to you." They disconnected. Reyna turned on the table lamp and rolled over. Hawk met her concerned stare. "That was Lily's father. He tried her phone, but she didn't pick up."

Hawk sat upright. "I'm sure she's fine. Tess would've reached out if there were an issue, but go ahead, give her a ring for your peace of mind."

She brought up the number and put it on speaker.

"Reyna, hi," Tess answered.

"Hi. Just checking on Lily. She didn't answer her phone."

"That's my fault. I had everyone turned their phones off. Several had their faces glued to their social media. Now they're all watching *Jingle All the Way*. Here, I'll send you a pic."

A moment, then the phone dinged. Hawk gave a look over Reyna's shoulder. Lily and the group were dressed in their pjs and stretched out atop a pile of blankets in front of the TV, laughing. Bowls of popcorn and other snacks were spread about.

"Looks like they're having fun."

"They are," Tess replied.

"Well, I won't keep you. Good night." She ended the call and turned to Hawk. "I need to speak to Lily's father. He'll worry if I don't."

As she did so, he lay down, resting upon the pillow, arms crossed beneath his head.

"Rey," Blake answered.

"Lily's fine. Kate's mother had everyone turn their phones off to watch a movie."

"Lily hardly knows this kid, and now she's at a sleepover?" Once again, he spoke loudly over the thudding drum of background interference, which made it easy for Hawk to listen in.

"Tess, Kate's mother, is the sheriff here. She's great. I've gotten to know the family. I wouldn't have let Lily go if I didn't trust she'd be safe."

"True that." Blake released a long breath. "I miss my sweet pea. You know we talk every night. I guess I'll have to wait to find out who's been a dweeb this week." Both chuckled. "I have a surprise for her."

"Blake, Lily has enough stuff. What did you get her this time?"

"Unlike our baby girl, you never liked surprises. Remember when you tore the bedroom apart searching for that necklace I bought you? You couldn't wait an hour. I'd planned to give it to you at the restaurant."

"I found it." A soft chuckle.

Hawk regarded their easy laughter and familiar comfort. In his silence, he stroked a hand up her bare back to her neck, circling his thumb with a methodically slow caress, while trying to discern if it was not only Reyna maintaining this peculiar relationship, but Blake as well. As though catching wind of his musing, Reyna looked over her shoulder. He was rewarded with a tender palm cupping his cheek.

"You'll find out the surprise when Lily does. Oh, the crew is calling me. Gotta get back to work."

"Stay safe." She sat her phone on the nightstand, clicked off the lamp, the glow of the clock giving off the only ray of light, and burrowed beneath the covers.

Hawk extended his arm, and she rested her head in the crook of his shoulder. A hand glided across his chest. A smooth leg hooked at his thigh, her warm body snuggling against him. She was in his bed. His arms. There was no need to be envious of her relationship with her ex. He decidedly put that to rest. But how could he make a connection with Lily?

Blake obviously adored his daughter—in Hawk's opinion, to the point of catering to her every whim. Where did that leave him with Lily when trying to establish a small branch between them, especially when she viewed her parents as a couple? Given the agreement of not allowing their child to see them in other relationships, Reyna and Blake, in essence, had set up this odd family dynamic for Lily. The only one she'd ever known.

Hawk expelled a weary breath, his thoughts bearing down a bit heavier now. "Lily's father calls her every day.

That's good. Sorry, I couldn't help listening. He was practically yelling."

"No telling what that banging sound was. He's a chemical engineer. He's in Alaska on an oil rig somewhere in the middle of the ocean." Light fingertips played in his chest hairs, swirling around one nipple, then the other, trekking slowly downward across his abdomen, then returning, a soothingly warm touch. "He got called in to help fix a problem, which is why he couldn't take Lily this holiday."

"Sounds like you and he are in a good place. I suppose you two talk every night as well."

"He calls Lily, but yes, we talk. Not every time."

"Maybe you could help me find common ground with Lily, offer some pointers in how I might gain her trust. Her likes and dislikes, for example. Blake's her father—that goes without saying—and I'd never try to interfere with his role. But there must be something I can do outside of bribing her with gifts, giving her whatever she wants. I think you and Blake have that covered." He chuckled.

Reyna's head reared back, her frame going taut against him. Hawk didn't need to see her face to know she was steadily regarding him and that his teasing wasn't received well. She came out of the circle of his arms and clicked the lamp back on, then braced herself up on an elbow, facing him. "What are you trying to say?"

He had to be cautious here. "I only meant . . ."

"Go on."

"Well, in my short observation, from what I've gathered, Lily can be a bit . . ."

"A bit what?" Lines crinkled her otherwise smooth brow.

"Spoiled. I get it, she's your only child," he supplemented.

"I'll admit Lily can be stubborn and maybe even mouthy at times, but what thirteen-year-old isn't? It's a phase. I went through it, as I'm sure you did too. Are you trying to say I'm a bad mother? That I don't properly discipline my daughter?" The creases in her forehead etched deeper.

"No, not at all. I'm only saying, perhaps you might try to set a few boundaries."

"I wanted to reprimand her for erasing the text, but you asked me not to. So, set boundaries only when *you* don't have to suffer any repercussions. Got it." She glowered and sat back against the headboard, jerking and tucking the heavy down comforter beneath her arms, setting a definite boundary of her own between them.

"Reyna, you're right. I shouldn't have asked that of you." He tried to take her hand, but she wrenched it away, crossing her arms tight at her chest, her expression just as tight. "Nick and I are hosting our annual Christmas party at the center tomorrow. Maybe you and Lily can come lend a hand. It's usually a lot of fun. It'll give Lily another chance to see what I do there. Plus, it's an opportunity to show her how those who don't have much appreciate the kindness of others."

"I'll think about it." Her features remained taut.

"On another matter"—Hawk paused, considering for a moment, then decided to swallow and choke on that foot he'd lodged in his mouth—"have you told Blake about us?"

Her dark lashes fluttered before she looked away.

"I take that as a no. How will Lily ever get comfortable with me dating you when you're uncomfortable dating me?

Seeming almost guilty."

Her eyes flashed to his. "That's not true."

"Isn't it?"

"As I mentioned, I was fifteen and Blake was seventeen when we got together," she said after a long, tense silence. "An awkward girl entering not only a new school but an entirely new environment—it was scary. School turned out to be nothing like the books I'd read. Clothes, hair, shoes, you name it, and I got it all wrong, according to my peers—kids can be brutal. Blake was the school's fast-rising star football athlete. We met by chance in the library, where I spent my break period, and Blake had been forced to catch up on chemistry or risk sitting out several games.

"I had my head in a book when I turned a corner, and it was as if I'd hit a wall. Even then, he was massive. We became best friends. Everyone found it odd that he'd be interested in me. Lily was born a year later. We got married. When he went to college, something changed . . . with both of us. We grew into different people, wanting different things. I think we simply matured into the individuals we were on the path to become. That road was leading us in opposite directions. I said all that to say we managed to find our way back to where we started—as good friends, which has been great for Lily's upbringing."

"But as a result, Lily sees you two as a couple."

She threw back the covers, swung her legs over the side of the bed, and started to rise. "I don't expect you to understand. I should go."

"Reyna, wait." Hawk caught her hand and held on against her resistance. "You're trying to raise a healthy, well-adjusted child, which requires a good co-parenting relationship with your ex-husband. I get that. I only meant you deserve to have someone too. Please stay," he urged, and hooked an arm at her waist when she tried to leave the bed again. "We're talking things out. Sweetheart, let me hold you. Reyna?" He tugged lightly and managed to get her to lie back down.

"I have to do what's best for my child," she said through a shaky whisper.

"I know," he uttered between tender kisses on her tight lips, which gradually softened around his persistent nibbling, and the tension left her body with it. There was more he wanted to say, but clearly it wasn't the time to say it.

She clicked off the light, then brought the covers up to her shoulders, turning away from him.

He tucked himself in close, breaching the barrier she'd erected, fitting her snug within the angles of his body. As he offered up gentle kisses at the nape of her neck and along her bare shoulder, attempting to soothe her upset, she started a slow caress of his arm cradling her waist, gliding her hand down, entwining their fingers on a gust of a sigh. When he was sure she'd settled into his embrace within a deep slumber, he let go of the tension coiling and squeezing every muscle. In that moment, he tried to resign himself to the idea that their involvement should come to an end, but the notion caused a flash of panic that clenched his gut and sent a jabbing pain through his chest.

What was he to do?

"You're sneaking out on me?"

Reyna froze at the sound of that lusciously husky voice. It had been the plan, but the noisy zipper on her boot gave her away. Seated on the edge of the bed, she turned her head, addressing him in the dark. "I didn't want to wake you." He reached over and turned on the lamp, then stretched out on his back. The slate-colored bedding complemented beautiful pale-gray eyes that were heavy from sleep. Waves upon waves of thick, dark hair spread upon the pillow. The sculpted wall of his bare chest expanded even more with a deep inhalation, rippling down tight abs. Thick, muscular thighs slightly spread in a relaxed sprawl, tangled within the rumpled bedding. He was strength personified and truly a feast to her appreciating gaze. How could he wake looking so cover-model gorgeous?

"It's still dark out." He scooted closer and caught her waist, tugging. "Come back to bed."

Simply looking at him sent a warm shiver through her. Reyna was so tempted. "I want to get back to Harbor Mist before everyone starts to rise. Is the door locked at this hour? It's not a hotel." Another thought slammed her brain, throwing her into a state of panic. "Geri. I wonder if Tess told her we were meeting tonight . . . last night? Oh God, I can't let her see me trotting in at five in the morning."

"The day staff relieves the night crew at six a.m. I'm pretty sure Geri doesn't usually arrive until around seven or seven thirty. She and Tess are best friends, but I doubt Tess would've told her about our date."

"Well, if she catches me strolling in at the break of dawn, she's surely to put two and two together."

He captured her hand between both of his then pressed his warm lips into her palm before resting back upon the pillow. "Yesterday, Geri asked me to come by for dinner, but I told her I had plans. Her asking is nothing new. The few times I do show, half the meal is spent with her inquiring when will I settle down, get married, and have kids. I don't know who's worse, her or Tess. Such things don't happen in an instant."

Reyna's heart now skipped a beat for a different reason. Was he looking for a wife? Was she ready to be one again? Not that the thought hadn't crossed her mind. But fantasizing was one thing.

She zipped her boot the rest of the way and stood. "I need to shower and check in with my drivers before Lily returns for breakfast."

He slid out of bed. Powerful arms went around her waist, drawing her flush against his comforting frame. "You can shower here with me."

"I can't. I don't have any of my things." Gentle nibbles on her neck was all it took for her to whip her arms around his strong back. She sank into the pleasure of his lips against her throat and enjoyed the close-cut hairs of his bearded cheek brushing against hers.

"About what was said last night," he voiced softly at her ear, then tipped her chin up with a light touch of his fingers. "I'd like to see where things go between us. In other words, I'm in this fully. Completely. If it's not what you want, I'm a big boy and can take the rejection. Not saying I'd be happy about it, but I'll accept it."

Her heartbeat quickened. It must have registered on her

face. His buoyant expression disappeared, and his brow lowered, dimming the light in his eyes.

"Is that too heavy to hear at five in the morning? I can't tell if you're wavering whether to join me back in my bed or make a run for the door."

"Right now, it's the latter. I really need to get some work done. I want to reach out to a few companies to try to find hangar space." It wasn't a lie, but not the only reason why she had to get out of there. She needed time to think, which was impossible with him near.

A soft sigh. "I'll walk you out." There was a solemn intensity to his demeanor as he lugged on his slacks and followed her, bare-chested and barefooted, downstairs.

Reyna stuck the book of sonnets in her handbag. She turned to see Hawk with her wool coat opened wide, prepped to dress her. After sliding her arms in the sleeves, she accepted his ministration of buttoning her up. Then he pulled open the door.

"You stay put," she ordered when he looked ready to follow her outside. "I won't be responsible for you catching a cold." Heavy arms curled around her from behind while once again his warm lips teased that knowingly sensitive spot behind her ear. Before she could insist that he end his bold, sweet torture, he broke the contact.

"Drive carefully. The side roads can become a sheet of ice. You won't know until you're sliding. I should follow you. I'll grab my coat and boots." He pivoted.

"No." Reyna caught his wrist. "I'll be fine." His lips pursed, likely to object, but instead, took her chin in another light hold between his fingers and tipped it up for a quick peck on the lips.

"Text me the second you park."

"I will." She hurried down the five steps to the walk, got behind the wheel of her car, and backed out of the driveway with him standing half dressed in the door of his home, watching her the entire distance to the street. His heartfelt declaration struck like pebbles skipping across a fast-moving stream.

*He wants a wife.*

# Chapter Thirteen

THE GUESTS' BLENDED chatter and the clink of dishes became background noise to Reyna's jumbled thoughts. *I'm in this fully. Completely.*

Heaven help her; she'd asked for this. For him. Even had the *list* to prove it. Then why did it suddenly frighten her so?

With her mug in both hands, she sipped her coffee, appreciating the warmth licking her fingers as apprehension and uncertainty continued to churn her belly into tight knots.

A discussion with Blake about Hawk would need to happen. Was she ready?

Reyna looked up, drawn out of her headspace by thick Belgian waffles, fluffy scrambled eggs, sausage links, Canadian bacon, cheesy hash browns and a large, icing-coated cinnamon roll. Lily had come to the table with a small sampling of just about every item from the breakfast bar.

"Young lady, I don't see one piece of fresh fruit on that plate," Reyna scolded and nursed her small bowl of mixed berries.

"I didn't have room." Shrugging and munching on a strip of Canadian bacon, Lily grinned.

"You would if you didn't have—"

"Good morning."

Reyna's head snapped up, her heart slamming into her rib cage at the sight of Hawk stepping up to the table. The moss-green flannel shirt beneath his parka lay unbuttoned, revealing a gray T-shirt. Loose faded denims and heavy-sole black boots completed his new day apparel. And he smelled wonderful, a pleasant earthy spice. She'd been swaddled in his scent mere hours earlier. He rotated to speak to someone calling out to him a few tables over. His hair was tied into a knotted ponytail at the nape, fine strands damp and curling at his neck. She loved his no-nonsense style . . . his soft lips against her skin, his strong hands caressing her body. She loved—

Her pulse punched harder.

He turned back, wearing a broad smile, and she *loved* the way it reached his eyes. Her heart raced faster still.

"Someone has a big appetite. Good morning, Lily."

Lily cut him a mere side glance. "Hey."

Reyna exchanged a subtle look with Hawk and recalled their talk about boundaries. "Lily, show your manners!"

Her attention popped up from her plate. "Good morning, Mr. Hawk."

Satisfied, Reyna smiled. "Hawk, what brings you by?"

"Thought I'd grab breakfast before I head to the shop. Then I'm off to the veterans' center."

"You're welcome to sit with us." Reyna tilted her head at the adjacent empty chair by the window. "The view of the iced lake is so pretty, and the snow covering the branches on the other side. I can imagine how beautiful it is with the blue water and heavy foliage in summer."

He removed his jacket and draped it over the back of the chair. "It's definitely something to see. I'll go grab a plate. Be right back."

"Why does he have to sit with us? Can't he go somewhere else?"

Hawk gave a look over his shoulder, evidently not out of earshot to escape Lily's rudeness. Reyna sent him an apologetic nod. "There aren't any vacant tables. And it's the polite thing to do—something, young lady, you've been lacking lately. What is it about him you don't like?"

Lily shrugged. "He's always staring and smiling at you. It's weird."

"Would you rather he scowls when he sees me?" Reyna pinched her brow and scrunched her face while crossing her eyes.

Lily snickered. "No. More like this." With her tongue hanging out the corner of her mouth, eyes crossed, she hunched her small frame and crooked her neck.

"No, this," Reyna challenged.

"Now that's a look to cause nightmares." Hawk sat his plate down and took a seat opposite Lily.

"We were just clowning around." Reyna regarded his full plate over the rim of her mug. "Goodness, *that's* a hearty appetite."

"I had a vigorous workout last night. Need to refuel." He winked subtly, wearing that wide, white smile amid cutting into his stacked blueberry pancakes drowned in maple syrup.

Reyna choked around the mouthful of dark-roasted blend and accepted her water glass that Hawk handed over. A sudden tightening clenched her stomach, her toes curling within her boots, reminding her of the wild, hot passion unleashed between them last night. She brought up the napkin from her lap, pressed it to her lips, and looked at Lily. Rapidly working thumbs tapped away on her phone.

"No texting at the table. You know that."

"It's Dad. He sent me this TikTok." Laughing, Lily held the phone out. "He said to tell you good morning." Reyna gave a glimpse at Hawk and could easily read his study of her. *Lily sees you two as a couple.* She was starting to see the evidence. More to the point, Reyna was believing it. "Tell him you're at breakfast. He can call or text later."

"But he's about to go to bed. He worked last night. We didn't get to talk."

Reyna sighed. "Five minutes." She turned another awkward look at Hawk, but he concentrated on his hash browns, his expression a blank mask, though she was certain he was quite tuned in. "Lily and I will help today at the center."

"Do we have to?" Lily pouted, typing away.

"Tell your dad you'll chat later." Getting a huff, Reyna watched as Lily sent off the text.

After Blake replied, shoulders slumped, Lily set her phone on the table as text alerts continued to pop up, one after another, from her circle of friends. "Do we have to go to the center? Everybody's going out to the creek to ride snowmobiles."

"Sweetheart, it's important we give back. With all the donations that come in, I'm sure we can be useful."

Hawk wiped his mouth on his napkin. "Extra hands are always welcomed. Especially today. We have families visiting. The boxes of clothing and toys you all helped pack will be handed out this afternoon. Nick and I make it an event with games, food, and music. The kids seem to really enjoy themselves. For the parents, it lessens the stigma for them, you know."

Reyna understood. Staring at him, her heart bloomed wide. She swung her head in the direction of her daughter. "Mr. Hawk spends a lot of his time helping those in need. He's also an Army veteran himself. These are his brethren." She looked at Hawk once more, simply awed by his generosity. His kindness. "Lily, the Christmas tree here in the lobby . . . it was Mr. Hawk's idea to have guests hang an ornament. He donates it to a needy family each year." Beneath the white tablecloth, Reyna rested a hand on his knee briefly, feeling a mix of admiration and attraction, then turned back to Lily. "Isn't that a nice thing to do?"

"Yeah," Lily mumbled around a bite of her cinnamon roll. "Mom, can we at least not stay all day? I'll still have time to ride."

Reyna sat back, tension in her shoulders. "You've never been on a snowmobile. You need lessons first."

"I already know how. I ride ATVs. Can't be any different," Lily argued.

Reyna bit the inside of her jaw to fight against the rising tide of frustration and not to show herself growing annoyed in front of Hawk and the room of guests as a whole. The child was as stubborn as they came. With a stern eye on Lily, she asked, "Hawk, is there a difference between riding an ATV and a snowmobile?" He'd been sitting quietly, eyes shifting between her and Lily as he ate. When he was slow to reply, Reyna turned her head and read the reluctance in his gaze. The question would pull him into the battle—one he didn't appear eager to join.

Hawk cleared his throat and took a sip of water, followed by another swipe of his napkin across his mouth. "Snow is an unpredictable beast. It reacts differently than dirt and sand. For example, there can be ice pockets. If you're unfamiliar with any terrain, whether it be snow or otherwise, it can be treacherous. A couple of lessons wouldn't hurt."

If looks could kill, there was no mistaking Lily's irritation, and Hawk received the full weight in her glare. "My dad would let me do it. He's not scared of anything." She pushed back from the table and got up.

"Where are you going?" Reyna palmed a hip. "You hardly finished your food. That's wasteful. Sit."

"But I'm full. Some of my friends are here. They're hanging out in the game room. Can I go?"

Reyna regarded her daughter's peeved expression for a long moment and decided to spare Hawk the disdain. "Yes. And stay within these walls. Um," she added, and Lily pivoted. "What do you say?" Reyna angled a nod at Hawk.

"Have a good day, Mr. Hawk."

"You do the same." He smiled. It wasn't reciprocated.

After Lily cleared the room, Reyna sighed, shaking her head. "It's her father's fault. He has her thinking she's invincible. That girl isn't afraid of anything."

"I see I have a steep hill to climb." Hawk chuckled and shook his head, stroking the hairs on his chin. "She really doesn't like me, does she? All kids like me." He laughed lightly again, but the furrow of his brow betrayed him. "I think her position is pretty clear where I'm concerned."

Another weighted sigh—part frustration, part disappointment—and Reyna gave his hand resting on the table a light squeeze before taking hold of her mug. "Sorry for her behavior. I know you're trying. As I said before, she's not used to a man showing interest in me." He merely nodded. Given Reyna's reaction last night to his accusations, she couldn't blame him for treading with caution. "Lily also said you're always staring and smiling at me . . . like you're doing right now." She smirked over the rim of her tepid coffee.

"I enjoy looking at you. Your hair's curly today." His gaze roamed over her face, settling on her eyes. "I find you stunningly beautiful. Hot. Sexy." Those flirtatious sentiments were said in a low, throaty timbre, stroking all the right pulse points. "I want to kiss you."

"What?" Reyna blinked rapidly. She followed his eyes upward to where a clump of mistletoe dangled over their table, then around at a few guests who were laughingly partaking of the tradition before taking their seats. "We sho—"

A waiter approached to collect the dishes, then went on his way.

"Not being afraid to try new things is not a bad trait to have. Unfamiliar and scary, we tend to let fear rule us as we get older," Hawk remarked.

"Are you referring to Lily or me?"

"Between the things I said last night and this morning at the crack of dawn—judging by your swift exit, I scared you, didn't I?"

"It was a lot to digest." *More than a lot.* Reyna took a large gulp from her mug, her emotions a jumble of nerves.

His warm palm stroked her denim-covered thigh beneath the table. Those beautiful unwavering eyes, so calm and patient, yet so deep and determined.

"I discovered something last night too," he whispered. "My heart is yours if you want it." Neither looked away as the slow-moving hand on her leg kept up a soothing caress, so daringly intimate, she couldn't complete a full breath.

"Good morning."

Their heads turned. It was as if Amelia had appeared out of nowhere. She stood beside the table, holding a cup with wisps of steam and a packed bowl of fruit. Her expression taking on a quizzical look. Then her lips twitched a grin. "Am I interrupting? Hawk, Geri said you were here, having breakfast, so I thought . . ." She paused, appearing as though caught by some invisible tug, taking a step back. "I'll leave you two—"

"No." Reyna cleared the knot in her throat and swallowed hard to try to steady the rapid beat of her heart. "You're not interrupting. Good morning, Amelia." She glanced about at the still-packed room. No vacancies. A few more minutes to savor having Hawk all to herself would have been a small treasure. "Would you like to join us?"

"Thanks." Amelia set her cup and bowl opposite Reyna, then angled her cheek toward Hawk with a point upward while drawing her long, rich-brown tresses over one shoulder. "Do I get a kiss?"

With a side-glance at Reyna, Hawk came out of his chair and delivered a peck. The action was about as innocuous as it could get, though she noted his unease and gave a light touch on his knee before directing a smile across the table.

"Amelia, I didn't know you were staying here."

"I'm not. I had a delivery. Geri offered breakfast. I've opted for fresh berries. Got to fit into my gown for the ball."

"Amelia has been providing the baked goods to the Mist for about six months now," Hawk supplied.

"Nearly nine actually," she corrected and rotated her head to Reyna. "Sweet Amelia's—it's my store. I'm about a block from Hawk's. We host an afternoon tea on Saturdays. You should stop by."

"Sounds fun. I will."

"Have you gotten your dress? I hear every boutique is sold out of anything decent. Hope you have."

"I managed to find something suitable. I haven't worn a gown in ages."

"It's the one time of year I get to dress up. I'm looking forward to it." Amelia turned to Hawk. "I almost forgot. I'm having my uncle over this afternoon for lunch. You should join us. I know it's been hard to pin him down. Maybe bring along the agreement. He's happiest when he's munching on apple pie." A small chuckle. "You might be able to get him to sign it."

"Though our meeting went well, it has been a challenge to get him to finalize our verbal agreement," Hawk explained to Reyna.

"Then there's your opportunity." She decided to cut through the edge of indecision she could see on his face and tried again to convey she had no qualms with his and Amelia's friendship. She folded her napkin, placed it on the table, and came to her feet. Hawk followed suit. "I'm going to check on Lily, then finish up with work before she and I head over to the center later."

"Today will be a lot of fun," Amelia remarked.

"So I hear. I'm looking forward to it."

"I'll see you there," Hawk told Reyna.

"You will." She gave a scant look up and no other hint was needed. He leaned over and gave her a kiss on the cheek, adding a surprisingly light caress of fingers up and down her arm. It took everything within Reyna not to turn her head ever so slightly to catch a brush of his lips against hers. When he drew back, she noted the smirk Amelia wore as she concentrated on dicing up her fruit. Reyna couldn't discern whether Hawk's subtle show of affection was done on purpose in some small feat of reassurance . . . or defiance.

She went on her way but paused at the door and looked back. Hawk inclined his head, eyes trained on her, and she returned the same.

He'd said his heart was hers if she wanted it. Fact was, he'd already stolen hers.

# Chapter Fourteen

THE SOUND OF music and laughter was such a cheery sight.

Reyna and Lily entered the center's recreation room to children running about with sticky hands and fruit punch-stained lips, courtesy of the overflowing snack table in the corner. Some guests claimed seats on the mismatched sofas and chairs. Others mingled about.

"Wow, so many people," Lily said.

"Yes." Reyna tried to see over the many heads around her.

"Reyna?"

She turned. "Nick, hi."

"Glad you could come out. Lily, it's great to see you."

"Hi." She smiled.

Nick ushered them across the room and through the rear double doors, continuing down the hall to the cafeteria.

The aromas met them at the threshold. Sweet and savory. Volunteers carried out from the kitchen large foil-covered, steaming-hot, deep-dish aluminum pans and placed them on the back tables.

The cold industrial space had been transformed into a holiday haven. Paper tablecloths with red-and-green checkered patterns adorned the rows of white folding tables. Wooden bowls filled with acorns and holly served as centerpieces. Overhead, twinkling white lights strung from the drop ceiling added to the festive décor.

Nick gestured to the boxes they'd packed with donations, now stacked along the side wall. "I was worried we wouldn't have enough for everyone, but I think we're good."

"Mom, I did a lot of those small ones." Lily seemed proud of her handiwork.

Reyna took note of the boxes with a red bow atop. "Sweetie, you did a great job." She turned to Nick. "I didn't expect there'd be so many."

"Hawk and I have been doing this for about six years now, and we're always surprised by the sheer number of our vet families that need help. That's why it's important that for Christmas, we try to make it a bit special."

The amount of effort and care that went into it all swelled Reyna's heart. "What would you like us to do?"

"The food is almost ready. I'll have everyone file in soon." Nick grabbed two aprons from the few draped across the back of a folding chair and handed them over. "Find a spot behind the table to serve, if you don't mind."

"Not at all." Reyna and Lily took their stations alongside several others prepped to assist. They were handed serving utensils, then began uncovering warm pans of sliced ham, turkey, and tender roast beef. Farther down the table, steaming mac and cheese, mashed potatoes, smooth gravy, candied yams, mixed veggies, and a horde of other eats were revealed.

Over at the entrance, Nick signaled a thumbs-up, then

pinned the doors open wide. As the guests came in, Reyna, Lily, and the other volunteers filled their sturdy paper plates with healthy portions.

Reyna found herself chatting with each person who came before her and noticed Lily was doing the same with the younger guests. One in particular, who couldn't be more than four, and who was proud to say her name was Jessica, stood with her small hands cupping the edge of the table. One leg swung back and forth as she chattered away while individuals skirted around her. Her stubby red ponytails stuck out at the sides of her head. Adorable, plump, freckled, pink cheeks. The child's mother sent them an apologetic smile before she scooped the tot and carried her off.

When everyone was seated, some of those who'd been serving fixed themselves a small plate and found a seat among the guests.

Reyna kept an eye on the door. Hawk hadn't shown. It was half past three. He said he was all in. But would he decide she wasn't worth the complication? Lily hadn't made things easy. Why should he burden himself when he could find a woman who didn't have a headstrong, moody teen? Though it all rested at the outer corners of her thoughts, she tried to focus on the smiles and laughter around her as trays of sliced cakes and pies were brought out and set where everyone could help themselves to the confections.

The sudden jingling sound came from somewhere within the building. Then there was an intermittent pause that grew louder and louder until . . .

"Ho, ho, ho, Merry Christmas," said the man standing at the entrance and decked out in full Santa garb, round belly and all.

Children released ear-piercing shrieks and rushed Santa as he tried to make his way into the room and over to a chair where Nick stood near the boxes of donations, now wearing a green elf hat and pointy ears.

Reyna smirked when she and Santa made eye contact. She watched as Hawk perched on his knee a little girl about five years old and patiently listened to her long Christmas list. One after the other, little ones got a turn to tell Santa what they wanted, then Nick handed each a small box on their departure. The larger boxes, he announced, were gifts for the parents to take home later.

"Lily, here's your opportunity to tell Santa what you want for Christmas," Reyna said low, watching her enjoy a slice of chocolate cake.

Lily rolled her eyes, though a small smile caught the corners of her lips. "Mom, I'm thirteen. I know that's Mr. Hawk," she whispered back.

They both looked down at the little girl, Jessica, her cheeks now covered in cake crumbs as she tugged on Lily's sweater. "Come," was all her high-pitched, baby voice commanded while trying to drag Lily along to sit among those now gathered around Santa as he told them a story.

Reyna returned her daughter's shrug. She'd made yet another friend.

Back in Miami, her baby struggled with fitting in with those at her new private school, often saying they were stuck-up dweebs. Here, she blossomed. Lily even started her mornings bright and early. Though completing her school assignments was never an issue, now textbooks lay open and term papers were drafted well before Reyna cracked open an eyelid. This assertive side of Lily was pleasant to see.

"Hawk's like a magnet with kids. They're drawn to him."

Startled, Reyna hitched a quiet breath and turned her head to Amelia. When had she arrived? "I can see he enjoys being Santa." They shared a chuckle at watching a little boy shriek with laughter at getting tossed over Hawk's shoulder and spun in a dizzying circle. He'd be a terrific father. Reyna had no doubt.

"We dated briefly. But I'm sure you already know that."

Amelia's tone seemed matter-of-fact, as though sharing the latest weather forecast. In observation, there was clearly a friendship she and Hawk shared, but Reyna didn't detect anything more than that. It did, however, provoke a question. "Why did you two break up? And when, if you don't mind me asking?"

"It's been a little over two years. The short answer, he wasn't ready to commit, and I wasn't patient to wait. When I was given the opportunity to run a pastry kitchen in New York, I took the job. We tried to keep things going long-distance for a couple of months. Let's just say absence didn't make the heart grow fonder. Hawk pulled away. You might say, out of sight, out of mind." She jerked her head to Reyna. "That doesn't mean you and he . . . to be truthful, we both fizzled. So we ended it. We do better as friends."

Their attention swiveled to the call for extra hands in the kitchen. "I think they're starting to clean up." Amelia stepped away, but then turned back. Her features were subdued, but her eyes were warm. "It's seldom you find a man with a heart as big as Hawk's. I'm glad he's found someone he's willing to share it with."

"We're not—" Reyna started to spout her practiced fib, but Amelia's tentative, gentle hand clasped hers.

"Just know he's a good man."

Watching her stroll away, the woman was unaware of the two-ton anvil she'd just dropped, one that left Reyna prying her tongue from the roof of her parched mouth to swallow the knot in her throat. A long-distance relationship was about all she and Hawk could have, of which, according to Amelia, he wasn't a strong proponent. Where did that leave them?

She wouldn't think about it. At least not now.

But that was nearly impossible. Could a relationship with Hawk survive over a thousand miles apart, or would theirs suffer the same fate? Add to it Lily's unwarranted aversion to Hawk, another battle Reyna would have to contend with. It all seemed hopeless.

Cleaning always helped to distract her. Reyna went into the kitchen, rolled up her sleeves, and got to work scrubbing pots and pans, loading the dishwasher, taking out the trash, mopping the floor, doing just about anything to keep herself busy. After a little over an hour, she checked on Lily. Seated on the floor were five kids and little Jessica on her lap, thumb in her mouth, quietly listening as Lily read from her cell phone, no less, *'Twas the Night Before Christmas*. Her spirit brightening a touch, Reyna took out her phone and snapped a picture, then sent it off to Blake with the text:

*Our daughter...*

She saw Hawk talking with Nick over by the exit. When he stepped out, she hurried after him. Aside from sharing long glances and subtle smiles sent her way, he'd kept his distance, respected her wishes to keep their relationship discreet.

"Hawk, do you have a minute?" He spun a bit wobbly in that portly Santa getup. A smile greeted her, one so radiant, so genuinely happy to see her, it felt as if he'd reached inside her chest and hugged her heart. To have him look at her like that gave her pleasantly warm chills. "Can you lend me a hand?"

"Anything for you."

They strode down the hall. Reyna glanced left and right before pushing open the storage room door, pinning herself against it to allow him entry.

He scanned the packed shelves. "What do you ne—?"

She silenced him with the hungry crush of her mouth, holding nothing back. Wisps of his thick white beard interrupted her tasting of his lips. He broke away long enough to yank the furry, fake hair down beneath his chin, then he brought both hands up to palm her face, angling her head back. The hot, greedy, opened-mouth kiss he demanded of her, kissing her like she was his oxygen, sent shock waves through her, shifting every thought, every modicum of indecision. Her parents often said when the stars align themselves, take the path offered. She would do just that.

With reluctance, Reyna pulled away from his tantalizing mouth.

"That was a nice hello." Hawk grinned, puffing for air.

"When I see you . . ." She looked away for a moment, surprised herself by the level of attraction she had for him. "I missed you."

"I missed you too. That said, would this little tryst that has me now sweating even more underneath this suit have anything to do with whatever it was you and Amelia were discussing earlier?"

She blinked. "You saw us? You were telling a story to the children."

"I can't focus on anything else fully when you're in the room." On a low chuckle, he tugged at the white furry lapel of his coat, fanning himself. "I need to get out of this before I combust. Woman, you got me scorching under here."

Reyna snickered with girlish laughter. It'd been a long time since she felt these butterflies of giddy delight. "By the way"—she pointed at the Santa suit—"this, all of what you do, it's wonderful."

"The kids love it, and the parents appreciate it. Now, care to share what you and Amelia were talking about?"

"How did your lunch go with Amelia's uncle?"

"Good. He signed the agreement to turn over the vacant space."

"That's great! Congratulations!" If only finding a garage hangar were that simple.

"Thanks. Glad to finally be able to get things moving forward. I was hesitant about spending the money, but if I want to grow my business, I must bite the bullet and invest to do it. Now, you and Amelia's little tête-à-tête, care to share?"

Reyna pulled open the door. "Go change before you sweat out twenty pounds."

"Ah." He nodded, grinning. "Deflecting 101."

"We'll talk about it another time. Oh!" He hooked his

arm around her waist, the movement sudden and swift, jerking her against his body, taking her breath as his mouth claimed hers. "Hawk, we're in the hall. Someone might see us. Lily might," she whispered, as he nibbled at her neck.

"I love your fragrance." He pressed a light kiss at the column of her throat. "Your silky skin. Your sweet mouth"—a soft peck—"your beautiful eyes"—a brush of his lips over her lids—"you, Reyna."

The declaration was so tender, so devastatingly wonderful, she trembled. "We-we, have to stop before someone catches us." Her legs struggled to keep her upright when he released her.

"Maybe tomorrow I could prepare dinner for you and Lily at my place . . . oh, right, that won't work," he said before Reyna could point out the optics it would suggest of the three of them together.

"Thanks for understanding. I better get back."

He delivered a quick kiss on her lips, then broke into a low harmony, still smiling, "I saw Mommy kissing Santa Claus."

Reyna chirped a laugh. "You're ridiculously silly."

"I'm guessing that's what you love about me."

"I do." They both blinked. An even wider white smile added to his jolly gray eyes. He turned and strode on down the hall, unhurried, whistling that notorious Christmas melody. Unable to stop smiling herself, still floating from his sweet words, still recovering from the passion of his kisses, Reyna pivoted to head back to the cafeteria and found Nick standing at the threshold. His head angled, looking past her to Hawk, then back at her, and his eyes flared in recognition.

"You two?" His entire face displayed his surprise. "I'll be . . ."

"It's . . . we're not—"

His hand came up, palm out. "It's okay. I'm sure you both have your reasons for keeping it a secret."

Accepting his proffered arm, she kept up with his measured, uneven gait.

"All I want to know is, how did he get so lucky?" Nick whispered and pressed a chaste kiss across her knuckles.

Reyna blushed.

Amelia's words still hung in her mind like fingertips gripping the edge of a cliff. Hawk said they'd work out the long-distance matter. But what about Lily? Did she really view her parents as a couple? One way to answer and resolve that issue was to tell Blake about Hawk.

Why was her heart suddenly racing?

# Chapter Fifteen

"Oh! What was that for?" The kiss on the cheek and lovable shoulder hug from her daughter took Reyna by surprise. Standing before the bathroom mirror, she paused in taming her curls and turned, as Lily planted herself on the edge of the soaking tub. "What's going on?"

"Nothing. I just wanted to give you a hug and say thanks for bringing us here. It's been really great."

"I'm glad you're having a good time. There will be lots to share with your friends when you get back to school."

"You mean friend. I've made more friends here than back home after being at that school for nearly four months." Lily sighed. "The kids suck, and I wish we didn't have to wear uniforms, but my classes are okay, especially biology and chemistry—we get to do lots of experiments—so, I guess it's worth it. When I graduate, I'll be an entire college semester ahead."

Reyna agreed. Lily had a knack for science. Blake wanted to nurture her gift. The stellar STEM program the academy offered was why Reyna agreed with him to send her there—that, and the fact Blake fully covered the exorbitant tuition. But Reyna understood what it was like at that age to not have friends, that core circle of teens to relate to, share thoughts, and bond with.

She turned back to the mirror, saying, "Jacob seems nice." She caught Lily's full blush in the reflection. "He's cute. Is he your boyfriend?"

"Mom!" Lily gaped.

"Have you told your dad about him?"

Hazel eyes stretched wide as a saucer. "No way! Dad would lose it. He said I'm not allowed to date until I'm twenty-one."

Reyna swung her head around. "He said that?"

Lily shrugged. "It doesn't matter, anyway, because Jacob and I are just friends." Her small shoulders drooped, the cheery air a second ago replaced by features suddenly crestfallen. "It's just . . ."

"What is it?"

"All the girls are getting asked to the Mistletoe Ball, but no one has asked me. Maurice asked Kate. Tyler asked Brooke."

"Maybe Jacob will ask you soon."

"The ball is next week. What is he waiting for?" Lily's phone buzzed. She bounced up and out of the bathroom to catch it on the nightstand.

"Is it Jacob?" Reyna teased and stood in the doorway, observing her daughter typing away.

Lily looked up. "Everybody is going to the ice rink around eleven, then grabbing food. Can I go?"

"Who is everybody?" Fresh from the shower and still in her robe, having spent the morning catching up on work, Reyna went to the armoire for simple tan leggings and her comfy, oversized cream sweater. The start of the day had been spent conferencing with Danielle, but also scouring the short list of companies to approach for possible lease space. So far, she was unsuccessful. Every business she'd reached out to either wanted to bankrupt her with their ridiculous cost to lease or simply gave her a firm no thanks, not interested. So, an unproductive morning.

But she hadn't gotten this far without having to leap over major hurtles. It'd taken three banks' rejections before she'd landed the loan to start her business. She didn't give up then and she wouldn't now. There was a home for North Star out there.

"Everybody—Kate, Brooke, Tyler, Maurice, and the rest of the group I always hang out with," Lily continued.

"Jacob too?" Reyna playfully waggled her eyebrows.

"Mom." Lily rolled her eyes. "Can I go? They're meeting here, then we'll walk to the rink around eleven."

"Walk?" Reyna looked over her shoulder at the clock on the nightstand—10:20 a.m.—while hooking her bra at her back and putting on her sweater. "The rink is at least a mile from here. Walking . . . Lily, I don't know." This was new territory for Reyna. Her baby's independence had sprouted along with her confidence. "I'll drop you off."

"Mom, that's lame. We're like four blocks from Main Street. The rink is only another five blocks to the square from there. Not far at all."

The chime of Reyna's phone distracted her. She went to the nightstand to check it. An instant flutter tickled her belly like that of a giddy teenager. She opened the text from Hawk and read:

**Hawk:** *Morning, beautiful. Hope you slept well.*

**Reyna:** *Good morning. I did. How about you?*
**Hawk:** *Yes, because you were in my dreams.*

"Mom!"

Reyna looked up. "Sorry, baby, what is it?"

Lily's sigh was packed with impatience. "Can I go to the rink?" She frowned. "Why are you smiling?"

"I'm not." Reyna pressed her lips flat.

"Maurice and Kate are already downstairs. The others will be dropped off soon."

Loosening the tether a little on her baby girl was something Reyna understood she needed to do. "Yes. But you are to go to the rink and back to Main Street for food. What are you doing?" She watched Lily yank off her gray sweatshirt, switching it out for one of her new thick sweaters, a green cable-knit that heightened the prisms of emerald hues behind amber gold in her eyes.

"Jacob will be there."

Reyna suppressed a smirk as Lily hurriedly removed the single hair band, freeing her heavy curls, then shook her head, fluffing and finger-combing her hair before donning a white knit hat. Reyna stepped over to her and tenderly brushed the coiling tresses touching her shoulders, wishing she could stop time, so she could squeeze and cuddle her baby close to her breast a little longer. But she wasn't a baby anymore. "You look adorable."

Lily dropped down on the edge of the bed and put on her boots. She then snatched her parka off a hanger in the armoire. "Bye, Mom." She dashed out.

"Have fu—" The sound of the main door in the other

room banged shut. A moment later, Reyna turned toward the sound of the door opening again. In rushed Lily, delivering a quick peck on the cheek. "Love you," she said, then once again zipped out.

Smiling, Reyna sent off a text to Hawk:

**Reyna:** *Are you free for lunch?*

His response was almost immediate.

**Hawk:** *Definitely. What are you in the mood for?*
**Reyna:** *You.*

No response. Staring at the phone, she chewed the corner of her bottom lip. The three dots appeared. His reply flashed up.

**Hawk:** *The key is under the mat by the side door. Meet you there in thirty.*

It was her turn to wrench off the baggy sweater.

---

THE KNOCK AT the door jolted Hawk into a sprint around his bedroom, gathering bed linens and dirty clothes from the floor. He glanced out the window at the Bentley parked beside his truck, then hurried downstairs to the laundry room and stuffed the bundle into the hamper, before continuing across the hall to the mudroom. The knock came again amid him grasping the knob and pulling open the door around catching a breath.

"I see you're not one for tardiness." He relieved her of

her coat. A pale-pink fitted cashmere sweater and cream-colored, body-hugging leggings. Her outfit was simple yet accentuated her soft curves.

"I believe in being punctual. Everything okay? You seem a bit short-winded."

"I was upstairs trying to tidy up before you got here. The kitchen was a mess the last time you came. I wouldn't want you to think I'm a slob. I had an early start this morning and didn't have time to clean."

"I'm not here to do a home inspection." Those brown eyes were penetrating, studying him beneath the perfect arch of her eyebrows as she took a seat and began removing her boots.

"I'm very clear on that." And he loved that sensual side of her.

She stood. Her gaze, piercing, traveled a slow path from the top of his head to his chest, over his denims, and down to his socked feet. "You're gorgeous."

Hawk grinned. "Glad you think so."

"I do."

They headed into the kitchen. "Can I get you something to drink? I picked us up some takeout."

"Later." She captured his hand and led the way to the stairs, getting right to her afternoon lunchtime objective.

"Where's Lily?"

"At the ice rink with Kate and her other friends." She turned to face him in his bedroom, lust gleaming like a laser pointer as she walked slowly backward for several smooth paces while drawing her sweater over her head, tossing it haphazardly to the floor. "In the meantime, you think we can find something to do for a few hours?" She winked with a tilt of her head in the direction of his messily made bed.

Seduction. Passion. Fire. And she was his. This was a side of Reyna Star no one else would get to see. There was an intoxicating rush of attraction in that.

Hawk smiled wide. "Oh, most surely. How did I get so lucky?"

"I did sort of put you on my Christmas list, more or less."

He lifted an eyebrow. "Your list included a man?"

"It was all in fun. A game my girlfriend and I played. You make a list of the attributes you wish to have in a companion, then place it under your pillow."

"Do I meet all your bullet points, Ms. Star?" He approached and palmed her hips, drawing her to him, marveling over the fact to have found the woman of his dreams.

"Mr. Swan, I wouldn't be here if you didn't." With a smoldering flicker of mischief coloring her expression, she began the bewitchingly slow task of unbuttoning his shirt.

"Now I'm hungry," Reyna said an hour later, gazing up at him as she threaded her fingers through the silky strands of his hair, moving in slow swirls, and watching as his eyes shuttered from her ministrations.

"Good, because as I was about to say before you whisked me up here and had your way with me, I picked us up pecan chicken, which is surely cold by now."

He rolled off her onto his side, but brought her with him, spooning, maintaining the warm connection.

They lay in the quiet room, a reflective ambience, her arm over his at her waist, their fingers laced together and their breathing calm as they stared out the window at the breaks of rays trying to squeeze through the ribbon of gray clouds.

"I could stay like this all day." Squirming ever closer within the cocoon of his big body, Reyna angled her head back to accept his light press on her lips, then her brow. She regarded eyes that were a shade cooler than the winter clouds crossing the skies. The level of her contentment matched the lull in his countenance. "What are you thinking?"

"That I'd love nothing more than waking every morning to you beside me. You and Lily could stay here. Three spare bedrooms, a large sun porch for her to hang out with her friends, and the lake out back where they all can swim. I more than have the space for her. The schools here have great track records. Tess can back me up on that."

"Hawk . . ."

"I want what we have here, Reyna. That's heavy, I know, but it's where I'm at."

The longer she held his intense stare, the faster her heart raced. She did feel the same. The emotion like nothing she'd felt since first being with Blake. Even that couldn't compare to the wild, dizzying quiver that reached down to her marrow when she looked at this wonderful, caring, beautiful man.

"Hawk, I have a business to run in Miami, one that's starting to show promise."

"Yes, but you said you need to find hangar space for your vehicles by the start of the new year. Maybe you could relocate your business. There are peak seasons here in the summer, and as you witnessed, it's a hotspot in winter."

"But it's nothing compared to Miami. There, my services are needed year-round. It's where the wealthy comes to play or just escape to their private residences from all around the world. I didn't learn the magnitude of it until I got into the business of hauling them about. I can no more move here than you could uproot and relocate your store in Miami."

"Yes, I'm scheduled to start renovations on the vacant space the week after Christmas."

"Your type of business works here. Tourists spend boatloads on the kind of items you make." Though somewhere, deep down past the barrows of common sense, Reyna had considered Miami might be an option on his end. "So, the long-distance issue—this is what you meant by 'we'll work it out.' I'd simply move my business here. Problem solved."

The longer the stretch of silence, the weaker his embrace became until he was lying flat on his back. An arm went beneath his head as he stared up at the whitewashed planks of beadboard making up the vaulted ceiling.

*We tried to keep things going long-distance for a couple of months. Let's just say absence didn't make the heart grow fonder. Out of sight, out of mind. Hawk pulled away . . . we ended it.*

Amelia's words hummed on a continuous loop. Reyna's situation mirrored Hawk's ex-girlfriend, which, if she was to go by the evidence, meant Reyna and Hawk had no future.

Her chest constricted, a stabbing ache that sent her upright. She brought her legs over the side of the bed and took in slow, even breaths before trusting her limbs and crossing to the bathroom. When she came out, he was seated on the edge of the bed in his jeans and thick socks, hands braced on his knees. A brick didn't need to clunk her on the head to know that their afternoon lovers' tryst had come to an end. Or was it even more than that?

"I'll warm up the food," he offered with almost no inflection, no emotion, as if it was the mere polite thing to do and snagged his shirt from the floor.

"I'm not hungry."

With both arms stuck in the long sleeves of his T-shirt, he paused in bringing it over his head. "You were a few minutes ago," he said, then continued, dragging it down his thick torso in one smooth motion.

"Well, I'm not anymore." It came out terse as she jerked on her clothes. Reyna wanted to be sensible, but her frustration that lay behind the hurt was too acute at the moment. "I should go."

He followed her downstairs and into the mudroom, neither saying a word. He didn't bother to object. No attempt to compromise. Nothing.

She retrieved her phone from her coat pocket before taking a seat on the bench to don her boots. "Where is this?" She held the device out to him, where he stood with a lean against the doorjamb, looking about as frustrated as she felt. "The map is trying to pin Lily's location, but the signal isn't working properly. She's at the ice rink. Maybe it's me. Your place is surrounded by trees. That could be the issue."

"No, the signal here is usually strong." He took the device and expanded the map. "That's east of Rushing Peak.

The area is blocked off because with the angle the sun hits the lake, the ice can be thin in spots. Plus, with the amount of snow on the ground, the downed trees, and surprise drops, the terrain is unpredictable. There are always thrill seekers out there, though." Both stared back, realizing what became the obvious.

"Shit." Hawk gave her back her phone, jogged into the kitchen, returned with his cell phone, and grabbed his boots.

"Lily wouldn't . . ." Reyna tried calling her. "She's not answering." Her head jerked to Hawk snatching his coat from the hook on his way out the door, his phone to his ear. "Where are you going?" She grabbed hers and raced after him.

"To get my sled," he yelled back. Then he spoke into the phone. "It's Hawk. Get me the sheriff."

Short minutes later, he emerged from the garage. "Tess is headed out there now. We're closer."

Reyna tried to keep a hold on her panic as she watched him hurriedly unfold a ramp and attach it to the tailgate of his truck. He got on the snowmobile, started the engine, and on a wide girth across his snowy lawn, circled and aligned the skis with the ramp, then slowly accelerated, driving it up into the truck's bed with precision, as if he'd done it a thousand times. After securing the sled with locking straps, he hopped down and removed the ramp, placing it in back as well.

"Get in."

Reyna rushed and hopped into the passenger seat.

# Chapter Sixteen

"IT'S TOO DENSE."

"Then what do we do?" Reyna had fought to keep her mounting fear at bay by watching the map the entire drive over rough, wooded ground. "Lily's position hasn't changed. The search wheel keeps spinning, not locking on a signal."

"We will have to ride the sled from here." Hawk threw the truck into park. He unloaded the vehicle. "Put this on," he said, handing her a helmet.

"Maybe Lily dropped her phone." Reyna worried as he straddled the seat and had her climb into position behind him. When he was certain she was situated, they rode out through the woods, dodging downed trees and circling around steep sloping grounds. They came to the spot where the map indicated Lily should be, but she wasn't there. It didn't take long to find her phone peeking up through the drifts of snow.

"Oh God, what if something happened to her?" Reyna choked on the fear splintering her control.

Hawk snatched off his glove and caught the tears on her cheeks with his thumb, his chilled hand cupping her face, his calm eyes centering her focus. "Remember what Tess said when she called? None of the kids were at the rink. They're likely all out here together. You saw the tracks. There were many. Let's keep going."

They rode out about another mile and could hear the rumbling of engines as they came upon a frozen lake within a short clearing up ahead. Teens were zipping and sliding about, kicking up high drifts within reckless swirls and spins.

"There they are!" Reyna peered and got off the sled. "That's Lily in the pink ski jacket."

On their right, Tess broke from the dense trees, lights flashing. Her sled came to an idling stop beside Hawk's. "Wait until I get my hands on every single one of them, Kate first. She knows better," Tess gritted before she unclipped a megaphone from a side strap.

The second the teens heard her blaring voice, they raced off at breakneck speed for the woods across the lake. Lily's snowmobile took a severe lean. She tried to regain her footing, but the sled only seemed to accelerate and spin.

"Hawk!" Reyna screamed as Lily nearly flipped before barreling for the trees. "Oh God, she's going too fast!"

"I got her," Tess hurried off.

"No, get Kate and the others. I got Lily," Hawk hollered, already heading toward her, easily leaving Tess's government-issued snow vehicle in his drifts.

With her heart in her throat, Reyna looked on as Hawk sped past Lily and slowed as she came toward him at a severe side angle, like an out-of-control train off its track. In that same moment, someone emerged from the trees and was heading straight at Lily on her right. Though his helmet covered his face, Reyna recognized the brown curly hair sticking out at the nape. Jacob. Before he could get close, Hawk came up out of his seat, reached with a hard side bend and whisked Lily off the sled, settling her across his own. Her vehicle left the ground briefly, flipped, and slid into the wide trunk of a tree, the metal nearly splitting in two.

It took Reyna a long moment to exhale as she bent forward and gripped her knees, trembling, her head in a dizzying spiral. Lily's birth. Her first steps. First scrape. First word. Remembering Lily's excitement when she happily skipped off to her kindergarten class on that first day, and so many other points in her daughter's life. Every scene, happy and sad, everything she'd ever done, flickered like an old movie reel within that short space in time before it went black, cutting her child's life short. Shaking, Reyna choked on tears, her breathing ragged, near hyperventilating. It took effort for her to stand upright, swiping the wetness from her cheeks and drawing a clean breath.

Tess had the entire caravan of five other delinquents rounded up behind her. Hawk rode back at a slow haul with Lily seated upon his lap, her head pressed against his chest, arms cinched around his waist. When he came to a stop, Lily continued to clutch onto him. Hawk soothed her with whispered words, then managed to peel her away. She got off the sled, and Reyna hugged her tight, but said nothing, her nerves shot.

"Every single one of your parents will hear from me!" Tess bellowed. "I also want to know who drove you out here. Tyler"—she pointed a stiff finger—"was it that brother of yours?"

He delivered a soft nod. "And a friend of his."

"They're going to get what's coming to them," Tess barked.

While the sheriff interrogated the others, Reyna turned to Hawk. "How will the three of us get back to your truck, seeing as Lily's transportation is wrapped around a tree?"

"Lily can ride with me. I'm parked next to Hawk," Tess said.

"Can I ride with Mr. Hawk?" Lily asked Reyna.

Reyna regarded the tear-filled fear in her child's eyes, fear that might have only little to do with facing Tess's wrath and more from the near-death experience she'd just escaped. "Tess, I'll ride with you, if you don't mind," Reyna said.

"Not at all."

Two other police vehicles were waiting back at the truck. Tess must have radioed them at some point. She and one of the officers transported the teens. The other stayed behind to see to the sleds.

With Lily safe in Hawk's truck, he drove them away from the area. Reyna leaned back against the headrest and closed her eyes, her heart beating so loud, she could hear it.

"Mom?"

"Don't say another word, young lady," she growled low around her deep breathing. "You're grounded."

"For how long?" Lily's voiced quivered.

Reyna snapped her eyes open and whirled the fury of her glare to the back seat. "Until I see fit to lift your punishment, that's how long! Right now, I'm considering ending this trip and driving us back to Miami tonight, so don't ask me again! You have disappointed me beyond reason. I don't know what has come over you lately. And who do I now have to compensate for the sled you destroyed?"

"Jacob," Lily answered, barely above a whisper.

Reyna turned back and saw Hawk staring at her, his features pinched. Not in the mood to care about his concern, she brought her attention to the snow-covered road outside her window.

---

"Such foolishness." Geri shook her head. "Reyna has every right to be upset."

"I know." Hawk had brought her up to speed on all that had transpired that afternoon while awaiting Reyna's return from her suite. She'd asked him to hang around, so she could retrieve her car from his place after she got Lily settled. That was nearly forty-five minutes ago.

"Are you two dating?"

Hawk narrowed a harsh look at Geri. "Don't start."

"What? It was merely a question. I like Reyna. You—"

"Sh, here she comes." He came out of his lean against the counter. "Hey."

"Sorry for taking so long. I was on the phone with Lily's father. We spoke together with her, so she'd understand her punishment was coming from the both of us. She sometimes calls him for sympathy when she can't get her way with me. This way, it's clear."

"Makes sense."

"Thanks for waiting. My purse and keys are also at your place," she said low.

As they headed out, Hawk gave a glance over at Geri.

Her attention was on her papers, though she wore a subtle grin, no doubt had her ears perked. He pulled the passenger door open for Reyna, then rounded the front and got in. "I can assume Blake wasn't happy," he said as they drove off.

"Livid. I've never heard him raise his voice to Lily. That changed today. She was shocked as well. Blake did suggest that I not cut the trip short. I'll stay as planned, but Lily will be working on her school assignments for the next three days. No other activities."

Her not leaving was a relief. And yet . . . "Blake's suggestion is all it takes for you to stay put?" Hawk regretted it the second the words left his mouth. Between the dilemma on where things stood with their relationship riding alongside the situation with Lily, his insecurity had reared its ugly head at the absolute worst possible time. The sharp, narrow-eyed glare she delivered sliced down to the bone.

"What is that supposed to mean? With Christmas so close, Blake felt it would be best for Lily and me to celebrate it here as planned. Quite frankly, the entire purpose of this trip was meant to spend it with her for the holidays. The incident wouldn't have happened had I been with her. I was in a man's bed instead of seeing to my child."

His gut clenched at the off-handed dismissal. "I thought we were a couple making love in the middle of the afternoon. But I see we view those hours differently."

"My company is in Miami. Yours is here. I don't see us working out."

Hawk's head jerked so hard it just about snapped off his shoulders. The temper reflecting in her features was still boiling at one hundred. "It's been a long day. Maybe we should put this discussion on hold until things settle down some."

"What more is there to discuss? You made things very clear this afternoon. Since I'm not relocating my business, you saw no need to pursue whatever this is between us any further."

"I never said that." He pulled into his driveway next to her car. She'd already used her phone to start the engine.

"It was implied. The second I said I couldn't... I wouldn't... relocate my company, you were half dressed and practically shoving me out your door." She climbed out of the truck and moved with hurried steps to her vehicle. "You did the same to Amelia, so why should I expect any different?"

The situation was spiraling out of control. Hawk went quickly to her as she got behind the wheel and caught her hand when she tried to close the car door. He brought her palm to his lips and delivered kisses before pressing it against his cheek, his eyes regarding hers, that were solemn, yet final. "Reyna, you've had a lot to deal with today. Get some rest. Your head will be clearer tomorrow."

"My head is very clear. Bye, Hawk." She snatched out of his hold and slammed the car door shut. The wheels on the Bentley rolled back.

"Reyna, don't do this. Reyna?" The numbing bite of the cold cut through his shattered world as the red flare of her taillights disappeared beyond the trees.

# Chapter Seventeen

"Surely, she can't blame you for what happened."

Hawk finished up with his customer at the register, then responded to Ash, who was relaxing back against the counter beside him. Dressed in a smart-looking suit and tie, as a real estate broker, his cousin had spent the morning lugging around a couple on the hunt to find a house to purchase. "I think she mostly blames herself. I just happened to be the easiest scapegoat." They stepped aside when Noah entered, returning from his hour-and-a-half-long break, carrying a pizza-for-one size box.

"It's about time." Hawk glowered.

"The line at Tony's was out the door. They're running a free slice promo from noon today til one o'clock Christmas Eve. Here, I got you one. Might need warming up. It's been sitting. Couldn't chance getting back in that line."

"No thanks." Hawk waved Noah off and went to the storage room to get the boxes of blankets to bring to the center. When he returned, Ash was stuffing his face with the last of the crust. He followed Hawk outside.

"So, she breaks up with you because of her daughter's disobedience. This is why I don't date women with kids. I warned you."

"You date women with kids all the time. And no." Hawk exhaled through the weight of his heavy heart and closed the door of his truck, then turned to Ash, who was hovering behind him. "If she hadn't been in bed with me, she would've prevented Lily from doing such a foolish thing. She prides herself on being a good mother. I'm a distraction."

"Ah." Ash nodded. "When did you become philosophical?"

"That wisdom came from Tess. I picked her brain for advice. She suggested I give Reyna space. I'm trying, but it's damn hard. It's been three days and—"

"Mr. Swan?"

Hawk and Ash turned. "Hey, Jacob." He, too, held a Tony's pizza box. "Surprised to see you out." Tess had been true to her word. Though she hadn't written up the incident, she'd called all the teens' parents and had them retrieve their child from the precinct, so they'd have a firm understanding of the severity of what their little lawbreakers had been up to. The reprimands across the board had been swift and firm.

"Only to get a bite. I'm still grounded. My mom is at the hair salon down the block. As part of my punishment, I must go wherever she goes. Even to her book club meeting." His face screwed up, as though he'd tasted something bitter. "Like taking my phone, computer, Xbox, and having lights out by nine weren't enough," he groused.

"You earned it, son."

"I know." Jacob stared down at his boots, tendrils of curls beneath his knit hat shading his eyes from view. "I thought Lily was behind me. When I realized she wasn't, I went back to find her and saw her having trouble steering on the ice." His head came up. "I tried to get to her. I swear."

"I know you did."

"I want to apologize. I should've made sure she was okay."

"Shouldn't you tell that to Lily, and perhaps her mother?"

"I would . . . will . . . when I get my phone back. Anyway, I didn't want you to get the wrong impression about me, and not let me hang out with Lily."

Hawk angled his head, puzzled. "Why would my opinion matter? That's not my call. I'm not Lily's father."

"I-I know, but Kate said you and Ms. Star—"

"Kate likes to talk." The last thing he needed to add to his rickety situation with Reyna was a public rumor, though true it might be in this case.

"Oh. Okay." A short sigh. Tentative eyes darted between Hawk and Ash.

"What is it?" Hawk could see he had more to say. The thirty-something temps and easterly winds were surely doing a number on that pizza slice.

"Do you have any advice on how I might ask Lily to the Mistletoe Ball? Every time I think I have the right words, then I see her and my tongue freezes up. I'm grounded until the day before Christmas Eve. Without my phone, I can't even text to ask her. I really screwed up any chance I had."

The young man always appeared so confident, bordering on cocky, the alpha among his peers, yet here he stood, struggling on how to ask a girl out.

"Step aside, Hawk." Ash came forward, linking his fingers and cracking his knuckles before draping an arm about

Jacob's shoulders. "He needs an expert. Jacob, my man, here's what you do. Order Lily a box of chocolates and have it delivered. On the note, ask her to the ball. It's that simple."

"It's a decent idea, but with one flaw. He doesn't have access to any electronics." Hawk shoved Ash out of the way. "Jacob, perhaps share your dilemma with your mother and ask her to reach out to Ms. Star."

"I can do that." His tawny-tan face brightened. "I better get back before I get even more grounded." He gave a sigh and an eye roll. "Thanks for the advice." He turned and headed back toward the salon.

"Girl crushes." Ash rested an arm atop Hawk's shoulder. "Ah, to be fifteen again."

"Speak for yourself." Fifteen or thirty-four, relationships and heartbreak, it was all the same. Hawk got in his truck and drove off.

As the day wore long, between helping at the center and working until well past closing at his store, Hawk kept himself busy to the point of exhaustion. Now, with the time creeping toward eleven p.m., lying in bed, his body was worn out, but his mind raced. It didn't help that for the past hour, he'd hovered a thumb over Reyna's name on his phone, seesawing whether to call her. Space was relative. He just needed to hear her voice, get the small reassurance they would be okay. He tapped. By the fourth ring, he disconnected and waited another ten minutes, then tried calling again, only for it to jump straight to voicemail. It was a strong indication she'd turned her phone off.

An unwanted, stark reality delivered him a one-two

punch. His brain served that soul-crushing blow his heart refused to accept. They were over.

※

With Lily under suite arrest for the past three days, Reyna used the time to focus on her business. Freshly showered and wrapped in her fluffy terry cloth bathrobe, she sat with her computer at the café table situated by the picture window in the parlor. The bright moon lit the dark night like a beacon and aided the small, low-wattage table lamp that was a mere ambient glow.

She opened North Star's daily report Danielle had sent over. The company was running smoothly with Dani at the helm. Rico had been a smart choice as well. Feedback from clients were all five stars.

Concentrating on work helped Reyna pretend she wasn't in a constant state of internal torment.

She'd pulled out of Hawk's driveway with firm resolution—she'd made the right call when it came to their involvement. But as the minutes turned to painful hours and excruciating days, that concrete resolve had crumbled into fine micro-dust and her heart along with it. To see Hawk's name pop up on her phone tonight only made the hollow space in her chest ache all the more from the grave sense of loss.

Unable to help it, she turned her phone back on for a mere glimpse of his name to feed her starving heart. He'd called again.

The time displayed on the computer screen showed it

was nearing eleven thirty. She tapped on Danielle's number in her favorites list, getting a short ring before it connected.

"Hi, Rey."

"Hi. I won't keep you. I was reviewing the report and just wanted to say thanks for handling things in my absence."

"I've enjoyed sitting in the boss's chair. Though, I'd never want to give up driving. The tips are too sweet. Yesterday, Mr. Brum dropped me three hundred dollars. And he was a one-way fare."

"Yes, I saw it in the log." Offering gratuity-in-hand was prohibited. Reyna found it tacky, diminishing the company's otherwise posh appearance. Clients added their tip to their payment instead.

Reyna held small regret about pulling the Bentley out of service for these three weeks away. The cars were kept fueled on her tips alone. But had she not taken the trip, she wouldn't have reconnected with Hawk. Eyes shuttered, she rested her forehead against the cool windowpane. If only not being with him didn't hurt so much.

"Rey?"

"I'm here. You have an early day tomorrow. I'll let you get to bed."

"I know you're worried about finding lease space. It'll happen. You'll see."

Reyna brought her gaze to the gently swaying trees off in the distance. Brisk winds stirred the wintry white covers resting upon branches. "It's not that. Well, it's that, too, but . . ."

"What is it?"

"It's about Hawk."

"From what you told me, rescuing Lily the way he did is commendable. He definitely doesn't deserve the stick-up-the-butt title I gave him." Danielle chuckled.

"He's a good man, Dani. A really good man. Things had gotten serious between us. But... I ended it." Reyna exhaled slow and even and cleared her throat to stifle the quiver in her voice. "He lives here. His business is here. It would never have worked out." The threat of tears started to cloud her vision. "I have Lily to think about. She's crossing into those years where she could pivot in the wrong direction if I lose focus. The sled incident is a prime example."

"Rey, girlfriend, you're being too hard on yourself. You became a mother very young and haven't had any time for you, no attention given to *your* needs. You can allow space in your life for Hawk."

Her friend didn't understand what it took to raise a child. Nor had Danielle witnessed her child nearly careen into a tree at racing speed, headfirst. A chill of fear rushed down Reyna's spine whenever the vivid image surfaced from that day.

"As for hangar space, why not buy Ace yourself?"

"I can't afford it right now. Don't get me wrong, North Star is doing well, but financially, I'm not there yet to put up the level of capital needed."

"Just give it some thought. I'm sure you'll figure something out. You always do. Have a good night."

"You do the same."

Lily was top priority. Reyna had made that choice at fifteen with no regrets. She'd fallen short in her responsibilities lately, allowed her need for companionship to come before her responsibility as a mother.

There was plenty of time for her to meet someone. Besides, Hawk didn't do long-distance relationships. He will meet a woman and get married and have babies . . . Reyna's breath hitched. A stabbing pain pierced her chest, so sharp, it brought literal tears to her eyes, an ache ebbing into excruciating despair.

She bit her lip to once more battle against her anguish, went into the bedroom, and retrieved the book Hawk had given her. Then, she took a seat at the table by the window there and clicked on the small lamp. Angling the book to catch the low light across the pages, she began reading random passages. Some were cruelly beautiful, others complicatedly wonderful.

Another page was dog-eared. She brought it near the light. With each word that spoke of undying love, she could no longer contain her sadness, her pained cry expressed in choked breaths.

She hurriedly dried her eyes on the fluffy lapel of her robe before turning her head to Lily rolling over in slumber. An even snore pushed past her slightly parted lips. The upsweep at the outer corners of her eyes. The cute button tip of her nose. A hand pillowed beneath her cheek. The shadow glow of the moon cast an angelic air to features the color of warm wheat and that still possessed a hint of soft roundness, that juncture just before the full reins of adolescence lay claim.

Every sacrifice had been for her.

Light gleamed from the silent ring of Reyna's phone in

the pocket of her robe. She got up, padded back into the parlor, and slid the double doors closed before answering, "Hi, Blake."

"Hey. I know it's late, but I figured you'd be up. You were always a night owl. I'm on break. Just wanted to check in on Lily."

"She's asleep."

"How is she handling being on punishment while on vacation?" He laughed a little. "Can't be good."

"Actually, she's okay. I think the entire incident frightened her. If it weren't for Ha—" Reyna's pulse skipped. "If it weren't for the man who rescued her, she could've been . . . I don't want to think what might have happened."

"From what you described to me, neither do I. I still can't believe she'd do something like that. She'll sass us sometimes, but it's not like her to be flat-out disobedient. I guess we're rolling into the unpredictable teen years."

"It was over a boy."

"Come again?"

It had taken a full day for Reyna to find her calm from both fear and anger to allow Lily to explain her actions. Lily didn't want her dad to know and had refrained from sharing. Reyna felt it was time he faced reality. His baby girl had a crush.

"I know you didn't say what I thought you said."

With the click of the remote, a cozy fire danced in the hearth. Reyna curled up in the armchair, preparing for his outburst. "She wanted to impress a boy. Jacob Gagneaux. He's fifteen and—"

"Fifteen!" Blake's deep baritone thundered.

"Yes. There's this Mistletoe Ball event that apparently is all the rave here."

"I'm aware. Lily mentioned it. She didn't say anything about some chump, who I see got her out there acting a fool."

"Blake, calm down. First, it was our daughter who decided to perform for the boy. All her girlfriends have been asked to the ball, but she hasn't. She likes Jacob and thought if she showed him how well she could ride, he'd think she's cool and ask her out. She hadn't anticipated spinning on slick ice and losing control of the vehicle. She thought she could treat it like an ATV."

"Reyna, Lily's too young to be talking about dating, and especially to some fifteen-year-old delinquent."

Reyna almost chuckled. "He's not a delinquent."

"Oh, no? Was he one of the kids out there in an unrestricted area? Trespassing?"

"You mean the area where our daughter was as well? Yes. Look, Blake, I don't like the fact that our baby is growing up so fast, either. But whether we like it or not, Lily's starting to notice boys. It's normal around her age."

"Well, you didn't have this trouble back in Miami, nor when she's with me in Texas. It's only now out there in the Berkshires this person I don't recognize has emerged. I don't like it, Rey. Maybe you should've returned home like you wanted. I shouldn't have encouraged you to stay there for Christmas. That place and evidently the people in it are bad influences."

"Haven Creek is a nice town and the people have been really friendly. I think Lily has done well here. She has made friends, unlike the four months in that private school you insist we send her to. Aside from her science courses, she's not happy there." Reyna sighed when he huffed. "Blake, it was one poor decision. I think she has learned her lesson."

"Yes, well, we'll see if this behavior continues," he grumbled. "Gagneaux. What kind of a name is that?"

"What do you mean?"

"You know what I mean."

"I don't know, French maybe. I think he's biracial. His mother's African American. I've spoken only briefly with her at the skating rink when we first arrived. She seems nice. She's a teacher. I haven't met Jacob's father. But I know he's an international commercial pilot. Not home much."

"That's obvious. He's not properly seeing to his son, that's for damn sure. By the way, where were you when Lily was on that snowmobile, out where she shouldn't be?"

A heaping dose of guilt returned, packing Reyna's gut like a heavy meal. She chewed her bottom lip with no intention of sharing the truth. Not specifically, anyway. Given that she'd ended things with Hawk, what would be the point? It would only leave her sobbing, which was the last thing she wanted to do with her ex. Yet her eyes watered, and that suffocating tightness started to crush her airway as it was. She swallowed to relieve the pressure and found herself saying, "I met someone. We were"—she swallowed again even harder—"having lunch when the incident occurred." The rhythmic, loud, pounding sound happening in the background seemed to get louder around the deafening silence.

"Is that why you didn't have eyes on our daughter? Because your attention lay elsewhere?" His tone was grating. "You let her go off with teens she hardly knew and look what it got her. Nearly injured . . . and arrested."

Reyna didn't need him to make her feel guilty. She'd achieved that all on her own. "The ice rink in the town square isn't very far from the inn. Lily asked if she could walk down with her friends. She's never given me any reason not to trust her."

"Until now. And about this *someone* you mentioned. Is it more than just lunch between you two? Do I need to remind you of our agreement? Is it something we should discuss?"

She'd broken up with Hawk, so the honest answer was, "No." She'd be lucky if Hawk would even speak to her at this point. "And I resent you questioning my commitment as a mother." Blake tended to push his authority. More times than not, Reyna didn't push back because she understood he was only looking out for their child's well-being. But she would on this.

"Apologies. I know you're a wonderful mother. I didn't mean to insinuate otherwise. It's just this situation with Lily has thrown me for a loop. And now you're saying it was all for a boy. It's a lot for me to unpack." He exhaled heavily. "I have to get back to work. Rey, with Lily, we need to revisit this dating thing. I'm not onboard with it."

They had an understanding. Both had to agree on any and every matter involving parenting Lily or it didn't happen. "The ball is Christmas Eve. It's one date. Jacob may not even ask her."

"Let's hope he doesn't. It'll save me the trouble of saying no."

Reyna sighed. "Blake, be reasonable here. You can't stop her from growing up."

"Yeah, yeah. I could lock her up until she's thirty." A small laugh. "Rey, I need time to think about it. We'll talk tomorrow. Good night."

"Good night."

Talk, he said. She wouldn't allow him to stifle Lily from trying to spread her wings. On the other end, Hawk felt Reyna was too lenient with Lily, and said she should set more boundaries. The sled incident validated his claim. Reyna now recognized that.

Hawk had jumped into gear the second he realized where Lily might have gone, and how he didn't hesitate when he saw her in distress on the icy lake.

Instead of thanking him, Reyna had turned him away. And now her heart hurt.

She clicked off the lamp, throwing the room into the glimmer of moonlight, and stared out into the cold night. Being alone was never a problem. No siblings, few friends as a child, and moving around a lot, she was comfortable as her own company, often preferring it. But for the first time in a long time, she truly felt lonely, hollow, as though a vital piece of her was missing. She'd never needed, never yearned so desperately for someone as she did Hawk.

She removed her robe, climbed into bed, and snuggled close to Lily, listening to her easy puffs of air and letting them soothe her to sleep.

# Chapter Eighteen

THE FAMILIAR WELCOME chime over the door ushered Reyna and a couple of others behind her into Hawk's Custom Woodworks. It seemed the store was packed at any given time of day. The last Saturday morning before Christmas brought out those who apparently got a thrill out of bumping elbows and bottlenecking aisles. She made her way forward, scanning over the many heads around her.

"Rey, how's it going?"

Reyna turned, surprised to hear her nickname called. Seldom had she heard it since she'd been here. "Good morning, Noah." He stood behind the counter, working the register. To his left, a girl packaged and bagged up whatever the previous customer had just purchased. Reyna approached, but stood off to the side, so as not to stop the machine flow they had as the next person in line stepped forward. "Is Hawk in? I was hoping to speak with him."

"He went next door to take some measurements before his contractor arrives. Can't wait until we get more space in here. It's like working in a sardine can."

"I can see that." The door chimed and a couple more bodies added to the confined square footage.

Reyna turned her head toward the familiar figures who

came into her periphery. Beyond the open door leading to the back office, Hawk and Amelia stood together, chatting, laughing. A small part of Reyna hoped he'd lost sleep and couldn't eat, the same as she'd suffered without him, but he seemed about as chipper as they came.

Amelia sobered and draped her arms around Hawk's wide shoulders. He enveloped her at the waist. Reyna gave a look at Noah, who shrugged.

"I guess he's back. I didn't see him come in. Next in line." He beckoned the person forward without a shift in his apathetic expression.

Reyna's attention moved back to the pair as they strode into the storefront. Hawk stopped short. Surprise flared in his eyes, and tension tightened his features. "Good morning," she managed.

"Reyna, hi," Amelia said with a warm welcome.

Hawk stared, unblinking, frozen like a still model being sketched by a painter. Only when someone had to wedge to get past did he blink.

They all moved out of the path to the door for patrons trying to exit. Reyna gave her attention to Amelia. It allowed her a minute to gather herself. "It's good to see you."

"You as well. Nick said I'd just missed you yesterday at the center."

"I spent a few hours of the morning there helping him box canned goods and other nonperishables."

"Hawk came across my aunt's old diaries next door." Amelia held up two small books and gave an awkward glimpse up at him. He continued to stand there stock-still without a word.

"That's great." Reyna lifted her gaze. His beard was neatly trimmed close, hair pulled back into a knotted twist at the nape. The dove-gray crewneck sweater hugged his bulky upper body and coordinated with sleek black slacks and buffed black shoes. Dark, scrumptious, and sexy . . . and no longer hers. How stupid was it to have let him go? And she wanted him back. But why on earth would he take her back after the ugly, serrated way she'd cut things off?

The unexpected vulnerability on a tumble of emotions started to surface. Reyna had thought she'd be able to look him in the eyes and accept his rejection if he chose not to accept her apology. But she realized now she simply couldn't.

"Hawk, I-I can see you're busy. I'll come back another time." She turned for the door, but he caught her hand. She wrenched free on reflex from the unexpected, heated current that shot up her arm and spread to the very tips of her nerve endings. The knee-jerk reaction caused her to slam her fist back into a man behind her, who in turn bumped a shelf, rattling the items on it. She spun. "I'm so sorry. I didn't mean . . . Are you okay?"

A kind smile. "No harm done."

Grossly embarrassed, she twirled back around to head for the door, but again, Hawk caught her hand, his grip firm.

"We can go to my office, get out of the way here."

"I better get back to my store." Amelia looked between them. Their tension seemed to become her tension. "Good seeing you, Reyna. Hawk, thanks for finding these. My uncle will appreciate getting them."

"I'm sure." He never looked away from Reyna.

"I should go as well." Reyna tried to break Hawk's hold.

"Let's talk." He tugged against her resistance, led the way back to his office, and closed the door behind them, not accepting any objection. "How's Lily?" he asked on a turn to face her, looking relaxed and well-rested, unlike her sleep-deprived mind.

"She's fine. Happy to be released from the suite."

"No doubt."

Silence ticked for a moment. "I just came by to say thank you for helping Lily that day on the snow and ice. I-I realized I hadn't done that."

"You're welcome, but no need to thank me." His stare piercing, he moistened his lips, and Reyna was reminded of their softness, how his kisses had left a mark on her soul that could never be erased nor replaced by another. "Oh, Jacob's mother, Lashelle, called me. She said you told Jacob to have her reach out to me to ask Lily to the ball."

"Not quite. Jacob asked for advice on how to go about it. On punishment, and without a way to ask Lily himself, I suggested he have his mother contact you."

"Lily was happy to get the invitation, no matter who delivered it." More deafening silence. "Okay. Well, that's all I wanted to say." What an enormous lie that was. She came to say so much more.

*I was a fool for letting you go. I can't eat, food tastes bland. I can't sleep. When I do, out of sheer exhaustion, you come to me in my dreams.*

Goodness, she was dying inside without him.

"I see the store is busy as usual. I'll get out of your way." She took a step. He blocked her path.

She looked up. To move his big frame out of the way, if

that were even possible, would require touching him, putting her hands on familiar parts of his muscular frame, reigniting that current of warmth from the power of his strength. "I should get back to the inn."

He moved aside.

Heart heavy, Reyna gripped the knob, but let go and turned back. "I haven't dated much. Married at sixteen and divorced by nineteen with a three-year-old, my focus has been on being a good mother to my daughter. I sometimes felt that I had to prove myself to those who saw me as a kid raising a kid. I've worked so hard to try to do all the right things. But I failed that day when Lily . . . She wouldn't have been out there on that sled if I—"

"If you hadn't been in my bed."

"Yes," she said low and turned to the door. The moment her hand met the knob again, he planted his palm flat against the solid wood surface. His other hand turned the lock.

"You want to be a good mother, do all you can for Lily, and keep her safe. I get that. But it doesn't mean you have to give up your life to do so."

"My needs aren't important right now."

"They're just as important."

He leaned in, the hard plane of his body pressing, imprinting, molding against her like hot, heavy steel. His head lowered. The way he inhaled deep on a soft rasp sparked a flutter of her pulse along the column of her neck. "I love your scent. Like delicate flowers."

Reyna took a slow intake of breath, hoping he didn't hear the slight quiver.

His teeth captured her lobe, nibbling, lips behind her

ear, tasting. Her will crumbling, she reached back, freeing his silken locks from its knotted twist, dark tresses sliding through her fingers.

"Hawk—"

His hand seized her beneath the chin, tilted her head back, and silenced her with his kiss. The second his tongue found hers, she surrendered to the feral, hot, hungry yearning overtaking them both. She turned and clutched his tense shoulders in a jolt of frantic longing.

Her head swam as he hoisted her up by the back of her thighs and brought her down atop the papers on his desk before she even realized it, their lips never breaking contact.

She needed to know she hadn't blown it with him. That his chest felt just as hollow, that he missed her with the same mind-numbing level of despair as she had missed him. Reyna closed her eyes, and the tears started. But he was there, kissing the wetness on her lashes away, soothing the panic drumming of her heart.

"I was afraid," she finally said when the ache in her throat receded.

"I know, baby." He brushed his lips tenderly over hers, then looked down at her face, his gaze roaming before holding hers. "You don't have to be afraid."

"Hawk, does this mean we're okay? I haven't lost you?"

"As long as I have you, we will always be okay. I'm aware Lily's father is heavily involved in her life. I would never try to step into his role. But I want to be there for her as well, in any capacity you deem suitable. Just know I'm here for you both."

Reyna palmed the neat hairs of his cheeks and brought

him down to her open mouth. She missed touching him, kissing him.

The jiggle of the doorknob followed by a row of knocks startled them back to reality.

"Hawk, your contractor is out front," Noah called. "He's been waiting for like fifteen minutes. You want me to tell him you had to take an unexpected meeting?"

Reyna detected small laughter in Noah's voice, which meant he knew what they were up to on this side of the door. "Does your brother know about us?" she whispered.

"He knows I'm crazy about you, but I haven't shared with anyone except Ash that we're dating. Well, I confided in Tess when you cut things off. They won't say anything. With that, I think Amelia suspects it."

Reyna nodded, understanding they wouldn't be able to keep it under wraps for long. "I'm sorry I interrupted your schedule by coming here unannounced."

"I'm not. To see you standing in my store, I thought I was imagining it." He angled his head over his shoulder. "Noah, tell him I'll be in my unexpected meeting another fifteen minutes." He smiled as he brought down the zipper on her coat. "Now, where were we?"

# Chapter Nineteen

"YOU BOUGHT THE child a snowmobile, and an Arctic Cat Sno Pro 600 at that!" Ash did a walk around the sled, looking it over. "Dude, seriously?"

"It's a rental and sort of an early Christmas gift. I have it for Lily until she leaves. I'm going to teach her how to ride it." Parked outside of his garage, Hawk slowly rode up the ramp, guiding his own sled into the truck bed, then strapped it tight and hopped down to swap out the ramp for the trailer. "The Pro 600 is about the best out there for a beginner."

"Yeah, and to lease it is costing you what, about five grand?" Ash shook his head. "I get you're trying to win over the kid while scoring points with her mother, but do you think you should be investing that kind of money when . . .?"

Hawk looked up from his crouch in securing the tow to the tailgate. Ash, with his head down, hands stuck in the pockets of his coat, his attention on his boots, was never one to hold back in speaking his mind, whether one cared to hear it or not. Hawk only needed one small win with Lily, a crack in her barrier to wedge himself in. She was a teen. He would approach her in a way she'd listen. Gifting her the sled for a couple of days, and more importantly, spending time teaching her how to ride it, would pave the way to earning her trust. He hoped.

"When what? Say whatever it is you know you want to say."

Ash met his stare. "Okay, I'll say it. Reyna breaks up with you. Then takes you back. But she still doesn't want anyone to know you two are hooking up. What does that tell you?"

"Remind me to never confide in you. We're not hooking up. We're in a relationship. I've already told you why Reyna wants to keep things between us quiet for now."

"It's so her ex-husband can give his stamp of approval on who she dates." Ash snorted. "If that's not the oddest thing I've ever heard. There has to be more to it. They're divorced, yet he's in her life on such an involved level. Come on, you don't find it the least bit strange?"

"The man wants to protect his daughter. I applaud him for that. Reyna has that same understanding from him when it comes to whomever he dates. Now stop being an ass and lock your side of the trailer. I'm meeting Reyna and Lily. With the overcast, there isn't a lot a daylight left."

Ash hunched to attach and secure the chain on his side, then helped to align the sled onto the ramp. "Why didn't you do this earlier? The sun was out this morning."

"Reyna needed to tend to her business."

"I know you're not planning to relocate to Miami since you're about to knock down a wall to expand your store. I guess this will be a long-distance affair. You forget how well that worked out between you and Amelia."

"I wasn't looking to settle down with Amelia." Hawk met his cousin's stunned face, then continued with his task.

Ash sighed. "Hawk, I knew you had a thing for this woman, but settle down, as in wedding bells? You two haven't been dating"—hard air quotes—"but a minute. Why not slow down, ease off the gas a bit to see if she's really the right woman for you?"

Hawk came to his feet. "What is it about Reyna you take issue with? Be upfront with it. Is it because she has a child?"

"Like I've said before, dating a woman with a kid, especially a teenager, is a lot to take on, but no. Though I can't fathom spending five grand on one I hardly know."

"Twenty-seven hundred. And I'm getting to know Lily. Teaching her how to ride is part of that. If it's not about Reyna having a child, then what? Is it because she's Black?" The scathing glare Hawk received wholly spoke to the contrary.

Ash's brow dipped low. "Given the united nation of women I've dated, I won't dignify that asinine question."

"Well, if it's not that, then tell me why you oppose her so strongly."

"It's not her. It's you. There's fluffy white snow on the ground, warm fires going, it's snuggling season. Throw in Christmas, and Reyna showing up in Haven Creek was perfect. I felt she'd scratch your itch and that would be the end of it. This whole settling down talk came out of nowhere. A couple months ago, how many women was it? Two? No, three. You were seeing three different women. No shade here. I sing your praises."

Hawk shrugged. "I went on a few dates."

"My point is, you weren't talking about settling down. I even ran into you out with Amelia."

"I wasn't out with her in that way. It was a late lunch. Amelia asked if I'd eaten. I said no and grabbed a bite with her. Nothing more to it."

Ash brought up a hand. "Fair enough. That said, now Reyna is the one you want to hitch your wagon to after only knowing her a short time. Dude, we flipped a coin for her. It could've gone either way."

"*You* flipped a coin. She intrigued me from the moment I saw her."

"And if I'd won the toss?"

"I would've ignored the outcome and asked her out anyway." No hesitation in Hawk's decree.

Ash drew up, wide-eyed. "You would've broken the bro code!" He shook his head. "My friend, I fear you're jumping headfirst without a parachute, and when the newness wears off, you will find yourself hitting cement instead of Reyna's soft breasts to break your fall."

"You don't know what you're talking about. Here's a thought—concentrate on your own love life instead of kicking mud all over mine." Hawk moved to the opposite side of the ramp and shoved Ash out of the way to check the chain around the ski. The man needed to get a life, preferably in the next four seconds. Hawk's patience was starting to wear thin.

"Hawk, man, think," his cousin went on, unfazed, intent on landing his annoying point. "Reyna has a high-price-tag business in Miami. No way she'll give that up or even move it to live here with you. That sort of business is more lucrative there. Did you ever consider that maybe she's the one getting her itch scratched with you?"

"We'll work it out. Enough on the subject." Hawk held his cousin's regard, not letting his features betray those same concerns.

"Okay, but one last thing. Has she told you how she feels about you?"

When their bodies joined as one, Reyna expressed her feelings for him in her kisses and in her touch. But the actual words that could reshape his entire being and make him forget how to breathe? She'd never said them.

"No surprise," came Ash's quiet comment as Hawk silently slid into the driver's seat. "Cousin, this is me looking out for you."

"Noted." Hawk shut himself in and drove off.

Snow, a fluffy featherbed of white powder, covered their boots calf-deep. The landscape was a cascade of slight mounds and humps. Where the sun touched, it melted, reflecting like diamonds, and disfigured the pillowy ground beneath intermittent blue skies. In the distance, wind drifts whipped the boughs of evergreens laden with thick snow layers so remarkably beautiful, Reyna felt the scenery appeared straight out of a winter fairy tale.

Hawk had driven her and Lily about ten miles north to an open field of untouched snow that stretched far and wide to teach Lily the fundamentals on how to ride a snowmobile. He'd brought along his own, but Reyna was shocked that he had rented a sled for Lily, as well, for the short remainder of her stay in Haven Creek and would spend time riding with her. The action and impulse resembled her ex-husband; she wasn't completely on board. But to see the joy it brought to his face upon witnessing Lily's reaction at the unexpected early Christmas gift, Reyna couldn't dampen the moment.

"The rider and the vehicle must work together. Throttle control and how to manipulate to have fluid acceleration is paramount," Hawk explained, seated on his sled with Lily stationed on hers beside him. "When you understand your throttle, you're never in doubt. You know exactly what your sled is going to do. Now, when trying to turn, take the optimal point of pivot angle and then bank your sled downward. You'll need to make a hard lean into the turn." Stationary, he simulated the motion. Lily followed suit.

"Mr. Hawk, can we go somewhere that has bigger hills?" She looked out at the vast landscape. "This area is mostly flat ground."

"No," Reyna voiced firmly, paying close attention to Hawk's tutelage, picking up pointers herself. "It's nice of Mr. Swan to take you out here to teach you the proper way to ride. Stay focused."

"How about you both just call me Hawk?" He sent a small smile Reyna's way, then rotated back to Lily. "When you've mastered the basics, how to come down these small slopes on a grade so that you don't flip over, for example, and when your mother says it's okay, I'll take you to the backcountry, the meadows, or the mountains, where it'll be much more of a challenge. Okay, put on your helmet."

"That day isn't today," Reyna made clear and took a step

back as Hawk started his engine. Lily once again followed his lead. The two rode off a good distance, their snow tracks at a comfortably slow, even pace. "Press on the pedal, but not too hard. That's it." Hawk's deep voice carried back on the chilled wind. Low gray clouds rolling in were bringing an early sunset. Unable to see the pair fully at the distance, Reyna brought out her phone to zoom in and took a video of Lily practically hanging off the side amid a one-eighty turn, one booted foot in the snow, guiding the sled precisely how Hawk had shown her, the pair in sync. They rode in, then made another wide half-moon whirl, kicking up snow walls on their reverse to go back the other way, repeating several times.

*Our daughter.*

Reyna sent the text with the video to Blake. Those two words were all that needed to be said whenever either of them had something to share about Lily. The video call that followed moments later was no surprise. She answered, "You saw our baby?" Reyna rotated the screen and aimed it toward Lily.

"I did. That's my girl. She nailed that pin turn. Who is that with her?"

Reyna flinched. So awed with Lily and her exceptional riding skills, she'd forgotten Hawk was in the live shot. She hurriedly flipped the screen. "Um, that's the man who rescued her. He's—he's Kate's uncle. Lily's friend, Kate. She told you about Kate. Kate's mother is the sheriff here. Really nice family," Reyna babbled, suddenly finding it difficult to breathe.

She had broken their ten-year pact. Videos didn't lie.

"Rey?"

She blanked, jolted out of her head. "Sorry, what was that?"

"I said it's nice of him to show Lily how to ride properly."

"Yes, it is."

"By the way, I've given some thought about Lily going on that date. It's a Christmas party. I guess one date won't hurt. You'll be there to chaperone?"

"Of course. Lily will be thrilled."

"Yeah, tell her we will talk later about all of it. I have some rules, like this Jacob kid is to have no touching below the shoulders."

Reyna huffed. "Blake, that's ridiculous."

He laughed. "I'm joking. On that note," his tone grew serious behind a heavy exhale. "Rey, I'm not ready for this. Dating. Next, she'll be talking about marriage. I'm so not ready for our baby girl to grow up. I was barely eighteen by the time she was born. I was freaked out of my mind, not sure what to do. Now, I'm freaking because I feel we're losing her."

"Back then, you think you were scared. I was hardly sixteen, remember? But we're not losing her, Blake. She's growing into the beautiful young lady we're raising her to be." Up ahead, Hawk and Lily were heading back at a slightly faster clip. "I'll let her know you'll call her later. And you weren't kidding about the no touching below the shoulders," she remarked, chuckling as the sleds came to a perfect stop before her, and the two removed their helmets.

"Nope, I wasn't." Blake laughed. "Talk to you later."

Reyna disconnected. There was a flicker of something she couldn't quite grasp in Hawk's steady study of her as his focus followed the motion of her sticking her phone in the front pocket of her coat. Not a smile nor a frown in the way he regarded her until he turned his head to Lily, where gray eyes lit vivid with admiration.

"She's a natural. Picked up the know-how with ease."

"That was awesome! Mom, did you see me?" Lily got off the sled, bouncing happily.

"I did. You were amazing. Dad thought so too. I sent him a video. Oh, I almost forgot," Reyna quirked a grin. "He said you can go with Jacob to the Mistletoe Ball." The running leap into Reyna's arms on a shriek that pierced the dusky night at an octave that could break glass nearly toppled her into the snow.

"Thank you!" Lily squeezed tight, then stepped back, still bopping excitedly. "I have to call Kate and Brooke. They're going to be so stoked." She whipped out her phone. "Oh, I must let Jacob know. He's allowed to text now. His mom let him off punishment early." She trotted off.

Reyna moved to Hawk. "Thanks for doing this for her. I know you could be at your store or the veterans' center." She walked alongside him as he rode his sled slowly over to the truck that was parked a few yards away. He then began setting the ramp, crouching to his knees to lock the clamps in place. His odd mood from the moment they had met up had been a constant barrier between them.

"She now knows how to maneuver enough so as not to panic if she finds herself in a situation like before." He glanced over. "But I also did it for you. It'll give you peace of mind whenever she's out riding."

Reyna got into the truck bed to help strap the sled once he had it loaded. They leaped down and hooked the trailer up next, then guided Lily's sled inside.

"Have you told Blake about us?"

His voice was just below a whisper. Reyna jerked a look over her shoulder to Lily, laughing with her phone to her ear. "No, I haven't." She struggled with the reason why.

On a faint smile, he turned and pulled open the front and rear passenger-side doors. "It's almost dark. We should get going."

Observing the quiet tension in his tone, she called to Lily, who jogged up and climbed in back. As they drove off, in the dark of the truck's cabin, Reyna stole glances at Hawk—eyes focused on the road, a forearm on the center armrest. One gloved hand was balled in a soft fist, the other coiled around the steering wheel at twelve o'clock. Something was shifting behind his impassive guise. What was bothering him, outside of the obvious? Not telling Blake about him, she knew, would remain a bone of contention between them.

Reyna shared the armrest and eased her fingers along his palm, lightly stroking. His fingers uncurled, responding to her delicate massage. He looked over. She tried to convey in her touch what she felt in her heart. His focus moved to the rearview mirror, drawing Reyna to give a subtle glance to the back seat. Lily's head was buried in her cell phone, her thumbs typing a mile a minute. Reyna brought her attention to Hawk's fingertips brushing hers as his features recovered from the grim concerns that plagued him.

"Are you hungry?" he asked softly, his eyes on hers.

"Starving!" came the reply from the back seat.

Hawk chuckled, as did Reyna. "I guess that's a yes." She gave his hand a tender squeeze before easing hers free.

"There's this event I think you both might enjoy."

"Where is it?" Reyna asked.

"It's not far. You'll see." The familiar smile she had come to love returned to his eyes.

"You're not going to say? It's a secret?"

He shrugged, wearing a smirk as he drove another couple of miles, then turned off the main road onto a narrow, well-traveled imprint of snow about another mile, moving through heavily wooded ground. Trees hung low from the strain of the snow weighing down their limbs.

She was pleased to see his disposition had improved, but Reyna never enjoyed surprises. Just when she was about to ask again about their destination, faint music could be heard that grew louder as they drew closer. Up ahead, clouds of smoke billowed into the night sky. The smell of sweet hickory wafted through the air. They entered a clearing where a towering, flickering flower of golden flames crackled and danced in the center, surrounded by hordes of people milling about. A cacophony of chatter and laughter mixing with the holiday tunes echoed into the twilight.

"Wow! That's so cool!" Lily came in between the bucket seats and stared out at the festive scene.

"There's a playful rivalry Haven Creek has with its neighbor here. We have the annual Christmas Ball. Sutton Springs has their Holiday Bonfire Night." Hawk brought the truck to a stop alongside a row of vehicles. They got out and walked to the gate, where he took out his wallet and paid the entry fee.

Food, music, dancing, singing, and children playing, surrounded by a backdrop of silky layers of pristine white landscape—Reyna felt it was all so overwhelmingly wonderful.

"Let's get you ladies something to eat."

They were led over to a line of grills putting out the typical burgers and hotdogs, but also among the delectable choices were sweet blackberry-glazed chicken, beer-braised beef, seared shrimp kebabs, mini aluminum tins of savory mac and cheese, hearty beans with chunks of bacon kept warm in cast-iron pots over a fiery spit, cheesy garlic potato wedges, and a variety of grilled veggies. Another long table held a smorgasbord of sweets to satisfy everyone's sweet tooth.

They found a corner spot to sit at a long wooden table.

"That's all you're eating?" Hawk asked, and Reyna examined her plate—a small piece of blackberry chicken and a bit of corn salad was plenty for her, unlike the hefty portions he'd loaded upon his plate.

"I had a late lunch."

"She eats like a bird." Hawk winked across the table at Lily, who grinned, chomping away.

They ate while observing young children line up to sit on Santa's lap. Teens were hogging the picture booth. Adults were dancing and singing.

"Lily! Oh my God, I didn't know you were here!"

Reyna turned her head to the girl jogging over, her long braids swaying beneath her knit rainbow pom-pom hat. She hugged Lily about the shoulders from behind, their cheeks pressing.

"Kendall, hi. This place is really cool."

"Yes. My parents left for their cruise this morning. I'm staying with my aunt here in Sutton. She's around here somewhere. Hey, my friends and I are about to make s'mores." Kendall pointed to the group of teens situated on blankets a comfortable distance from the fire. "Come sit with us."

Lily looked across the table. "Mom, can I?"

Reyna had a narrow view of the teens' location. "You've hardly eaten much off your plate."

"I'll take it with me."

She gave another survey of the group. Aside from a playful shove and a toss of wet earth now and then into the fire, they seemed to be behaving themselves. "I guess it's okay. But right there, where I can see you." The two hurried off. "Who is Kendall? I've never seen her before. I tell you, my daughter has become the social bee here," Reyna told Hawk, who'd just about cleaned his plate. "Lily started a new private school this year and doesn't like it very much. I plan to have a serious discussion with her father when I return home."

"You could stay here. Schools are great."

"Hawk." Reyna met his determined push on the matter. "I can't."

"I know." He smiled and bent near her ear. "Can't blame a man who's crazy about you for trying."

Her breath hitched at the light brush of his lips behind her lobe before he drew away, amusement leaving his expression.

"Is there a reason why you haven't told your ex about us? I understand if you're not at that place yet. It would only help to know where things stand with us. Right now, I really haven't got a clue."

Reyna wanted to tell Blake, but there never seemed to be a right time. Or was it that she was stalling?

"Hawk, one important reason why I haven't told Blake about us is because I broke the agreement he and I have had for ten years. That will not sit well with him. I did tell Blake I'd met someone, but I said it didn't go beyond a lunch date because it was when you and I had broken up—"

"*You* broke up with me," he stated firmly.

She nodded. "Right. I was with you when the incident occurred with Lily. That, too, he will take issue with, when he puts two and two together."

"So, you want to spare his feelings at the expense of mine."

"Hawk—"

"It's all right, Reyna. Would you like something warm to drink?" He came to his feet and gathered up their plates. "How about hot chocolate? We can go join the kids for s'mores."

"Okay." But she knew it was far from all right, though he was keeping things light after that heavy moment. Goodness, what was wrong with her? He was such a wonderful man, one who was willing to put up with her drama, her steadfast rules, and who had tolerated Lily's behavior. Few men would even bother.

On his return, she took the steaming cup and started to follow him over to those gathering by the fire, but then she caught his wrist. "Hawk, wait."

"Yes?"

Reyna looked around at the many bodies, then over at Lily seated among the group of teens. "Not here." She walked off, crossing over from cleared ground to snow beneath her boots, far enough away that the warmth from the fire didn't reach and shadows didn't follow.

A couple of sips from her cup helped to center her frayed thoughts.

"Should I be worried?" He smiled, but an edge of concern reflected in his handsome face.

"As I mentioned before, Blake and I were best friends. Now we're at a good place after the divorce and have been for about ten years. We're even friends of sorts now."

"I'm very much aware." He sighed and looked away. "Reyna, I see where this is headed and—"

"Please, let me finish," she cut in. "With Blake, we co-parent. We have history. It's easy. With you"—her intake of breath was audible—"with you, I'm scared to get my hopes up. I'm afraid. I know I've wanted to keep some distance from you until I talk with Blake. And you've been so patient with me. But my fear is what's holding me back, not my feelings for you. I want to be with you. It's all I can think about."

His head snapped around, facing her again. "You want me?" He stared, unblinking.

"Yes, and it's part of what scares me. Your life is here."

"You want me." His tone was solid that time, a smile brightening all the way to his gray eyes.

"In a few days, I'll be returning to Miami. This will have

all been a mere fairy tale. I will wake up and have only dreamed you. Long-distance relationship didn't work for Blake and me. Amelia said you two grew apart when she moved to New York."

"We did. But it had occurred long before she left." He took the cup from her hand and set it on the ground, then slowly removed her glove, her heart skipping when he pressed cool lips into her palm. "Reyna, I'm not going anywhere. Damn, I want to kiss you so bad."

"Behave." Smiling, Reyna snatched her glove from him while giving a look about. "I should check on Lily." She moved around him and headed back.

"I'll behave because I'm all you think about," he said low near her ear, following short paces behind her.

"Sh." Reyna laughed with shaky amusement as they came upon Lily and the group of teens. "Having fun?" she asked.

"Lily, there's something I want to share with you," Hawk said, shoulders low, legs spread, hands behind his back.

"Okay." She eyed him quizzically.

Reyna stilled, her heart racing. "I don't—" A flash of white whisked past her and hit Lily in the shoulder, bursting into a powdery sea of sparkling ice crystals. Reyna stiffened, observing the shocked look on her daughter's face before Lily ran off. The group stood in stunned silence.

"Hawk?" Reyna was speechless.

"I thought . . . I didn't mean—" The snowball caught Hawk smack in the side of the head, the soft flakes bursting on impact, followed by a second with precision aim. He turned and got pelted by several more, as Lily laughed while building her arsenal in the white fluffy snow a few yards away.

"Snowball fight!" one of the teens yelled and chaos broke out as everyone began pummeling one another, some trying to take cover out of the line of snow warfare. Amid it all, fresh snow began to fall in heavy clumps, which only added to the festive melee that had no rules, no respites, no mercy at all, just good old-fashioned snowball annihilation.

"This is so much fun!" Lily giggled, crouched behind the table while searching for her target. "He's right over there. When he pokes his head up, I'm going to nail him." She giggled some more.

"Get him good." Hunched low, Reyna laughed as she packed tight a large ball of snow.

"Your dad's really cool," came from the boy who was part of Lily's group and now shared refuge behind the table.

"He's not my dad. But yeah, he's awesome! I'm going in." A solid white ball in both hands, Lily leaped up and charged on a shrieking war cry of laughter. The young man followed.

Reyna came to her feet, bursting into a roil of amusement, watching the scene as Hawk met the snow warrior halfway, the two sending their projectiles head-on.

By the time the battle was over, when the coldness had numbed through their heavy thermal gloves, yet neither one would concede, Reyna called it a tie. They loaded their chilled bodies into the truck, and Hawk cranked the heat.

"That was the best! Hawk, I nailed you." Lily taunted from the back seat on a deep exhale.

"No way!" he countered, just as winded. "If I hadn't

slipped, it would've been all over for you."

"Yeah, yeah. Excuses, excuses." She snorted. "Mom, I really like it here. Can we come back next summer?"

Reyna exchanged a look with Hawk, who grinned from ear to ear. "Sure, we can come back."

"Cool."

# Chapter Twenty

THE PERCUSSIONS, HORNS, and strings ensemble's holiday medley welcomed the parade of guests into Cedar Rose's grand ballroom. There were those who took advantage on entry of the sprigs of mistletoe dangling from crystal chandeliers. Walls, consisting mostly of floor-to-ceiling windows with small sections of white exposed brick in between, revealed views of the surrounding gardens in summer and, as it was, the snowcapped forest in winter. In the far corner stood a towering Scotch pine tree decorated with an abundance of red and gold ornaments. Glimmering lights added even more brilliance to the spectacular Christmas display. Traditional red poinsettias centered the forty or so white cloth, round tables. Classic red stripe candy canes were velvet-ribbon-tied and served as napkin holders at every plate setting.

Hawk weaved his way through the crowd, surveying, searching.

"Your tie is crooked."

He turned while straightening the black bow tie at his throat. Ash and Noah stood on his left. "Never was a fan of these. Took me three tries to get it halfway decent."

"I hear you. That's why," Noah gave a tug at his own,

snapping it right off. "Can't go wrong with a clip-on."

"You would be considered fashionably late, by the way," Ash remarked.

"Not even," Hawk returned. The oversized antique patina clock across the room read eight forty. "Doors opened at eight. It's Christmas Eve. My store was packed with last-minute shoppers."

"I thought you might have been with Reyna."

"She and Lily aren't here?"

"I haven't seen them."

"We texted around noon, but I've been so busy at the shop, I lost track of time."

"Don't you all look handsome tonight?" Amelia said, as she joined them.

"Nice dress," Noah said and he, Hawk, and Ash kissed her cheek when she pointed up to the mistletoe above them.

"Everything and everyone looks so lovely tonight. I really enjoy the Christmas ball each year." She surveyed the room. "I haven't seen Reyna and Lily."

"I don't think they've arrived yet," Hawk replied.

"Well, they will surely have a good time when they do. Oh, there's MaryAnn." And off she went.

"Hawk?"

Tess's dark-auburn hair was pulled up at the crown in an elegant arrangement. Soft tendrils at the temples framed her face. Eyes the color of amber glass stood out beneath winged dark lashes.

"Sheriff, you clean up nice. Almost didn't recognize you," Ash teased.

Tess glanced down at the shimmery red, assertively low-cut, square-neck gown. "You're lucky I'm off duty or I'd arrest you for breathing." She smirked, elbowing his side in good humor. "Not sure how long I'll last in these heels. My feet are already protesting."

"Have you seen Reyna and Lily?" Hawk asked her.

"No. Wait until you get a look at her in that gown. She was hesitant to buy it, but I convinced her."

"You won't have to wait long."

Hawk and Tess followed Ash's gaping stare over toward the entrance.

"Wow! Now that's how you wear red to ring in the holiday," Noah remarked.

Tess touched Hawk's elbow. "What did I tell you? I did good, right?" Her grin was filled with pride. "If you think the front with that side slit is everything, wait until you see the back."

Hawk delivered her a side look. "The dress has an ulterior motive?" Not that he needed to ask the obvious. "There you go, sticking your nose where it doesn't belong."

"I think she's perfect for you, so sue me." Tess turned to Noah and Ash.

"Yes, I like her. Lily's cool too." Noah nodded.

"They've grown on me," Ash added.

"See, the entire family approves. I figured if you hadn't hooked Reyna by tonight, that dress would do the trick." Tess winked, confidence glowing in her rosy cheeks. "But you two are dating, so tonight, the dress is an added bonus."

Always the matchmaker, the *meddler*, but for once, Hawk would give his sister her well-earned credit. The ruby-red satin fabric imprinted over every soft, familiar curve.

Reyna's hair hung in loose waves, breaking over her bare shoulders. Crimson lips full and luscious.

"Doesn't Lily look adorable?" Tess remarked. "Emerald green is so pretty on her." Just then Kate, in sapphire blue, and Brooke, in pale pink, ran up and snagged Lily, the trio linking arms, giggling on their trot away.

"Yes, she does." Hawk's eyes moved back to Reyna, mesmerized, and observed her scanning the room. Their gazes met. The smile she sent his way nearly stopped his heart. They started moving toward one another, cutting around clusters of bodies, and meeting halfway.

"I thought I might have to go find you." Simply looking at her made him smile.

"We're a little late because I had a bit of trouble lacing and tying my dress. Thankfully, Lily was there to help untangle me."

"I knew you'd wear it well," Tess's voice came from behind him. "And the gold clutch purse and matching heels are perfect. Twirl for us."

Hawk glanced back to his sister, Noah, and Ash, who'd evidently chosen to follow him.

Reyna did a slow pirouette. The spaghetti straps that capped her shoulders crisscrossed at her bare back, looping several times all the way down to form a bowstring at the narrow base of her spine.

"You look beautiful."

"You're looking pretty smart in that tux yourself."

"Mm-hmm."

Hawk turned his head at the exaggerated sound of Ash clearing his throat and followed his glance up to the clump of mistletoe overhead. One couldn't escape the greenery—it was everywhere. He pressed a chaste kiss on Reyna's cheek and felt the light brush of her lips against his.

"Would you like to dance? This song is slow enough that I might not run the risk of stepping on your feet."

"Sure."

"I'll hold your purse." Tess took the small, beaded clutch from Reyna.

They found a square foot of space on the crowded dance floor. Nat King Cole's "The Christmas Song" serenaded them as Hawk fitted his palms at her waist and drew her in but remained forever mindful of her desire to maintain discretion in public. Her hands rested on his shoulders, solidifying a careful distance.

He imagined himself sliding a palm over the perfect curve of her buttocks, stealing a hearty squeeze, while sending her into a low dip backward with a deep kiss in front of the entire room. He also pictured the shock it would bring and chuckled. His hands traveled downward ever slightly.

Her brow puckered with a wary glint in her eyes, but her lips twisted into a grin. "Hawk, I know what you're thinking. Don't you dare."

"I see we're already reading each other's thoughts." He continued to smile wickedly at seeing hers grow. "We'll become that couple that finishes each other's sentences. For example, I'll say, 'Let's go to . . .'"

"The theater."

"I was going to say a movie, but it's close enough." He grinned. "Okay, what about, I'll have . . ."

"Blake!"

He cocked his head. "I'm pretty sure your ex isn't what I was thinking about."

"No." Eyes wide, her head tilted, looking past his shoulder. "That's Blake."

Hawk spun. It was smart that he'd refrained from looking the man up on social media. The short, stocky, acne-faced image he'd conjured was far more palatable than the tall, wide-chested man standing a short distance away with his legs slightly spread and hands unassuming in the front pocket of his precision-fitting dress slacks. A squarely perfect bow tie circled his thick neck atop a pristine white shirt and an impeccably cut tuxedo jacket.

Blake's lips turned upward at one corner. He sent Reyna a wink, then pivoted and sauntered off in an unhurried swagger. She rushed after him, the two exiting out a side door.

*Okay.* Hawk left the dance floor in much need of a drink. He brought up a hand to catch the attention of any one of the four bartenders serving those congregating. Among them, Ash stood along the bar a short distance away, pouring his charms out on an attractive brunette.

"What can I get for you?" the bartender closest to Hawk asked.

"Glenlivet, neat."

"Make that two," Ash said, approaching solo. "I don't get women. They say they want a man to be upfront, honest about his intentions, but when we do, they're ready to knee us."

Their glasses were set before them. Hawk took a deep swallow, his emotions waging war between insult and upset.

Blake arrives, and he was all but forgotten. "What did you tell her?" he asked, staring into his glass.

"That I found her attractive, and my objective was purely physical."

Incredulous, Hawk rotated his head over to the man. "Seriously?"

"What? Should I have lied and then later get stuck dealing with the crazy when I ghost her? My friend, we're not all scouting to find our soul mates. Speaking of, where's your better half?"

"With her ex-better half."

Ash frowned. "Come again?"

"Reyna's ex-husband is here. One minute we were dancing, then she spotted her ex, and off she went with him." Hawk tossed back what was left in his glass, then smiled tightly. "Merry Christmas."

Ash shook his head and finished off his whiskey in one gulp. "Damn."

"Hawk!"

They turned to Tess. A wad of her gown was fisted in one hand to avoid tripping as she rushed up to them.

"I stepped out to make a call just now. Reyna was there with a man. Whatever they were talking about seemed pretty intense. I can always tell by the body language."

"It's her ex-husband, Lily's father, Blake," Hawk muttered before signaling the bartender with a point at his empty glass.

"Did you know he'd be here?"

"No clue."

"Her ex is easy on the eyes." Tess shrugged at his scowl.

"What can I say? I have a thing for big shoulders."

The bartender refilled Hawk's shot glass, and he tossed it back in one swallow, then started toward the exit.

"Where are you going?" Tess called.

"To get some air." He was glad when they didn't follow. At coat check, he fished around his jacket pockets for his ticket, while trying to convince himself Reyna hadn't played him, deceived him.

"Hawk?"

The sound of her voice was like a siren song. He closed his eyes a moment, wanting to ignore her, but felt powerless to Reyna's allure, and turned, even though everything within him said not to. Blake was beside her, eyes hard and jaw tight with tension.

"You're leaving?" Her brow furrowed. They moved out of the way to allow a guest to check his coat and from direct earshot of many others funneling in.

Hawk saw no point in hanging around. She'd made her choice. "I'm stepping out."

Her questioning gaze conveyed her disappointment, yet she wrung her hands nervously. He'd almost believe she'd prefer he left, taking the pressure off her. "I want to introduce you to Lily's father, Blake Star. He decided to come here to surprise Lily."

"Yes, but it appears I'm the one surprised," Blake ground out. "You're the man I just learned has been hanging around my daughter . . . outside of teaching her how to ride a sled, that is." His deep voice was low, but no less harsh. "A man I know nothing about."

"That's not quite the case," Hawk said. "I understand

why you'd be concerned. I can assure you—"

"Do you have a daughter?"

"No, I don't."

"Then how could you possibly understand? I thought my ex-wife and I had an understanding, but apparently not."

"Blake, listen." Reyna reached out to him, but he jerked his shoulder hard, repelling from her touch.

"Reyna, there's nothing you can say. I've always trusted that you and I were a team, of one mind when it came to raising our child."

"We are. You know that."

"Did you plan this trip for Lily or for him? You said you two met in Miami. Now, you want me to believe this hasn't been going on long before you suddenly arrive in the very town of the man you're sleeping with?"

"As I'm sure Reyna explained, she and I met only briefly in Miami. I hadn't met Lily then." Hawk tried to offer reason, then frowned, cocking his head. "Your concern for your daughter, I get. But you sound more like a man who just found out he was being cheated on."

"Hawk!" Reyna gasped.

Blake's hazel eyes were about as sharp as daggers pinned on Hawk, signaling a world of menace before he slid that blade to Reyna. "I'm going to go find *our daughter* and check out this Gagneaux kid. If you give a care, you'll do the same." He turned, but paused a moment, locking eyes with Tess, then continued past her. She was draped in her heavy wool coat, a hand in the pocket, no doubt gripping her badge, standing a short distance away with a keen regard of them all.

"Hawk, why would you say such a thing?" Reyna chided.

"Why would I? The way you're acting right now, you seem like a woman guilty as charged. Did you know he would be here tonight?"

"No. As I said, he wanted to surprise Lily."

"Had you told him about us long before now, this wouldn't be an issue." He shook his head while patting and searching his suit pockets, finally finding his coat check ticket. "But I think I see now why you didn't." He crossed to the attendant and handed the slip over, then turned back to Reyna. "It's as I thought. You're not over him."

"That's not true."

Coat in hand, he said on his way to the exit, "Deny it all you want. Blake didn't."

"Because it's absurd," Reyna argued.

She started after him, but for once, Hawk was glad Tess hurried forward and ran interference. "Reyna, let him get some air."

---

THE SLIT OPENING of Reyna's gown swirled and fanned her legs with each swift pace back and forth across the bathroom floor of the venue's ladies' room. Her pulse was jackhammering. Her thoughts webbing in a dozen directions. She checked her phone again. Still no response from Hawk.

"Hey."

Reyna spun around. Buried deep in her turmoil, she hadn't heard the door open, or Tess come in. With a sigh, she came forward and leaned against the counter, crossing her arms with a silent, steady gaze. Worry twisted Reyna's nerves into tight knots. "Hawk's not returning my messages."

Tess tilted her head, studying. "Should he?"

"Yes. We need to talk. He was right. I should have told Blake about us before tonight. But now," Reyna's voice quivered. "He's gone. He wants nothing to do with me."

"I'm going to share something with you that I haven't said to anyone, not even my best friend, Geri. When I'm asked why I don't try to meet someone, get back out there, I often say it's because no one will match up to my Keith. That's partially true.

"But I've stayed single mostly out of fear. Fear of the unfamiliar. Keith was my everything. He knew the precise temperature I liked my coffee. He knew I hated getting in a cold bed, so he'd go to bed a few minutes earlier and lay on my side to warm it just so I'd be comfy when I crawled in. I knew what to expect with him. I think that's the same for you with Blake. It's easy. Familiar. Comfortable."

Reyna let those truths sink in, but she wanted to make this clear. "I'm not in love with Blake anymore. My connection with him is Lily."

"That's good, I suppose." Tess stretched her arms wide, looking out at the tasteful floor-to-ceiling white marble walls. "Yet, here we are. Rey, I'm not the one you need to convince."

Her heart caught between panic and anguish, Reyna cried, "I want to make things right, but Hawk left and now won't respond to my calls and text messages."

Tess snatched a tissue from the decorative box on the

counter and dabbed away the tears, then took Reyna's makeup compact from the small, gold-beaded clutch. "I had a nice, long chat with my brother. It took some doing—he tends to dig his heels in when he's upset—but I managed to get him to stay put." She lightly patted the sponge over Reyna's nose and cheeks, then put the compact away before giving her a comforting embrace. Tess drew back, but held on at the shoulders, meeting Reyna eye to eye. "Now the rest is up to you. If you care about my brother, show him."

Reyna nodded. "Thank you."

They made their way back to the ballroom and easily found Hawk with Ash over by the bar. Reyna came in cautiously. "Hawk?" He would hardly look at her. When he did, which seemed to take a lot of effort, the warm affection she'd grown accustomed to seeing in his eyes was no longer there. Her heart fell. She looked at Tess and Ash. Though silent, they appeared despondent too. Reyna read Tess's subtle nod before she said, "Ash, let's dance," and tugged her cousin away.

On a quiet breath, Reyna stepped closer and noted Hawk's bearing seemed to tighten as he eased back a foot, which validated where things stood with them. Her heart ached more. "I'm sorry for the way I left you in the middle of our dance. I was so surprised to see Blake standing there." She looked away for a moment, hating that she'd pushed him so far over the precipice of tolerance. "I should've told Blake about us."

She reached for his hand, but he filled it with the glass stationed on the bar and finished off what was left in one gulp. "If you won't talk to me, will you at least dance with me? I'd like us to pick up where we left off. You didn't step on my feet." She let out a nervous laugh.

"No thanks. I've had enough holiday cheer with you for one evening." His cold regard sliced deep.

Every angle of his tense body language reverberated that response. "Hawk, I made a mistake and"—she fought against the tears threatening to crest—"I will forever regret it. Can we finish our dance? Then I'll let you be." She wasn't beyond begging and simply wanted, needed him to hold her in some small way one last time. That fact tore her up inside. Though there was sheer reluctance in his rigid stare, he gestured with his hand for her to lead the way. She gave a glimpse over her shoulder to be sure he followed.

There were fewer couples crowding around them, but still a good number swayed to the music, keeping up an easy rhythm. With her purse that was only about as big as a cell phone in one hand, she hooked her arms around his neck, crossing them at the wrists, locking on to him. He rested his palms on her waist with the lightest touch. She coaxed him in, so close that her thigh brushed his, but he eased back, setting distance, a sure boundary.

His disconnect was soul crushing.

"I can't finish your sentence if you don't say anything," she said after staring up at him, while he looked everywhere else but at her. Talking helped to prevent her from bursting into tears. "Okay, then finish my thought. I want to…"

He sighed, as though watching a boring stage performance. "Reyna, I don't think you and I—"

"Of course," she rushed out. "We'll just dance." She couldn't bear hearing him say aloud they were over. He didn't need to say it. She read it in the hard set of his jaw and felt it in his unresponsive touch.

The music lowered to a background hum as the soft ambiance of the chandeliers rose to a sparkling brilliance. Guests turned their attention to the director of tonight's event over at the far corner of the room. He stood in the center of the dais where the band was arranged in a strategic arch. With a microphone in hand, he droned on in a rather lengthy speech, praising those who helped to bring the ball to fruition, then finally thanked everyone for coming out.

"Now, in following with tonight's theme, let us seal it with a kiss," he announced.

Reyna glanced up at the mistletoe overhead and at those around her in full merriment, then at Hawk. To dance with her out of sheer goodwill was asking enough of him. Despair jabbed through her.

"You don't have to."

He lowered his head and pressed a light kiss on her cheek. She caught the back of his head, unable to help herself when he attempted to pull away, and gave a peck on his lips, followed by another. Soft. Warm. Decadent. She wanted to put to memory his taste, the delightful, clean scent of his skin, the feel of his formidable strength. Yet with her, his touch was always incredibly gentle, as if she were as fragile as fine china.

"Don't. Please," she murmured, not caring how desperate she sounded when he tried again to break the contact. She palmed his bearded cheek, thumb stroking, kissing him sweetly, tenderly. "I'm sorry," she whispered against his lips and heard his shuddering intake of breath as his resistance slowly ebbed. His hands at her sides slid around her, their kiss heightening in intensity. Her head angled, wanting much more as the tip of her tongue brushed silkily over his, stealing a taste, and he easily acquiesced, joining her. The gesture so daring, so drugging, so devastatingly intimate, lost in the current of their shared exploration, it took a long, startling moment before the stillness in the room registered.

They broke apart, drawn back to the center of the dance floor, where they now stood alone. Everyone else had backed away, giving them a wide berth, leaving them on display. Both turned slowly in a small circle to the many faces who'd become their audience.

Reyna looked up at this beautiful, caring man and her rattled emotions simply took over. "Never would I have imagined meeting someone as altruistic, thoughtful, and wonderfully patient as you. You are an unexpected gift. I love you, Hawk. My heart is yours if you want it."

He blinked, then his stare steadied, that warmth she cherished returning in his gray gaze. "Oh, I want it. More than want it. I love you, Reyna." He took her into his arms and kissed her with every ounce of his affection in full view.

A sudden clap reverberated through the quiet space. Hawk and Reyna looked about. They seemed to narrow in on Lily at the same time. Blake stood behind her, hands in his pockets. The center of his attention mirrored everyone else's, but without a hint of readable expression. Lily clapped again and glanced up at her dad, who joined in with a slow smack of his hands. Cheers rang out and grew louder. Ash, Noah, and Tess sent up two-finger whistles between their lips. Several followed suit in the celebratory show of approval.

Reyna looked at Hawk and smiled. "I guess our secret is out."

"Looks that way." He grinned.

Hands linked, they crossed to Lily and Blake as the music returned to an upbeat tune, and the party resumed. "I can explain," Reyna told Lily.

"What's to explain? I saw Mommy kissing Santa Claus." Lily smirked.

Hawk threw his head back in laughter. "I suppose she was."

Reyna turned to Blake. "We should talk."

"Yes, it seems we should."

HAWK FOUND TESS out in the hall as she was putting her phone back in her purse.

"Let's move Christmas festivities to my house tomorrow," he said.

"What? Why? It's my year to host. I've already prepared and refrigerated some of the sides."

"Pack everything up and come to my place. I'm inviting Blake to join us. He'll get to see my home, our family. Well, we can make an excuse for Noah." They both laughed. "My point, Blake will see that he can trust me around his daughter, that I'm not some crazed individual with ropes and chainsaws hanging around my basement."

"Your entire garage is filled with ropes and chainsaws. It's part of your profession. You work with wood."

"You know what I mean. I want to show him I'm on the up and up."

Tess frowned, hands on her hips. She gave an aggressive tug on the thin leather strap of her purse hanging from her shoulder. "You have to get his approval to date his ex-wife?"

"No, it's not like that." Hawk broke down everything to his sister, who looked ready to bang some heads. Then her expression softened on a sighing *aww* as she pressed her hand over her heart.

"That's so sweet. Now it all makes sense. As young as they were when they had Lily, it shows how well they've done in raising her. She's adorable. Kate thinks she's terrific. She'll miss Lily when she's gone. I told her we'll visit in Miami next summer and . . ." Tess trailed off. "Reyna leaves the day after tomorrow."

"Yes." It was Hawk's turn to exhale heavily.

"Hawk." She clasped his hand. "Watching you and Reyna express your feelings in front of the entire room like that"—Tess smiled, then her amber eyes fell—"I got so caught up in seeing how happy she makes you, I guess I put aside the fact she lives in Miami. What will you do?"

"Build up my frequent flyer miles, I suppose," Hawk replied on a dismal grin. "What else can I do? My business here is growing. Things are good. Better than good. It would be foolish to uproot right now. Reyna's company is more lucrative in Miami."

"There you are."

They turned to Reyna striding forward. She slowed, eyes darting with a cautious look between them. "You two are trying to have a conversation. I'll come back." She pivoted.

Hawk caught her wrist. "No, we were talking about tomorrow's Christmas get-together, who's bringing what."

"Oh. Is there anything I can do to help?" Reyna offered.

"No need. We have everything under control."

"Yes, all good there," Tess added. She stepped to Reyna and enveloped her in a tight hug. "I'm so glad you and Lily came to Haven Creek."

"Me too."

"I'll go check on the kids."

"You'll find Blake nearby. He's keeping a close eye on Lily with Jacob."

When Tess went on her way, Hawk asked, "How'd your talk with Blake go?"

"He still takes issue with me breaking the agreement. With that, he'd like to know more about you if you're going to be around Lily."

"Then he'll accept my invitation to Christmas dinner tomorrow."

Her eyes brightened. "That would be perfect." She slipped her arms around his waist and kissed him, a deep, lingering kiss, no longer shying away from public shows of affection. "How did I get so lucky?"

She wore the sweetest, happiest smile. In less than two days, she would be on her way back to Miami, back to her life there. She hadn't even left yet, and he was already growing melancholy. How would he manage a long-distance relationship when the mere thought of being without her delivered an agony of emptiness?

"I'm the lucky one."

# Chapter Twenty-One

"Not bad." Blake surveyed Hawk's vast property from his passenger-side window. Light, fluffy snow fell from a sky saturated with thick blue-gray clouds, dancing on a gentle wind, before resting atop a white, pillowy landscape. Smoke billowed from the stone chimney, promising a warm fire kindled within. It was the perfect addition to a chilly Christmas late afternoon.

"What did you expect?" Reyna gave a look at him as she parked the car in the driveway behind Tess's black Chevy Tahoe.

"I don't know, some sort of lumberjack-looking hovel." Blake laughed and dodged Reyna's playful punch at his shoulder. "I'm kidding. I didn't think he'd have a spread like this."

"Dad, you're funny." Lily laughed with him from the back cabin.

"You two behave." Reyna snickered and popped opened the trunk. Blake retrieved the wrapped packages. The three had waited to exchange gifts to join in later with everyone else.

They strode the freshly cleared flagstone walkway and up the five wide steps. A beautiful wreath made of holly berries twined with acorns adorned the polished maple front door.

Reyna pressed the doorbell.

"It's open," came a voice from inside.

She turned the knob and entered to a gaiety of voices.

Lily and Kate immediately scurried off toward the sun porch through the kitchen.

"Merry Christmas." Ash came out of the recliner and gave Reyna a hug. "I'm Asher, Hawk's cousin. We met briefly at the ball," he said to Blake and shook his hand. "That's Noah, Hawk's brother."

Noah delivered an acknowledging nod from his lounging position on the sofa in front of the flat screen mounted above the fireplace.

"Over in the kitchen is their sister… my cousin, Tess."

"We met at the ball as well," Tess said with a wave, and Blake returned the same.

"Rey, are one of those for me?" Grinning his boyish charm, a bowl of potato chips before him, Noah munched while gesturing at the gifts with the video game controller in hand.

"Actually, yes. Where should we place them?"

"Under the tree." Hawk jogged down the stairs and crossed the room. He pressed a kiss on Reyna's lips with sturdy confidence, then helped her out of her coat. When Blake freed his arms of the packages, Hawk shook his hand. "Glad you came."

"Wouldn't have missed it." Blake started to remove his coat.

"Keep it on. I want to show you around the grounds." They went into the kitchen. "Dinner should be ready soon.

Right, Tess?"

"That'll depend on your smoked brisket," she answered as she prepped asparagus with a generous brushing of Parmesan butter.

"It'll be ready to serve in fifteen." Hawk turned to Blake. "How about a drink?"

"Sounds good."

"Tess, I'll give you a hand." Reyna grabbed the apron lying on the counter. "What would you like me to do?"

"All that's left are the mashed potatoes, if you don't mind." Tess sat the warm bowl before her.

"Not at all." Reyna went to work, adding softened butter and pinches of salt, then dashes of heavy cream. But she kept a keen eye on the two men talking, standing shoulder to shoulder at the bar credenza over in the living room. Glasses in hand, they left the house through the side door off the kitchen. She moved from the island to the counter to be able to see them out of the bay window behind the sink as they walked to the largest of the three garages at the back of the property and entered through a side door. The main door slid up to reveal a boat stored within. From Reyna's vantage point, it looked to be in repair.

Both hunched, focusing on something at the hull, then strode about the space, still talking, between sips from their glasses. Now they were laughing. About what exactly? *If only to be a fly on the wall at that moment.* The big door suddenly started a slow roll downward. They left the garage the way they entered, trekked across the snow-covered backyard, and came to stand facing the frozen lake.

"I think those potatoes are about the creamiest I've ever

seen."

Reyna blinked and looked down at the bowl she'd been stirring, then back to Tess standing beside her. "Oh. Sorry, I got distracted."

Tess gave a glimpse out the window. "Your ex-husband and your boyfriend out there yacking it up. I can see why."

"What do you think they're saying?"

"Hmm, maybe comparing notes about you," Tess joked on a dark chuckle.

"Goodness." Reyna laughed. When Tess wasn't wearing her badge, it would seem she had a pleasantly wayward sense of humor. "Look, they're coming back."

"Great. I don't like cold asparagus. Time to eat," Tess announced and took a couple bottles of wine from the shelf.

Reyna grabbed plates and utensils. The door opened. Hawk and Blake entered in the middle of their dialogue about sports. "Hey, you two, dinner's ready."

"Perfect. I'm starved." Blake smacked his hands together, rubbing vigorously.

Hawk saw to the brisket and set the perfectly cooked, finely cut beef in the center of the table, surrounded by the many other deliciously prepared dishes.

Everyone found a seat, with the dinner a relaxed, casual affair. As the meal progressed, Reyna listened to Blake across from her and Hawk beside her continue their debate about what team would likely end up in the Super Bowl, discussing players' stats and team injury count. Ash joined in, as did Noah. After the meal, the easy laughter and comfortable atmosphere continued as they all gathered in the living room to open presents. When the last gift was unwrapped, Reyna turned to Hawk seated beside her. "There's something I want to tell you."

"Should we go somewhere private?"

"No, I'd like everyone to hear."

"Now you have me cautiously intrigued. Or should I be concerned?"

Reyna looked at Lily, then Blake, and finally Hawk again. "I've decided to purchase Ace Car Service." She explained to the group the circumstances surrounding losing her hangar lease. "Hawk, I thought about what you once said about expanding your business. If I want to grow my company, I must bite the bullet and invest to do it. I've also decided to let my trusted employee, Danielle, continue to manage North Star going forward. She has done a great job in my absence. On that, Lily, sweetheart, how would you like it if we moved to Haven Creek?"

Lily stared, looking flummoxed. "I like it here, but what about my school? I can't leave. The program I'm in will allow me to finish a college semester ahead by the time I graduate. Mom, I want to do that."

Reyna thought her daughter would be thrilled by the news. She hadn't expected nor prepared for the contrary. "Well, I . . ." She was at a loss for words.

"Sweet pea, you can take extra classes at the junior college during your junior and senior year, which will keep you on track," Blake put in, and it seemed to help soften the look on their child's face.

"Your dad and I discussed the possible move, and I've been researching the schools here. I like what I see. I think you will too."

"I guess so. All right. Yes!"

Lily jumped up from the floor, dashed over to the sofa, and smothered Reyna in a near-suffocating embrace. "That's a firm yes!" she laughed. When Lily finally released her, Kate squealed, and the two girls hugged. Reyna turned to Blake. "And you're still cool with it?"

"I trust your judgement in this, Rey."

Reyna sent him an appreciative nod, then turned back to Hawk. His weak smile was not what she'd expected to see.

He stood. "Can we talk?"

"Um, sure." She followed him through the kitchen out to the sun porch. The late-afternoon rays poured in through the glass enclosure, making it warm and cozy. Reyna imagined the comfort in summer sitting upon the thick-cushioned lounge, watching the sun set beyond the trees on the other side of the lake.

"You purchased Ace Car Service?"

"I've been in communication with the owner for a few days now. I didn't want to say anything until we'd negotiated the sale. He was thrilled I'd be the one to take Ace. The purchase will stretch my finances a bit the first year, but I plan to sell off Ace's cars and use part of the money to pay off the loan. The rest will go toward upgrading the fleet to North Star standards."

"Does this mean you'll eventually relocate your company here?"

"No. As I said, my driver and good friend, Danielle, will continue to manage things in Miami. She's been handling the day-to-day in my absence. I'll fly down often to check in on things, but mostly, I'll run North Star from here." Still, his expression wasn't thrilled, to say the least. "Hawk, I thought you'd be happy about this."

"I am happy. More than happy. But I'm almost afraid to be. That you would do this for me. . . for us. . . I don't know how I became so fortunate to have found you. I love you."

"Wishes to Santa really do come true." Reyna brought her arms around his neck, and his circled her waist, drawing her in tight. Their kiss was soft and light. "We found each other. I love you."

He smiled wide, and she saw the wonderful promise of their future within the light of his eyes.

With one arm cinched around each other, they headed back to join their blended family.

## The End

Want more? Check out *See Me* by Michele Arris!

Join Tule Publishing's newsletter for more great reads and weekly deals!

## Acknowledgements

I really enjoyed writing this book and getting to work with my fantastic editor, Julie Sturgeon, once again while doing it. Julie, thank you for guiding this story through its building blocks. I'm so fortunate to have you in my corner.

A special thank you to the entire Tule Publishing team for helping to turn my many words into to book.

My heartfelt thank you to my family for their constant cheers.

Finally, dear readers, I'm immensely grateful for your continued support. It makes me giddy that I get to share another story with you.

If you enjoyed *Above the Mistletoe*,
you'll love the next book in the…

## Haven Creek series

Book 1: *Above the Mistletoe*

Book 2: Coming Soon!

*Available now at your favorite online retailer!*

# More books by Michele Arris
# The Tycoon's Temptation series

Book 1: *See Me*

Book 2: *Catch Me*

Book 3: *Return to Me*

*Available now at your favorite online retailer!*

# About the Author

Award winning author, Michele Arris, has always had a fondness for romance and happy endings.

When Michele isn't working on her next project, she can be found reading all types of romance genres or watching period classics. Even in her limited downtime, she's daydreaming about how her alpha hero and her strong-willed, hardworking heroine shall find their happily ever after together.

Michele lives in the Washington D.C. area. Get to know more about her by visiting her website at michelearris.com.

Thank you for reading

## Above the Mistletoe

If you enjoyed this book, you can find more from all our great authors at TulePublishing.com, or from your favorite online retailer.

Made in United States
North Haven, CT
29 November 2022